STRINGER

STRINGER

MELVILLE JONES

Matador
Unit E2 Airfield Business Park,
Harrison Road, Market Harborough,
Leicestershire. LE16 7UL
Tel: 0116 2792299
Email: books@troubador.co.uk
Web: www.troubador.co.uk/matador
Twitter: @matadorbooks

ISBN 978 1 805140 139

British Library Cataloguing in Publication Data.
A catalogue record for this book is available from the British Library.

Printed and bound in Great Britain by 4edge Limited
Typeset in 10pt Petersburg by Troubador Publishing Ltd, Leicester, UK

Matador is an imprint of Troubador Publishing Ltd

Also by the Author

Happenstance

ONE

London 1990

Natalie clung more tightly to Luke's arm. He looked down at her and saw the fear in her face. He tried to smile reassuringly. There was no point trying to speak: the shouts of the protesters; the wailing of sirens; the barking of ferocious Alsatians and the clattering of the hooves of the police horses, as they moved to pen in the crowd, made conversation impossible. Nelson looked impassively down on them but the fountains were not playing, probably turned off in case someone tried to drown one of the pigs, Luke had been told earlier, by a wild-eyed and dishevelled anarchist; one of a group of about twenty whom he was informed had travelled up from Southampton in a hired minibus. Luke had a problem with that. He had assumed anarchists were opposed to all forms of organisation; that there was a Southampton branch prepared to do the paper work to hire a minibus seemed to strike at the very heart of their existential philosophy, but wisely he had not pressed the issue.

This mixed constituency was the problem with demos he assumed, although this was the first he had ever attended.

He had seen plenty on the box in his youth; news coverage made the most of these dramas. He could remember vividly, footage of the women of the Greenham Common Peace Camp dancing on the nuclear silos and Yorkshire miners hurling bricks at the riot shields of their police tormentors. He had absorbed it all without comment. His father, the staunchest of Thatcherites, provided more than enough commentary for the whole household. The Greenham women were categorised as 'unwashed Lesbians' and the miners 'hooligans lead by a madman.' Whilst he fulminated, his two children, who were told it was good for their education to watch the news, sat silently. Mary, Luke's young sister, often absorbed herself in dressing and redressing her Barbie doll, whilst he tried to blank out his father's caustic comments in order to make sense of what was at stake in these violent clashes. His mother barely looked up from her magazines and when she did it was only to shake her head in despair at the wickedness of the world.

The only newspaper taken in the house was the *Daily Mail* and when his father had finished with it Luke was allowed to read it but it only seemed to reinforce his father's view of the world. It was his grammar school (one of those not swept away by the Comprehensive tide) which began to sow the first seeds of doubt. Not the school itself, which was the traditional and conservative institution his father told him on many occasions he was privileged to attend and how all the extra tuition paid out for extra cramming for the Eleven Plus had been money well spent. No, it was not the school but his friends. Not all were products of middle class conformity. There was Zack, in particular, whose mother was quite a well-known actress; not of Hollywood status but quite often seen on television. He had seen her once, briefly, quite by chance, in an episode of Dr Who. He had excitedly blurted out to his father, "That's the mother of one of my school friends." His father had not looked impressed. She sometimes picked Zack up after school and Luke used to wait at the school gate with him. He was never in a hurry to go home. He barely spoke to his father about anything other than his school progress which, fortunately, was generally satisfactory, and his Mother, whilst she fussed over him while he ate his supper, rarely spoke of anything but the weather and the rudeness of shop staff. Mary sometimes nagged at him to play with her but there was a four-year gap between them so he usually made excuses that he had too much homework. Zack, on the other hand, was fun to be around. He had a breezy self-confidence and had inherited his mother's histrionic gifts. He could mimic staff members with satirical precision but he kept out of trouble with his disarming charm. His school uniform rarely matched the stipulated requirements but if his tie was missing or askew and his shoes were Adidas trainers rather than the stipulated black brogues, he always evaded punishment by coming up with an explanation, delivered with heart-melting remorse: usually pleading dire poverty or 'family problems' (unspecified).

One afternoon – halfway though his first term – Zack's mother got out of the car and walked towards the two boys. She beamed at Luke. "Hello. You must be the friend Zack was telling me about. Luke isn't it?"

Luke could do no more than nod.

"Well it's lovely to meet you Luke. I was telling Zack you must come and have tea with us one day. Would you like that?"

Zack spoke for him. "That'd be great Mum. We'll fix it."

His mother put her arm round her son and steered him towards the car. She glanced back at Luke. "TTFN," she said and laughed and gave him a little wave.

Luke did not often lie to his parents; he usually managed to avoid close scrutiny by evasion and half-truths, but this time he felt he had no option. He knew his father would be unhappy for him to go for tea to the house of 'that actress woman'. So Luke said he would be late home because of Chess Club. His father approved of chess; one of the few pastimes he did favour. Rugby was acceptable too, 'character building', but soccer was beyond the pale; 'overpaid louts'.

"And, dear Luke, you must call me Sarah. Mrs Langton is much too formal. Will you do that?"

Luke found it hard to reply with his mouth full of chocolate cake. He managed a last swallow and nodded his agreement. "I'll try to remember but—"

"Langton isn't her name now, dear boy. Didn't you know that?" This from an elderly but elegant gentleman who sat with them at the pine kitchen table with his back to what Zack had told Luke was an Aga. He had been briefly introduced as Charles, who was staying a few days it seemed, but no more information than that had been proffered.

Luke blushed in confusion. "No I'm sorry. I thought as Zack is Langton."

Sarah smiled at him. "Zack's father was a Langton but when we," she paused to find the right words, "when we went our separate ways I reverted to my maiden name." She looked at Zack almost apologetically. "For professional reasons."

"Sarah Sanders," Charles declaimed noisily, "best move you ever made darling, relaunched your career." He looked suddenly thoughtful. "Perhaps I should try it."

Sarah reached across the table and patted his hand comfortingly. "Cheer up old thing. I'm sure your agent will soon pull his socks up."

Charles managed a half smile. "Well, there is talk of a Radio."

Zack nudged Luke quickly and gave him a broad wink before addressing Charles. "And there are always the chipolatas."

Charles groaned and buried his head in his hands in mock despair. "Those bloody sausages."

Luke had made little sense of anything that had been said at the table and was grateful that no one had sought to involve him. But now Zack offered some enlightenment. "You know that commercial on telly where the Bishop blesses the sausages?"

Luke was unsure how to reply; to admit that his father detested commercial television and never watched it on principle. Fortunately Zack did not wait for a reply. Instead he burst into song. "Bless them all, bless them all, they're tasty and porky and small."

Sarah smiled at him indulgently but held up a restraining hand. "I'm sure Charles doesn't need to hear that, dear."

Charles groaned in agreement. "And to think I was once with the RSC."

Luke pondered that. He knew his father belonged to the RAC but he could not imagine Charles as a roadside mechanic. Fortunately Sarah was keen to press another slice of chocolate cake on the two boys and as they munched away dutifully Charles resumed reading the newspaper he had been studying when they arrived. He suddenly slammed it down on the table in rage. "That bloody woman," he bellowed.

Luke looked nervously at Sarah expecting some shocked reaction but she simply picked up the discarded newspaper and looked at the page which had so incensed Charles.

She put it down after a few seconds' perusal. "How does she get away with it?"

"By appealing to all the Little Englanders; the Jingoists. To take their minds off ten percent unemployment; race riots; striking miners." He paused in his outrage to glare at the two boys. Zack smiled cheerfully back but Luke froze with a piece of cake halfway to his mouth. "Now we can forget all that and grovel at her feet because she boasts she's going to give the Argies a bloody good hiding. It's sickening."

Sarah sympathised. "It is ghastly. Some of us in the business are signing a letter to *The Times*; calling for reconciliation."

At that Zack turned conspiratorially to Luke with a stifled giggle and raised eyebrows.

Sarah may have sensed the scepticism. She folded the newspaper and got to her feet. "We must be getting you home Luke: time is getting on."

Luke had prepared for this. "If you just drop me off at the Common I can take a short cut. It's easier than driving all the way round."

Sylvia seemed doubtful. "Are you sure?"

"Yes. I do it all the time," Luke lied. "It's broad daylight still and there are plenty of people around."

"Well if you say so, I'll just get my coat."

Luke watched the car drive away. He waved cheerfully. He had thanked Sarah effusively and she had seemed pleased and said he must come again soon. As the car disappeared from sight Luke knew that would never happen.

The lies soon multiplied. He told Zack, shamefully, that his mother was unwell and needed to rest in the afternoons so he had to get home promptly to make his sister tea. Zack had sympathised but had not, fortunately, pressed for details but the deceit made Luke nervous and his friendship with Zack cooled. He took up with other boys whose background seemed more akin to his own. Perversely he became resentful of Zack; of his confidence and popularity. The tea party had become a defining moment in Luke's life. It had thrust him unprepared into an alien world where adults swore and expressed political views his father would have regarded as blasphemous. He felt almost physically sick at the thought of taking Zack home. No doubt his charm would be on full throttle but Luke knew behind that smile there would be amused disbelief for everything his father believed in and Zack would subsequently entertain his friends with accounts of his visit; complete with impersonations.

As Luke's schooldays passed he learned to compartmentalise his life. Academically he was bright and absorbed information and ideas readily. In particular he found in Literature and History the entry to a world of ideas and emotions which altered his perspective on life. He began to realise how complex human society was even if Mrs Thatcher had declared there was no such thing. He knew too that he could not share his father's views but neither could he denounce them. He was not sure if his acquiescence was compassion or cowardice. By the time he reached the Sixth Form his adolescent doubts and embarrassments had given way to a more reasoned maturity. His school life and social life (such as it was) occupied a parallel universe to family life. He passed on to his parents only unimportant scraps of information; a reassurance that all was normal conformity, which, in truth, it was most of the time. His father was pleased with his crop of exam results but had begun to ask questions about career choices which Luke tried to fend off; he had come up to the school once or twice to watch his son play rugby and Luke was surprised to find that his father's presence on the touch line was a source of pleasure to him and not embarrassment.

He berated himself for even thinking it might be. His father was not a bad man. He loved his family and his reactionary political views did not translate into any form of physical aggression. He had never raised his hand to his children or his wife; he had spent hard-earned money on education and provided a comfortable home. So, Luke convinced himself, almost, that his father's ill-informed prejudices didn't really matter; they were no more significant than hair colour or shoe size. So he played the role of the dutiful son; often escaping to his room on the pretext of study to avoid listening to his father's fulminations.

As an antidote to meek domestic conformity Luke wove another web of deceit. In his last year in the Sixth Form, on Saturday evenings, he claimed he went to the cinema. His parents didn't really approve but he pleaded he needed this break from his A Level revision and even his father conceded it was not an unreasonable request. Luke always checked the storylines of the films he never saw in case he was quizzed on them but in reality the evenings were spent in the back bar of the White Lion. The landlord must have known most of them were a few months under age but implied if they behaved themselves he would give them the benefit of the doubt. And they did behave; confining themselves to a maximum of two pints of weak beer. Freed from school uniform the boys sprawled in jeans, bomber jackets, loose T-shirts, white sneakers. Some veered towards Hip Hop with athletic caps and chunky faux gold chains. Luke, supposedly dressed for the cinema, did his best with a windcheater and dad jeans. As they drank their beers the mood was one of optimism. In spite of many years of Maggie Thatcher, or perhaps because of it, young people had a voice. Not a political one perhaps but a materialistic one. Many of them had Sony Walkmans to listen to, and then argue over the merits of the likes of

Spandau Ballet or Duran Duran. After they left the pub they would stop for a Big Mac. No one spoke much of politics: it seemed an irrelevance to them. Some talked about University but others were heading straight for the City. It was universally assumed that whatever route you took there was serious money to be made out there. Luke hoped they were right. He had no objections to earning well but could it be that easy? On his walk home, chewing on peppermints to sweeten his breath, he pondered on his future and wished he could be more confident about it.

Natalie looked at him pleadingly. "Can't we leave Luke? I'm getting scared," she shouted above the noise.

Luke bent his head to her level and struggled to make himself heard. "We're stuck here. We'll have to wait until the crowd thins." He tightened his arm around her shoulder. He felt guilty about persuading her to come along. She was not really a natural protester. Neither of them was. They were both reading English at university and found pleasure in that shared interest. That pleasure had never really progressed beyond many cups of coffee and occasional visits to the movies and college gigs. There had been a few awkward moments of faltering intimacy but it seemed neither of them had their heart in it. Neither ready to risk commitment and neither confident enough to settle for meaningless sex. Luke accepted he was not good at making decisions. He was in his second year now but still had no idea what he would do with his life. Whenever he went home to visit his parents, which was not often, his father quizzed him on his plans and he tried to fend him off with a few vague platitudes. Unlike many of his fellow students Luke did not hold firm views about Life. Perhaps it was the dualism of his childhood; the need to live alternate lives; to run with both the hares and the hounds. He had confided some of this to Natalie; the only person he had ever dared to confide in. She had been encouraging. She had told him not to fret; when the moment was right he would know which path to take. Luke had hidden his embarrassment with a joke. "Like the Damascus road you mean?" Natalie had not laughed. "Exactly: just like the Damascus Road."

The pressure from the crowd at their back was pushing them hard against the police lines. Luke was inches away from the riot shields. The police had drawn truncheons. The mood of the crowd was growing angrier at the stand-off. To begin with it had been quite amiable. The protesters had waved their banners and placards: it was more like a carnival than a demo. Everyone joined in the frequent chants of 'Maggie, Maggie, Maggie, Out, Out, Out.' Then the mood had soured. The anarchists had stormed the South African Embassy, always a target for protest, but, as Luke had told Natalie worriedly, a distraction from protesting against the Poll Tax. That was why they were there. It seemed iniquitous that the tax would fall equally on the rich man in his castle and the poor man at his gate. Many of his fellow protesters were students in rented accommodation who would be expected to pay as much as their grasping landlords. It was so obviously wrong that Luke had shed his wary caution and joined the demonstration. He was beginning to regret it. The attempt on the Embassy had been repelled but fires had been lit and smoke filled the air. The police were violently dragging away protesters and hurling them into the backs of vans. Ambulances sounded their sirens in frustration as they tried to forge through the crowd to reach the wounded. The mood had grown angry now. Bottles directed at the police lines were flying over Luke's head from the crowd behind him. Senior officers were yelling through loudhailers telling everyone to disperse but their words went unheeded. Then a police van suddenly drove into Trafalgar Square and scythed into a section of the crowd. There were screams of fear and pain from those mown down and a deep primal roar of anger from those who had witnessed the carnage. The crowd behind Luke surged forward chanting 'Pigs, Pigs, Pigs.' Their momentum impelled Luke and Natalie closer to the riot shields. He could see fear and panic behind the heavy visors of the officers. He felt his own rising panic and Natalie was crying. The police line must give ground or people could be crushed to death. Couldn't they see that? Instinctively he raised his voice and tried to shout above the tumult. He spreads his arms wide in a gesture of desperate appeal but the answer was an agonising pain in his right arm as a police truncheon cracked down on it.

Luke had never known such pain and he was sure he would have fainted if the packed ranks had not held him upright. His obvious distress and Natalie's tearful appeals eventually cleared an escape route for them. They managed to get away from Trafalgar Square and eventually found a taxi to take them back to the local Casualty Department near their lodgings. Luke had to explain the circumstances of his injury to the doctor who refrained from comment but expressed little sympathy. Four hours later Luke was almost comatose with painkillers but reclining on the sofa in the communal sitting room whilst Natalie brought him coffee. They watched the News which was full of reports on the demonstration. A Police Commissioner praised the professionalism of his officers, at which Luke pointed to his plastered arm; police estimates of the numbers participating were considerably lower than the evidence of his eyes in Trafalgar Square. A member of the government was wheeled out to say that whilst peaceful protest was the British Way violence would not be tolerated. Miles wondered where the footage was of the police van driving into the protestors or the indiscriminate baton beating. When the programme finished Luke looked at Natalie in despair. "They tell you what they like; they stitch you up."

A few weeks later, with his arm in a lighter plaster, Luke went home to see his parents. His mother fussed over him and pressed food on him and his father was sympathetic to what Luke told him was a rugby injury. After the roast lamb and mint sauce, as they sat at the table, his father, inevitably, brought up the subject of Luke's future. Had he decided what to do for a living? Luke had come prepared; his mind now firmly made up. So he told him and for the first time in his life he didn't care what his father thought.

TWO

Southern Africa 2015

The seat belt lights flicked on and the Captain's clipped Afrikaner voice told them they were preparing their descent to Johannesburg. Ruth welcomed the news. She had barely slept in the ten hour flight from Heathrow. She was stiff and her mouth was dry and her stomach uneasy from the plastic meal and duty free wine. However there was no question of joining the snaking queue for the lavatory. She could hang on until they landed. She had a couple of hours to wait for the onward flight to Bulawayo. "That's if they can find a plane that still flies," had been the reassuring text from her brother, Ben. He would meet up with her in Johannesburg. He had lived there now for over ten years: established a successful engineering company. He had a glamorous blonde South African wife – Charmaine or some such. Ruth had never met her or her two flaxen-haired sons but they had managed the occasional awkward Skype meetings at Christmas.

Ruth had not been back to Africa since she left as a guileless innocent straight out of High School. Her plan then had been to take a year out to explore Europe. It was what young Rhodesians did (she still found it hard to remember to say Zimbabweans.) Her parents had been anxious for her but she was travelling with a respectable and sensible girl friend who had an aunt in Bournemouth they would stay with initially. It seemed nothing could go wrong.

As the plane circled the airport in its holding stack Ruth though wryly of Bournemouth. The aunt had been unbearable; a prim suburban snob who tried to bully Ruth into enrolling at a local Secretarial College. Ruth had tried, and failed, to convince her she had not come to Europe to learn shorthand but to travel. She clearly needed to get away as quickly as possible and her plans were helped when the respectable niece succumbed to homesickness after three weeks and fled back to Africa. Ruth took herself off to London and found a job in a pub. She holed up with some Australian and South African guys in a grim tenement in Earl's Court. She had been nervous about taking the room in a houseful of men and knew her mother would be appalled if she knew, but there was no problem. Everyone was too busy working to get enough money together to pay for their next travel plan.

Ruth worked shifts in the pub and had the afternoons off. She used that time to explore London. She walked its streets and crossed its bridges and marvelled at it all and absorbed its history which brought to life the dry narrative of her school textbooks. Perversely, at her school the curriculum had been modelled on the syllabus of English Examination Boards. So Ruth knew all about the Tudors and Stuarts and the novels of Dickens and Shakespeare's plays but nothing of African history except for the colonisation of the continent by Europeans. Surely that would all have changed now? Zimbabwe had been independent since 1980. The year of Ruth's birth, so it was easy for her to remember the date.

When she was growing up political changes had not really impacted on her family too much. Looking back she could see she had lived a privileged existence. Whites could still enjoy a comfortable lifestyle; still drink their Sundowners on their verandas; play cricket and rugby and swim in exclusive clubs and be waited on by black servants who called them 'Boss' or 'Madam'. Ruth remembered being told with pride by the privileged few that Zimbabwe had no Apartheid. Not officially, perhaps, but she now understood that discrimination might not have been policy but it was still endemic in all walks of life. She did feel guilt now but not oppressively so. She had been too young to see beneath the surface. She could not deny hers had been a happy, almost carefree life, before she set out for Europe. Then, she had imagined, she would return after a while and 'settle down' as her Mother had urged in her letters to London. Ruth imagined that implied marriage and children. Before leaving she had half-hearted relationships with a couple of boyfriends: one a tobacco farmer's son and one a policeman; both regarded as eminently suitable by her mother.

Ruth could really find no enthusiasm for either. She had read enough to understand that there were wider horizons to explore and London had not disappointed. Of course she missed the sun of Africa and the wild open spaces of the Bush but she had grown from a naïve girl into a mature woman in the space of a few months. Her mind sometimes felt as if it was imploding under the weight of new ideas and perceptions. Life in a restless cosmopolitan city was light years removed from the strictures of narrow social conformity of white Southern Africa. Her wages from the bar went on visits to galleries, theatres, cinemas and especially jazz clubs. Listening in crowded smoky cellars to the Blues and Afro Jazz gave her an emotional connection to her home where none of these things would have been possible. In London she mixed with people of all colours and persuasions and laughed to herself about what her mother would make of her new circle of friends. Not that London was free of racial tensions; riots erupted periodically when the toxic ingredients of inequality, poverty and injustice, real and perceived, were mixed with colour prejudice. Ruth tried not to be too judgemental. She suspected some of her new friends were wary of her colonial background so she was careful to say nothing to offend. On the other hand she would not pretend to have attitudes she could not accept. Her family history was much more nuanced than most people knew; touched deeply by racism and oppression.

The Immigration Officer looked hard and suspiciously at her passport.

"German EU," he frowned. His voice carried the inflections of his native Nguni tongue even in his spoken English.

"Correct." Ruth felt disobliged to offer more. They had been warned on leaving the plane that immigration controls had been stepped up everywhere in the world after the Charlie Hebdo massacre in Paris earlier in the year.

The passport was now being waved at her. "But you are not German."

Ruth was used to this. "I know, but I have a German passport." She paused and the added helpfully. "It is allowed." She hoped she would not be required to offer a fuller explanation.

The officer seemed unsure whether she was being helpful or sarcastic. He made great play of studying her passport closely. He then took an eternity to check its details against his computer screen. Ruth was desperate to get to a lavatory.

She nearly lost her temper and was on the point of screaming, 'Do I look like a bloody Jihadi?' when the passport was suddenly handed back to her and with a curt nod she was sent on her grateful way.

A leisurely twenty minutes in the restroom and a cup of coffee had almost restored Ruth to a semblance of a functioning human being. She relaxed on one of the black vinyl sofas and tried to gather her thoughts. Ben had just texted. He was at the airport and would join her in the departure lounge soon. The indicator boards still showed the Bulawayo flight due to depart at the scheduled time. Mindful of Ben's views on Air Zimbabwe she had taken the precaution of double-checking with a badge – labelled Traffic Manager. He had dutifully consulted his files and assured her the flight was set to depart on time. Perhaps sensing her doubt he had smiled and said, "Must be your lucky day, Madam."

Ruth had nearly fallen asleep on her sofa when her hair was briskly ruffled from behind. "Sawubona, sister. Welcome to Africa!" Ruth leapt to her feet to greet her brother. "Kanjani, Ben. And I'm afraid that's all the Ndebele I can remember." They laughed and hugged then pushed each other at arm's length to take a good look. Ben was the one member of her family she had seen in the last fifteen years. Twice he had come to England on business trips and had stayed with her; first in her cramped and dreary flat in South London, and on the second occasion in the draughty and leaking old Vicarage she and Simon rented in Cornwall. On that visit Ben had met the two girls; Sarah and Esther: five and seven respectively. If Ben had concerns about his sister's circumstances he kept them to himself. He played with the two girls who clearly fell for him. He did his best to make conversation with Simon, which was very hard work. Only when he was leaving did he catch Ruth alone and ask her anxiously, "Are you sure everything's all right?" It was not a question she could really answer.

"You look great, Ben. Not a grey hair in sight." In fact he looked little different from the boy of sixteen she had left behind when she came to England. There was always a special bond between them. Her mother had left childcare to her black maids but as the children grew up they spent most of their free time together. They lived on the outskirts of Bulawayo and their house bordered wild Bush. In spite of their mother's nervous concerns they roamed freely amongst the thorn bushes and the spiky Acacia tree and often sought out the shade of a mighty Baobab 'upside-down tree', as they called it, to eat the sandwiches the maid had prepared. They trekked in the red earth imagining they were tracing the spoor of leopards although the only wild animals they regularly encountered were vervet monkeys and the odd baboon, which they observed from a respectful distance. They always made it home just before the swiftly descending dusk and assured their mother they were alive and well. Their father usually got home from his work soon after and listened to their stories of days in the bush with a smile as he sipped on a small bottle of lager; his only concession to alcohol.

When he was eleven Ben was sent away to boarding school. Ruth missed him terribly. He never spoke about school much but it was clear it was not his favourite place. He fretted at the rules and restrictions which landed him in trouble. His father spoke to him seriously after the end of one particularly rebellious term. Ruth hid on the veranda as her Dad took Ben quietly to task. Ruth could just make out from her father's muttered comments that he was reminding Ben that education was his only route to fulfilling his ambitions. There was no family money or land to cushion his future: finding the school fees was struggle enough. At one point her father had raised his voice to a new intensity. He warned Ben that he could foresee that in only a few years an unskilled white man in the new Zimbabwe would fall to the bottom of the heap; competing for fewer and fewer jobs with the black majority with no support from a bankrupt and oppressive government. Ruth remembered those words now and how prescient they had been. Ben too had taken them on board. He buckled down to the restraints of school; kept out of trouble and put all his energies into his academic work. When Ruth had left England Ben was about to embark on his A Levels and in her regular letters to Ruth her mother had spoken proudly of his success. He had even managed to win a scholarship to a prestigious South African University where he had taken a First Class Degree in Mechanical Engineering. It was not long before he had his own business and a trophy wife. On one of his visits to England he had explained to Ruth that there was much about South Africa he hated; particularly the artificial insulated life of the privileged white minority but he put up with that for the sake of his wife and children.

In an ideal world Ben would have liked to return to Zimbabwe where at least there was no tradition of gun crime and violence was generally the preserve of the government against its political opponents. But Mugabe's Zimbabwe was no ideal world. After the early pragmatism and even optimism the new republic had gradually fallen apart. The economy collapsed; the currency became worthless and famine a reality. Unrest was brutally put down. Those brave enough to speak the truth were imprisoned and tortured and in some cases even 'disappeared'. Ruth read about these disasters in the English papers and, when journalists occasionally managed to evade detection, watched heart-rending news footage on television. She became increasingly fearful for her parents' safety and confided her fears to Ben. Should she try to persuade them to leave? She would perhaps be able to sort something out in England. Ben told her bluntly not to think about it. He had spent hours on phone calls trying to persuade his father to come to South Africa; he would find accommodation for them. The answer was always the same. "I've already been driven out of my homeland by one dictator and I'm not letting it happen again."

Johan Kreutz had been two years old in 1938 when he had escaped with his parents from Nazi Germany. His father, Stefan, had been a successful Hamburg dentist and in normal times Johan could have looked forward to a comfortable bourgeois middle class upbringing; his mind would have been cultivated by exposure to music and literature and in due course, it had been assumed, he would have inherited his father's practice. Those assumptions proved as brittle as the glass in the shop windows shattered by Hitler's thugs on Krystal Nacht. Anti-Semitism had been stoked by the Third Reich for several years before it exploded in an orgy of violence and discrimination. Johan's father had tried to ignore it initially, unable to believe a sophisticated and cultured country like Germany would spawn such hatred. By the end of 1938 it was impossible to ignore the dangers. Violence against Jews on the streets was becoming commonplace. The windows of his surgery had been daubed with swastikas. Neighbours he had been on friendly terms with for years seemed to shy away from him but one, a particularly pleasant man, had stopped him in the street and, after looking around nervously, had whispered urgently, "You have to get out. Now. While you still can!"

Stefan stumbled as if sleepwalking through the next few weeks. His wife, whose health had never been robust, was paralysed by fear as the anti-Jewish street demonstrations grew more violent and more frequent. Stefan knew flight offered the only hope of survival. But where could they go? He had no relatives outside of Germany except for a cousin in South Africa whom he had not seen for twenty years; Cousin Ernst who had been something of the black sheep of the family and had run off at 16 to take his chance in the world. Stefan had dutifully maintained contact with Ernst with occasional letters and knew that his cousin had done well for himself in Africa. In desperation Stefan wrote to Ernst and asked for help and by return received a reply. "Come now. I will help you." In a few days Stefan was able to book passage from Hamburg to Cape Town where Ernst would meet them. The house had to be abandoned and such valuables as they could transport stowed away in several cabin trunks. Thus they abandoned their comfortable life and faced an uncertain future in a country of which they knew little.

Ruth's father had, of course, been only a baby and could remember nothing of the escape to Africa but she had listened with awe as a child when he pieced together her family's story. Ernst had been as good as his word and met them off the boat at Cape Town but then explained they could not stay in South Africa as their status as German Jews was unclear. He had told them in Rhodesia, where he had settled, regulations were less stringently enforced and so straight off the boat Ernst bundled them aboard the overnight train to Bulawayo. Exhausted and disorientated the three members of the Kreutz family were then driven in an open truck, their cabin trunks around them, some one hundred miles out in the bush to a lonely gold mine where Ernst showed them their new home. It was little more than a one-roomed shack with a cold water tap and an outside lavatory. Mrs Kreutz wept uncontrollably as she remembered the comforts of her house in Hamburg. Her husband awkwardly held her close in comfort and tried to reassure her: "We are together and we are alive."

Ruth found it hard to comprehend how her grandparents had survived. They had not lived long enough for her to have ever known them but they had brought with them from Germany a few family photographs which Ruth had been fascinated by as a child and had asked her father endlessly for details about these solemn-looking people posing awkwardly in sepia formality. She could barely imagine how her grandparents had coped with the hardship of life in the Bush. Sadly, Mrs Kreutz had not lasted long. Her asthma was aggravated by the dust of the mine workings and she seemed to fade away, as Ruth's father explained. Stefan proved more resilient. His dental qualifications were not recognised in Rhodesia and he even had to check in with the local police as a German alien once the war started, although why it should be thought a Jewish refugee from Nazi persecution might be a friend of Hitler was beyond him. Stefan was not really a practising Jew but Ruth, as she grew older and read more, wondered if somewhere in his psyche was the Jewish instinct for survival; for starting again after pogroms and diaspora.

Ernst had made his money by wheeling and dealing in gold and he frequently told Stefan that he had made every penny by his own efforts; his family had washed their hands of him as a boy and that only Stefan had bothered to keep in touch and that is why, Ernst implied, he had felt obligated to help. But the help was not unbounded. He had provided his cousin with basic accommodation and in return for it he expected Stefan to work. Fortunately his dental training had bestowed on Stefan certain mechanical and manipulative skills. He told Ernst that the drill he had used in Hamburg on his patients' teeth was but a miniature version of the drills used to extract the underground ore. He was an intelligent man and he quickly mastered the skills to maintain and adapt the mine machinery. Ernst did not pay him much but, after the first year, enough to afford to rent a better appointed home: a bungalow that had been built for the previous mine owner. It had a kitchen, a sitting room, two bedrooms and a veranda where at the end of a long day on the mine he and Mrs Kreutz would take a small glass of rough Rhodesian brandy, in the finest cut glass goblets they had brought with them in the cabin trunks, and watch whilst their son played in the red dust at their feet. It was only two years after their arrival that Mrs Kreutz died but Stefan bore the loss well. Perhaps the traumas of his recent experiences had numbed his capacity for grief.

A black maid and a gentle and dedicated houseboy, Joseph, saw to all the domestic chores. Every day Johan trotted off with his father and watched him working on the mine machinery and sometimes, to his delight, he would be allowed to make small adjustments with a screwdriver or spanner. But soon he was plucked from the environment of the mine to attend boarding school in Bulawayo. He put up with it uncomplainingly and was a serious and capable student but at the age of sixteen was happy enough to leave. There was no money for him to continue with his education and anyway he knew what he wanted to do with his life. He joined his father full time on the mine. There was a post war boom in the price of gold and Ernst was able to expand and invest in new machinery so there was no shortage of work. As time passed Stefan found some of the heavy work more taxing and was happy to leave more of it to his son. Johan was equal to the challenge and still found time to follow his own dream. He was determined to find gold. On Sundays when the mine shut down for the day he would head out into the bush in an old pickup he had restored and seek out old mine workings which had long been abandoned in the hope there were unworked seams still waiting to be discovered. Like so many before him he never found his gold but as he would later explain to Ruth the search for it had taken him into the wild heart of Africa. He had found a peace and a majesty there which could restore his soul. Ruth, as a child, never fully understood that but later she did. Sometimes, when she could get away and get out on her own onto the moors in Cornwall, she could sense something of her father's response to the empty solitude.

"Flight ZA 239 now boarding, Gate 4."

Ben turned to Ruth who was half asleep on the sofa. "Come on then, they must have found some strong elastic."

Ruth made a face at him and struggled to her feet. "Don't Ben. I hate flying at the best of times."

Ben just laughed and helped her stand and they trekked off to the departure gate.

To Ruth's great relief the short flight to Bulawayo was uneventful. The plane was less than half full. A group of high-ranking army officers occupied the front row of seats; their uniforms heavy with gold brocade and medals. The flight attendants hovered round them nervously and ignored the rest of the passengers who had chosen to seat themselves at the back of the plane as far away as possible from the military. Ruth and Ben had a row of seats to themselves; in front of them a couple of Indian businessmen were talking quietly as they examined spreadsheets and did occasional computations on their calculators. Ben whispered to Ruth that in his experience even in the most dangerous and difficult hotspots in the world you would always find Indian businessmen looking to do deals. He always found their presence reassuring; admired their ability to ignore anything that was irrelevant to their commercial focus.

In the rows behind Ruth and Ben sprawled a party of

middle-aged American men. Their clothes explained their journey. They wore expensive and pristine Bush shorts and hunting jackets and some had not even bothered to remove wide-brimmed Safari hats. All had expensive cameras around their necks. They spoke loudly and laughed noisily as they bantered.

"Mugabe is desperate for foreign currency," Ben explained in a low voice, "so the National Game Parks are touted as a chance for rich Americans to bag some of the Big Five which will be herded in front of them. Trophies to show back home and an exotic change from Elk and Bears or whatever."

Ruth shook her head in despair. "That's so sad."

Ben smiled wryly. "Don't worry. I doubt they'll shoot much. Poverty and famine means most of the game has been poached or eaten."

"It sounds desperate."

Ben was suddenly serious. "It's a desperate country, Ruth. You have to understand that. You know I've kept a small office going here, not that it does much but I guess it eases my guilt a bit for running away, so I came over once or twice a year to check up on Mum and Dad really, and each time you think it can't get worse it does."

"I don't know how they coped."

"Well, you know Dad. No tin pot dictator was going to shift him. And at least he had his German pension. The Euro could buy quite a lot here. And he had the sun and until the last few months he could still get out in the Bush." He laughed. "And still look for gold."

Ruth smiled. "He never lost that yearning did he? He loved the excitement of it; the freedom of the Bush. He told me once he had to thank Hitler for his life. But for him he would have been condemned to be a Hamburg dentist." She paused and looked at her brother. "Did he enjoy life, Ben?

I've always felt this guilt that I never came back. Never saw them after I was eighteen. I could have come; found the money from somewhere I suppose. I wrote to tell Dad I would come but he always said the same thing; told me never to come back because it would break my heart."

Neither of them spoke for a few moments. When Ben spoke it was in reassurance. "Dad never asked for much, you know that. I think he was conscious of how close he had been to suffering the fate of the millions of German Jews who couldn't get out. He said he was lucky to have a life and he was determined to make the most of it. And he did."

Ruth nodded. "All by his own efforts. He was a tough one. Becoming a mining engineer and then raising a family."

"And then," Ben reminded her, "when the Independence war made it too dangerous to work on those lonely mines he moved into town and started again; fixing broken machines; mending cars; paying our school fees and coping with Mum."

Ruth laughed. "That too." Their mother had been difficult. Life continually bewildered her. It was not her fault. She had been one of a large family with no money. Peggy's education had been basic and had not equipped her to make her way in the world. She was young, pretty in a doll-like way, and vulnerable, when she met Johan. One of her brothers worked on the mine and she came to live with him when her mother died. It was not a suitable environment for a young naïve girl and she was desperately unhappy. Johan befriended her out of pity, Ruth suspected, and became her protector and provider. As a sort of logical procession to their relationship they quietly got married, persuading two passers-by in the street outside the registry office to act as witnesses.

Perhaps surprisingly, the marriage worked. Peggy had found a protector. When they moved into town she could aspire to a life beyond her early dreams. The German government belatedly acknowledged their debt to the Jews forced to flee Hitler. There was compensation for Stefan and, later, a pension for Johan. The money enabled Stefan to buy a comfortable Bulawayo house where he lived out a peaceful retirement looked after by the faithful Joseph. When he died the house passed to Johan and Peggy. Joseph came with the house and with the help of black maids took the burden of homemaking off Peggy's grateful shoulders. That left her free to shop, to get her hair done, and become a staunch member of the Baptist Church where she even overcame the shock of a black Pastor. She fussed over her children: trying, in vain, to force Ruth into pretty dresses and demure behaviour and forever nagging Ben to slick down his hair.

Thinking about her mother now Ruth felt an empty sadness. She had to accept she had run away from the life her mother had planned for her. She knew it was a sort of betrayal. She turned to Ben for reassurance. "They were all right weren't they? In spite of everything?"

"They coped. Dad had his German pension which meant they could still afford the basics: when they could get them. He could still drive into town when there was any fuel. And they could afford to keep Joseph on for a bit."

"What happened to Joseph?"

"Aids I suspect. Mum said it was pneumonia, of course."

Ruth sighed. "Poor Joseph. I remember he was such a sweet guy."

"They had to manage without servants after that. Not a problem for Dad but Mum played the martyr."

Ruth laughed. "She was good at that."

Ben nodded but then looked away from Ruth and out of the smeared window at the far distant emptiness of the Bush below them. "Except at the end. After the stroke. She was helpless; bedridden, could hardly speak. But she never complained then. She had her faith of course but I think she knew she had been lucky in life. Lucky to have met Dad."

Ruth felt the tears pricking her eyes. "I should have come."

Ben turned back to her. "No point. She didn't recognise me. Fortunately she didn't last long after the second stroke."

"I spoke with Dad on the phone but you never really knew what he was feeling. He always told me he was OK."

"Yes. He never allowed himself the luxury of feeling sorry for himself or complaining about life."

"I suppose he was always aware that but for the grace of his Jewish God he would have had no life."

"He never spoke about his Jewish God; never went near a synagogue."

Ruth shook her head. "Maybe, but he knew what he was. It set him apart. He never really fitted in with the English Rhodesians. I think, to be honest, he found them a pretty crude lot. He may only have been a baby when he came here but I think there was something in his cultural DNA which set him apart."

"'How shall we sing the Lord's song in a strange land'?" He laughed. "Bob Marley."

Ruth poked him playfully on the shoulder. "The Psalms before that I think." Her mood changed. "You know Ben I sometimes feel that."

"Feel what?"

"That I am stranger in a land to which I don't belong. Am I English? Am I Jewish?"

Ben shook his head. "Or just a wild colonial girl?"

"I'm serious Ben," Ruth protested.

"Well don't be. Just be like Dad. No agonising self-appraisal."

"Is that how you cope, Ben?"

Ben fixed her with an unsmiling stare. "How else can you survive on this bloody continent? Every day you see stuff which could wrench your guts out if you let it. If you stopped for a minute to doubt or to question you would be lost. You just have to keep running."

"But where to, Ben?"

Ben shrugged, "In my case Australia or New Zealand perhaps. Canada even."

Ruth was shocked. "I didn't know you were planning to leave."

"I don't want my sons growing up behind security fences; afraid to go out of the house. What sort of life is that?" He smiled at Ruth. "You remember the freedom we had?"

Ruth grinned at him. "Tracking imaginary leopards."

They were both quiet for a moment in remembrance. Then the engine noise changed and the plane banked. Ben looked at his watch. "Nearly there." He lowered his voice and spoke intently to Ruth, "Now remember, the less you say and the less you know the better. The story is we are here to clear up our father's affairs."

Ruth protested. "But that's true."

Ben permitted himself a mirthless smile. "Up to a point."

"And you have all the documents? Death certificate; power of attorney and so on?"

"I do. And I can tell you they cost a small fortune to get. Luckily, Temba, the guy who runs my office here, knows the right palms to grease."

"Is he the one who arranged the funeral?"

"Yes. Very simple affair. He was the only mourner. I couldn't get there."

"He died so suddenly."

"Just like him. Didn't want a fuss. The certificate says heart failure, but I wonder."

"What do you wonder, Ben?"

"Whether he had just had enough. Since Mum died he had no need to carry on. He couldn't drive anymore because his eyesight was going. Couldn't get out prospecting. There was growing violence everywhere. He had no social contacts. He told me he had taken to sleeping with a gun by his bedside."

Ruth buried her head in her hands, "Dreadful."

"I pleaded with him to come to us; told him I would fetch him anytime but he wouldn't have it, said he wouldn't run for a second time in his life."

"You did all this Ben and I did nothing." Ruth looked at him in despair.

Ben shrugged. "What could you do?" He paused and looked quizzically at Ruth, "In your situation."

Ruth found it impossible to answer. She looked away.

Ben continued. "The last time we spoke, about a month ago, he said he was coping but his voice was different. He sounded weary; didn't really want to talk much. I was worried so next day I asked Temba to go round to check on him."

Ruth remembered. "He was the one that found him?"

"Yes, just slumped in a chair." Ben sighed. "Nothing out of place but he had that photo of Mum in his hand."

Ruth made no attempt to hide her tears now. Ben took her hand and held it firmly, "He had just had enough. It's not so sad, Ruth. At least no one drove him out; that would have been sad."

Within minutes the wheels were down and the shuddering reverse thrust of the engines slowed them to a taxiing pace which took them to the basic and shabby terminal building. The mood in the cabin changed. The hunters began to noisily unload their gear from their overhead lockers and the Indian businessmen put away their calculators. In the front seats a few of the generals stood and stretched and straightened their uniforms. One or two of them seemed to stare questioningly in Ruth's direction so she turned her head and fumbled with her seat belt.

The Army Officers did not demean themselves with Immigration formalities but strode straight to the black limos awaiting them, complete with their motorcycle outriders. As Ben waited in the queue for Passport Control and watched the Generals depart, he whispered to Ruth, "The next snouts in the trough."

Ruth raised her eyebrows in question.

Ben kept his voice low. "Mugabe is 91 for God's sake. He plans to carry on but the vultures are circling. Give him a year or two at the most."

"Then what?" Ruth asked.

Ben shrugged. "More of the same. You remember what Dad used to say? 'There is no hope for Africa.'"

"I tried not to believe him. Thought people would see what was going on; how they were being betrayed."

Ben shook his head. "No chance. They are fed lies and false promises. Question anything and Mugabe's goons will come for you. It's hard to be brave when you're powerless isn't it?"

Before Ruth could reply they were called forward for the laborious passport examination and then form filling at Immigration Control. They explained several times to various officials the purpose of their visit was to settle the affairs of their recently deceased father. Ben produced the necessary documentary evidence of their relationship to the late Johan Kreutz. Ruth could sense her brother's growing impatience with the protracted bureaucracy and at one point she laid a restraining hand on his arm. Finally, Ben asked, with exaggerated politeness, if he might speak with the

Chief Immigration Officer as a matter of extreme sensitivity. This had the effect of unearthing a besuited and perspiring functionary from an inner office. Ben made a show of lowering his voice but Ruth was able to hear the odd word. There was talk of meeting with an Air Marshall Ovanga and business crucial to national security. Ben invited the official to contact the Air Vice Marshall if he required corroboration but the offer was declined and he and Ruth were waved through without further delay.

Standing in the burning sun outside the terminal, Ruth looked questioningly at her brother but he merely grinned and tapped the side of his nose. Before Ruth could press the point a loud voice hailed them. Waiting by the open door of a spacious and polished saloon car was a large African man. He was dressed elegantly; his jacket and tie incongruous in the heat and dust. Dark glasses could not hide a livid scar on his right cheek. "Mr Ben?" he shouted.

Picking up their bags Ruth and Ben walked towards the car. Ben stretched out a hand in greeting and he and the African exchanged the traditional reverse handshake. "You must be Mobil. Temba told me to expect you."

Mobil nodded and opened the rear doors for them. He made no acknowledgement and offered no greeting to Ruth. He quickly got behind the wheel and soon they had left the airport behind and were speeding along the empty road towards Bulawayo. Ruth tried to ask Ben what was going on but he shushed her and she fell silent, aware of Mobil's scrutiny from his reflection in the driving mirror. Ruth began to recognise some of the landmarks as they neared town. It was more than fifteen years since she had left but the broad boulevards of the town seemed unchanged if a little more pot-holed. The stores where she had shopped with clothes for her mother were largely gone; shuttered or operating as basic African markets. There were long queues at some of these with people waiting patiently for the few commodities on offer. There were even longer queues outside banks. The pavement cafes, where Ruth and her school friends had sipped frothy coffees in pretend sophistication, were gone. A few bars remained open but looked depressed and uninviting. There were people about but the bustle and vitality of the street life she remembered as a girl was absent. People looked worn and dejected: no one seemed to laugh or smile. They shrank back on the pavements when groups of armed soldiers patrolled amongst them. Ruth remembered her father's words telling her she should never come back. Now she knew why.

Mobil swung the car into an empty parking lot in front of a hotel. It was an outpost of a major international chain but clearly just about hanging on. The paint was peeling, the pool full of stagnant water, security guards stood at the entrance. Mobil killed the engine and turned back to speak to Ben. "I will wait here. Be quick. There is much to do." He paused. "It will be expensive."

Ben had clearly been expecting this. He reached in his jacket pocket for his wallet. Ruth could see American Dollars of high denomination. He counted a wad out and handed them to Mobil who counted them again and nodded. Ben returned his wallet to his jacket and smiled briefly at Mobil. "The rest when we leave."

"Who the hell is Mobil?" Ruth demanded angrily. She and Ben had checked in and she had quickly stood under the lukewarm trickle of the shower and changed out of her travelling clothes. She found Ben in his room. He was sitting on the bed sifting through various documents.

"He's a fixer. Temba says he's the best."

Ruth shuddered. "He looks like a crook."

Ben laughed at her naivety. "Of course he's a crook. But he's our crook."

"And why is he called Mobil?"

"It seems he worked as a fixer for the oil company in Mozambique. He's also supposed to have been one of Mugabe's elite bodyguards for a bit. He knows everybody and everything and how much everyone costs."

"It's terrible we have to use people like that."

Ben put down his papers and looked grimly at his sister. "Look, Ruth. You left this place as a girl. You have no idea how things work here now. Tell me. Do you want this money or do you want to hang on to your liberal conscience? If you do we can get the next plane out now."

Ruth felt both shock and shame. Ben had never spoken to her like that before but she knew she deserved it. She did want the money. Why else was she here? And Ben was doing all this for her. He didn't need to. She could not hold back tears of despair. She moved to Ben and as he sat on the bed she stood over him and put her hand on his shoulder. "I'm so sorry Ben. I must seem so ungrateful. I'm so useless. If my life wasn't such a mess I needn't have put you through all this."

Neither of them moved for a moment, then Ben stood and gave his sister a reassuring hug. "Come on, Ruth. Better wash your face. We don't Mobil to think we're a soft touch."

The rest of the day passed in a blur. Ruth felt she was a spectator most of the time. Mobil ignored her and Ben was totally focussed on the minefield he told her he needed to navigate. First they had gone to a Solicitor's office where at least Ruth felt she knew what was going on. There, Ben had assigned his share of their father's house to Ruth and she had the documents proving sole ownership. The next step was to get a Judge to put his stamp of authentication on the new document. Mobil had lined up a likely judge. He drove them to the meeting in the Judge's chambers. They filed in before a small shifty-eyed old man who bizarrely kept his full wig on as he spoke to them. His desk was piled high with papers thick with dust. He must have known full well what Mobil required of him but he obviously decided he might milk a bit more out of the situation. Ben explained to him the need for his stamp of approval for the house sale documents. The judge looked as if this was the first he had heard of the matter and pointed apologetically to the dust-gathering piles of papers on his desk. He explained these things take time and he had more pressing matters to deal with. Ruth felt defeated by this. Was the whole situation hopeless?

Mobil politely asked the judge if he might discuss this new development with his client in private. The judge happily nodded his agreement. Mobil led them out into the corridor and conferred urgently with Ben. The wallet came out and Ben counted out more dollars. Mobil returned alone to the judge. Ten minutes later he re-appeared with a wide smile on his face waving the duly stamped papers.

Ben told her as they drove across town that this was now the really tricky part of the whole business. They left the outskirts of Bulawayo and after a few miles pulled off the main road and drove down a private drive past well-manicured lawns to an imposing mock Gothic mansion. Ruth remembered it. One of her wealthy school friends had invited her to a birthday party there. In those days it had called itself something castle – she couldn't remember the precise name – but it had been the exclusive watering hole of affluent white Rhodesians. She reminded Ben of that. He remembered too but explained that it had been acquired by the ruling party as, ostensibly, a conference centre. But in reality it was a pleasure dome for the ruling hierarchy; a place to entertain their mistresses or eat expensive meals with delicacies often paid for from the foreign aid fund. As Mobil brought the car to a crunching halt on the gravel Ruth wondered what on earth they were doing there. She was still wondering half an hour later. Mobil and Ben had been met at reception by a hard-eyed security man who had checked his list of expected visitors and beckoned the two men to follow him. He had called out to a young woman in formal if incongruous waitress attire to look after the lady. So Ruth found herself sitting with a pot of rather good coffee in a faded chintz armchair nervously asking herself what the hell was going on? A few others sat about taking tea or coffee. Ruth could imagine herself in a 'seen better days' English seaside hotel out of season: except there was no sea and the clientele was black and mostly in heavy and bemedalled military uniforms.

When Ben and Mobil returned they seemed tense and anxious to be away. Ben beckoned and Ruth quickly put down her cup and followed them out to the car. Only when they were nearly back in Bulawayo did Ben begin to relax. He told Mobil to drop them off at their hotel and to meet them there in the morning to take them to the airport where, he reminded Mobil, he would 'sort out the money'.

Ruth and Ben dined in the empty hotel dining room. The food was indifferent but neither had any appetite. Ruth wanted to ask Ben about the meeting but he told her it was best she knew nothing yet. He would tell her on the plane once they were safely away. Ruth did not sleep well and it was a relief to see Mobil appear to drive them to the airport. The flight to Johannesburg was only an hour delayed and it took most of that time to clear the lumbering security checks. Ruth noticed that Ben seemed particularly relieved to get his passport back. Before he had left them Ben had handed over the balance of Dollars to Mobil who had gripped Ben's hand and assured him they would always be brothers. He continued to ignore Ruth who fervently hoped she would never see him again.

Ben undid his seatbelt and relaxed. The flight was practically empty. With no military to attend to the cabin crew were happy, when Ben produced a few dollars, to find some whisky. Ben raised his miniature bottle in toast to Ruth. "A bit early but well deserved."

Ruth sipped her drink; relishing its fierce comfort. "So, Ben, can you tell me now?"

Ben looked around. The cabin crew were chatting to each other at the back of the plane. He spoke softly. "Air Vice Marshall Ovanga."

"He exists then?" Ruth asked.

"He exists all right. One of the rising stars."

"So what about him?"

Ben took another sip of his whisky. "He bought your house."

"What?"

"Not at a price you might have hoped for but real money. Not worthless Zim Dollars."

"What does he want with the house? Is he going to live in it?"

Ben laughed at the idea. "Of course not. He wants to add it to his property portfolio. He's bright enough to see the way things are heading; the economy going tits up. It's his investment against that or against losing favour with the party fat cats."

"So how was it done? Isn't it illegal to send dollars out of the country?"

"It is. But not if it is for Government procurement."

"Buying a house?"

"No. Purchasing high-tech hardware items for the air force." He laughed. "We make them."

Ruth stared at him. "Sorry, Ben, you've lost me."

"Simple, really. He ships out a hundred thousand dollars to a South African bank from a government account and I provide invoices for that amount."

"But no hardware?"

"Of course not. Nobody checks on him. So your house is purchased with Mugabe's money. That make you feel better?"

Ruth looked at Ben in astonishment. "And the money is really there?"

"It surely is. I've got your English bank details so I'll send it on. Be there when you get back."

Ruth took Ben's hand. "How can I ever thank you for this?"

"No need. You watched my back when I was a kid. Payback time."

"This gives me a chance, Ben."

Ben seemed to consider his words carefully. "Take it. Just for you. You and the girls."

Ruth was aware he did not mention Simon. She looked away and stared out of the window. The plane was floating above a cushion of white clouds. It was hard to believe that a different reality lay beneath.

THREE

CORNWALL 2023

In the cramped studio which Luke hired for an hour each week the recording light still showed a steady green. Luke held up one palm to Dave to indicate the time left. Dave took a quick sip of water and composed his features in the look of furrowed concentration he claimed enabled him to play his gormless character with conviction. It may only have been a podcast but he drew on his theatrical training; a one-time devotee of method acting he could not just read the lines Luke had written for him. He had, as he put it, to actually be Pasco; the dim-witted good old Cornish boy who, in their weekly exchanges, was the hapless foil to Luke's cerebral scalpel.

"So let me get this clear, Prof," Dave pondered in his exaggerated Cornish burr, "you're telling me that our lads down in Newlyn can't catch no more fish than they was catching before this Brexit business."

"No, Pasco," Luke replied with patient condescension. "They can catch a small amount more; a slight increase in the quota."

"That's good isn't it?"

"It would be if they could sell it."

"Why can't they? I like a nice bit of Cod, or Pollock even. Tamsin does a lovely fish stew—"

Luke cut in as the script required. "I dare say, Pasco, but the home market is less than one percent of the potential market."

"Well they can sell it to the foreigners then. They like our fish the boys tell me."

"Indeed they do. In fact the industry was totally dependent on the export market."

"Well, there you are then. They can catch more fish and sell it to the Frenchies. No problem."

"I'm afraid it's not that simple Pasco."

"Why not?"

"Since the Brexit fishing deal the EU has introduced new regulations. The industry was totally unprepared. Fish is rotting on the quayside waiting for Vets' certificates and hundreds of new forms to be completed. The price has collapsed and skippers are being urged to catch less."

"Yeah. But they'll sort it out won't they?"

"Your faith in our Government does you credit, Pasco."

"Thank you."

"But I have to tell you it is totally misplaced. The EU says the new regulations are permanent. Our leaders are huffing and puffing and hoping it will all go away. A cynic would say no one at Westminster really cares because the fishing industry represents less than one percent of our GDP."

"That's not what they said when we voted. All the boys went for Brexit: all those promises."

"That was then, Pasco. This is now."

Luke mimed cutting his throat and held up one finger.

Dave gave it his thespian all. "Don't seem right to me,

Prof. They tell you one thing and then they tell you something else. I get fair mazed with it all."

"Welcome to the real world, Pasco."

Luke held up a restraining hand for a few seconds and then switched off the recording machine.

Dave flung down his script and looked at Luke accusingly. "'Fair mazed'. Surely you can do better than that, Luke?" His accent now had lost any concession to Cornwall. He spoke as the classical actor he had once been.

Luke grinned at him. "It tests your range, Dave, and you do it so well. You know you have quite a following now. Our little podcast does not go unheard."

Dave seemed mollified by that. "It keeps one's eye in I suppose."

"Until the call comes, Dave."

Dave groaned. "I gave up on that years ago. I am reconciled to my fate."

Luke began clearing away the equipment. "Not that bad is it; running the Arts Centre?"

"Put it like that it sounds very grand, but as you well know putting on amateurish dross in a converted Methodist Chapel is not the equivalent of being Director of the National Theatre. And I doubt in that job you have to run the bar as well."

"Talking of which can I buy you a pint? I accept it is pitiful reward for your talents but—"

"I know." Dave stood. "Leave it for another time."

Luke gathered together the discarded scripts. "For when the ship comes in."

Dave did not make a move for the door. He looked quizzically at Luke. "You still get a buzz out of this don't you? This telling it as it is."

Luke shrugged. "The nature of the beast I suppose."

"But," Dave persisted, "you were at the centre of things once. Cutting edge and all that." Dave put on his declamatory voice. "You stalked the corridors of power."

"Is that what I did?"

"Don't deny it, I've been Googling you, Luke. You had it all once, didn't you? I've never asked you this before and it's none of my business but tell me Luke, where did it all go wrong?"

Luke looked at Dave as if deliberating his response. Then he turned away and put all his papers in a shabby briefcase. When he looked up Dave was still standing; awaiting reply. Luke smiled at him. "Let's say I flew too close to the sun."

Peter Rawlings passed a sheet of paper across his desk to Luke. "Not much I'm afraid. Our new owners are not big on culture."

Luke studied the paper he had been handed for a few seconds and then folded it and put it in his jacket pocket. "Two gallery openings and a one man Dickens evening at the Arts Centre. Is that it?"

"Afraid so, and no more than five hundred words on each. Advertising space is at a premium now."

Luke shrugged. "Soon you'll be a freebie; pushed through letterboxes with the pizza ads and the takeaway menu from the local Chinese."

The Editor of the West Cornwall Clarion managed a thin smile. "Thank you. And when that happens we certainly won't be able to afford the luxury of our freelance Arts Correspondent."

"Then what will I do? Have to look for a real job I suppose."

Peter sat back in his chair and looked quizzically at Luke. "As we both know, Luke, your problem is that you don't need a real job." He paused. "Do you?"

Luke returned Peter's stare. "Perhaps not the money."

"Certainly not the money, Luke. You forget I was there too. Not in your league perhaps but finger on the pulse and all that. Well in the picture."

"True." Luke held up his hands in mock surrender. "And I do appreciate your discretion, Peter."

"Good." Peter laughed. "I wouldn't want to be the one to unmask you; to let the world know there is more to you than the apparently penniless scribe scraping a precarious living as a part time hack."

"I don't think the world would be very interested. Not down here. Nobody really cares what you did or where you came from."

"That's why you chose Cornwall, was it?"

"That, and the fact it was as far from London as I could get."

Peter understood that. "Of course. They kept you on as a Stringer didn't they? Part of the deal."

Luke nodded. "Which means there is no need for them to send a staffer all the way down here to check out a story if I can do the leg work for them."

"Good thinking. Has it worked out?"

"The odd commission now and then. Nothing really."

"Well, as the editor of the Clarion I know only too well what a struggle it is down here to find anything newsworthy to print each week."

Luke grinned. "I had noticed." Then he looked thoughtfully at Peter. "Don't you miss it? The buzz. The feeling you might be making a difference."

Peter took a moment of reflection. "Of course I miss that but," he sighed, "what I don't miss is living on adrenalin; the crazy hours; the drinking. It was killing me. That's what my doctor said so Judith gave me an ultimatum. It was her and the kids or the job."

"No choice really."

"None. So when this came up I jumped at it. Came to Cornwall; the graveyard of ambition."

"No regrets?"

"Not a bit. The last couple of years have been great. The kids love it; Judith and I get time together."

"That's good." Luke got to his feet. "I'd better get on."

Peter looked at him. "None of my business of course but what about you? Has it worked for you?"

Luke shrugged. "It had to. I've had a few years to get used to it. Down-shifting I think they call it."

"I must say it was a surprise to come across you down here. I knew vaguely what happened but had no idea where you had gone."

"That was the point I think."

"Anyway, I'm pleased I persuaded you to freelance for us."

"Keeps my hand in, Peter."

Peter nodded. "Whilst you wait for the big break."

They both laughed at that. Luke made for the door but Peter had not finished. "If you ever did come across something major I would be the first to know, wouldn't I?"

Luke opened the door but turned back before leaving. "Probably the second Peter, or maybe the third." He smiled and closed the door behind him.

There was some warmth in the air now. It was still only early Spring but people were taking the air on the promenade, some in short sleeves, and a brave few even in shorts. Luke spotted an empty bench and sat facing the sea which shimmered and winked at the midday sun. He loosened his jacket, leaned back on the bench and stretched out in casual relaxation. He told himself, as he had many times before, there were compensations in his exile. Talking to Peter had stirred some of the old misgivings; the doubts and anxieties which he generally managed to keep at bay. He took himself to task now; telling himself he was past fifty for God's sake and he must accept that he had run his race: had his time centre stage. Of course it had not ended well. It was hard to forgive and forget; hard to shake off, even after nearly ten years, the feelings of bitter resentment which sometimes he imagined he could almost physically taste as bile in his mouth. But he had to remind himself that he was not an innocent in the whole wretched business. He had been naïve; or, worse than that, he had been selective in his moral judgement, ignoring or pretending not to see what was uncomfortable to confront.

The cackle of a gull distracted Luke from self-reproach. He sat up straight and took a deep breath of the sea air. Life was not so bad he reminded himself again. He had enough money to get by; a comfortable house which, albeit, he shared with his two tenants. He had cut down on the booze and he didn't smoke, so he could occasionally manage stiff walks on the cliff path without too much agony. He had no family to provide for and he had friends; perhaps not many and none too close, but enough to pass the time of day with. Only Dave and Peter had some inkling of his past life and that was the way Luke liked it. His pieces for the Clarion, and sporadic Stringer output, enabled him to pretend he was still a journalist and his recent Podcast – 'Pasco and the Prof' – had satisfyingly got under the skin of a few local politicians and Councillors. Dave had ironically remarked he was back in full cry as the crusading investigative Journalist he had once been. Luke's response was that he was not so much a Crusader any more but perhaps a Don Quixote. He smiled at that now as he buttoned his jacket and looked at his watch. Lunchtime; Paula would be expecting him.

FOUR

"Hold that stretch. If your balance is a problem grab the back of the chair. That's right Eileen... now we hold it for three. One, two, three. Good. Now straighten up and breathe deeply; from the diaphragm. Well done. Now relax. Good session ladies. Same time next week." Ruth switched off her CD player and began to collect in the exercise equipment from the class, chatting encouragingly to them as she did. She was glad she had started a class for seniors. They were more appreciative, even grateful, that anyone bothered with them. Ruth had to admit she was happier these days working at the slower pace pensioner classes demanded. She was over forty now and had to push herself to the limit to drive on the already super fit and toned young Lycra brigade who came to her classes at the Leisure Centre. She was not sure for how much longer her body would be able to cope with that. So, whilst Simon had grumbled about the expense, even though he wasn't paying, it had been a good investment to go on a course to retrain as a Fitness Instructor for the over fifties. This class was going well now and that helped with the mortgage. But Ruth needed more work. Simon had really stopped contributing; muttering vague promises and excuses which Ruth knew better than to believe.

"That seemed to go well, Ruth." Helen, who managed the Day Care Centre, handed over the cash she had collected from the class members and gave it to Ruth, who put it in her shoulder bag without counting it.

"I think they liked it."

"Well, they've all signed up again for next week. And a couple of new ones."

Ruth smiled. "That's good."

Helen moved to switch on an electric kettle next to the sink in her small office. She turned to Ruth. "Time for a coffee or tea? You must be parched after all that jumping about."

Ruth glanced at the clock on the office wall. "Thanks. Coffee would be great. I think I've got time."

Helen poured out two cups and handed one to Ruth. "Another class?"

Ruth hesitated. "No." She looked nervously at Helen. "Don't laugh but it's an interview for a part time job."

Helen did laugh. "Sorry, Ruth: but a job interview? How can you possibly find time for another job? You always seem to be running from one class to another as it is."

Ruth shook her head. "It might look that way but it's not enough. Not the way things are."

Helen had known Ruth for nearly five years now, since she had moved to Penzance and started classes there. They were not particularly close friends: Ruth didn't seem to have many of those and seldom talked about her life outside of her work but Helen had gathered the impression that there were domestic tensions. She chose her words carefully now. "Things difficult at the moment are they?"

Ruth sipped her coffee and looked away. "Not great."

Helen felt she should offer more. "If I can help."

Ruth put down her cup and managed a smile. "Thanks,

Helen, but I'll sort it." She looked again at the clock and then stood. "I'd better get on. Won't do to be late."

Helen stood too and carried the empty cups across to the sink. "Well good luck with whatever it is."

Paula Price was standing with one foot in the kitchen and one in the back yard; leaning against the frame of the open door. She flicked the ash from her cigarette into the yard. This was her one concession to Health and Safety regulations. She was virtually a chain smoker, pausing between cigarettes only long enough to stir the soup or put the quiche in the oven. Making cakes required frequent breaks to fit in alfresco puffs. When she was not smoking, because indoor attention was required for the completion of some complicated food preparation, she refreshed herself with frequent swigs from an always available bottle of strong cider. The smoking and the drinking would surely have taken its toll on even the sturdiest of individuals but Paula seemed indestructible. She proudly boasted that she was a functioning alcoholic; as if claiming membership of an exclusive club. In a town not short of eccentrics she stood out. Nobody was quite sure how she had washed up in West Cornwall and none dared to ask. There were rumours that she had been a high-powered businesswoman and rubbed shoulders with the movers and the shakers and that some scandal had forced her to make a run for it. Or perhaps, more prosaically, the drink had become too much of an embarrassment for her corporate colleagues.

Luke had been amongst Paula's first customers. They had both arrived in Cornwall at about the same time and Luke, with a long established habit of eating out, had found in Paula's an establishment which chimed perfectly with his new lifestyle. The food was good and cheap and the company suitably raffish and unconventional to be of interest. He seemed to pass some test of acceptance in Paula's mind. She did not ask about his life or work: she was always too busy talking about her own concerns. She appeared to know he was some sort of journalist and that, apparently, was sufficiently different for Luke to be looked upon as 'not too boring' which was not an accolade she attributed to many. Over time Luke became a bit more than a customer. Paula, unsurprisingly, was not very good at retaining staff. Luke had seen a succession of kitchen assistants and waitresses come and then more quickly go; often in tears. Only last week a young girl had walked out in the middle of a busy lunch session after Paula had yelled at her for serving tepid soup. In these frequent crises Luke had taken to lending a hand if things got desperate. He cleared plates from tables and put them in the dishwasher. Paula, without comment, one day showed him how to use the coffee machine and when it was quiet she would simply nod to him and point to the back door in the kitchen to indicate she was going out for a proper smoke whilst he kept an eye on things. No formal discussion was ever held to define Luke's role but after a year or so of his unofficial help Paula had brusquely said to him, "If you're going to make yourself useful you might as well have a free lunch." And that is how matters remained. Luke would spend a couple of hours at the café over the busy lunch time doing what was required and, in recompense, at two o clock he would sit down and eat his free lunch. If things were quiet Paula would sometimes join him and with no captive audience for her to perform for they would chat easily, even if Paula did most of the talking, but their conversation never ventured beyond the mundane: never became personal. That seemed to suit them both. Only once did Paula ever publicly allude to Luke's status in her cafe. He managed to spill a cup of coffee over a customer and stood in helpless apologetic embarrassment but Paula sailed over to the table where the accident had happened and breezily sponged down the damp casualty. She announced to the watching punters. "You must bear with him: he's a writer not a waiter." Even the sodden customer joined in the laughter.

Paula ground out her cigarette as Luke entered the kitchen. "How did it go?"

"OK. I think. Dave gave it his best shot."

"I'm sure he did," Paula grunted.

Luke looked at what was simmering on the stove. "What is it today?"

"Celeriac and apple. Pearls before swine."

Luke sniffed the air. "And in the oven?"

"Beef and courgette bake. Enough for ten."

"You expecting it to be busy?"

"Well, the sun is out." Paula stirred the soup with one hand and raised her glass of cider to her lips with the other.

"Right. Best get my pinny on." Luke unhooked a long Butcher's style apron from the back of the kitchen door and wriggled it over his head.

Paula looked at him appraisingly, "Hm." She took another generous mouthful of cider. "Just the two of us again I'm afraid."

"No response to your ad?"

"Only one. No one wants to work down here Luke: you know that. Sign on and surf is the Cornish mantra and as for—"

Luke interjected before Paula could work up a head of steam. "But you said one. One reply."

Paula stopped stirring the soup and fumbled in her apron pocket for a packet of cigarettes. She flipped one out and put it between her lips and then walked half out of the kitchen into the yard to light it. She drew in a deep lungful of nicotine and looked back at Luke. "She's coming at two. I don't hold out much hope."

"Why not?"

"She's not that young for a start."

Luke was puzzled. "Well that's good isn't it? Mature, experienced and all that."

Paula took another drag on her cigarette. "Set in her ways more likely. Untrainable."

Luke permitted himself a smile. "Well you didn't have much luck training some of the young ones."

Paula scowled at the memories. "Thick as two short planks most of them. Couldn't teach them anything."

"Maybe an older person will be different."

"I'm not holding my breath." She threw down her half smoked cigarette and stamped on it. Still holding the glass of cider she resumed stirring the soup. "You can sit in if you like."

Luke frowned. "Sit in on what?"

"The interview; if you want to call it that."

"I'm not management," Luke protested with mock humility.

"You certainly aren't but another opinion might be useful I suppose." She gave the soup a vigorous final whisk and then looked at Luke with something approaching a smile. "Even yours."

The café was nearly empty now after the busy lunch session. Just a couple of 'lingerers' as Paula dubbed them, finishing off their coffees. Paula used the lull to disappear into the back yard for an uninterrupted smoke and Luke sat with his plate of beef and courgette bake, idly thumbing through a newspaper one of the customers had left behind. He looked up from his paper when the tinkling bell rigged to the café door announced the arrival of a new customer. Luke, trying not to express any irritation at this unwelcome interruption to his lunch, got up and arranged his features in a professional smile of welcome. He registered that this was not a regular customer; in fact she looked totally out of place in the louche ambiance of Paula's café. For a start she was wearing trainers and a close-fitting track suit which, Luke couldn't help but notice, suited her. Her legs were long and shapely, her posture upright and her brown hair was tied back in a neat ponytail. She wore no makeup but her complexion was clear and as she looked at Luke he registered disconcertingly wide almond eyes which now narrowed in uncertainty.

Luke pulled himself together. "What can I get you?"

"Nothing. Sorry. That must sound rude." She looked around nervously. "I am supposed to be meeting Miss Price."

Luke now understood. "Right. About the job is it?"

"Yes. The advert in the Clarion."

"Of course. I'll get her." He paused. "She's just taking a breather out the back." That seemed more tactful than announcing Paula was on her twentieth cigarette of the day. "Why don't you take a seat?" He gestured to the table where his lunch was now congealing. He hastily scooped up the plate and was aware of those wide brown eyes watching him as she sat.

"I'm sorry. I've interrupted your lunch."

"No problem."

"Do you work here?"

Luke laughed. "In a funny sort of way." He could see the confusion in her expression. "I'm Luke by the way. Luke Collins." He held out a hand in greeting.

"Ruth. Ruth Kreutz." She took his hand and managed a wary smile.

Luke carried his plate to the kitchen and put it on the draining board. He walked through the open kitchen door into the yard where Paula was perched on an upturned milk crate smoking. She looked up and muttered some obscenity under her breath as she reluctantly jettisoned the cigarette. She pushed herself upright and walked back into the kitchen. She turned and glared at Luke. "Come on then, let's get this over with."

Ruth got to her feet as Luke and Paula entered the café. She stood awkwardly as Paula stared in unconcealed dismay at her. "Don't tell me you're a fitness fanatic," she barked, by way of introduction.

Ruth looked down at her track suit. "I'm sorry but I've come straight from work. There was no time to change."

Paula slumped down heavily in a chair and gestured to Ruth to sit. "So what work is that, may I ask?"

"I'm a fitness instructor," Ruth said half-heartedly, as if anticipating the likely reaction.

Paula did not disappoint. "Well, I suppose someone has to be. So why do you want to swap that for working in my café?"

Ruth spoke more assertively now. "Not swap: combine."

"Two jobs? Well that's not unusual in Cornwall I suppose, for those who can be arsed to work," Paula conceded. "Do you have any experience of catering?"

"When I first came to England I worked in bars and restaurants for a couple of years."

"Came from where?" Paula seemed more interested in that than employment details.

"Rhodesia. Sorry, I mean Zimbabwe."

Luke, who was standing self-consciously observing the so called interview, could sense Paula's interest quicken slightly at the mention of Ruth's African connection. Paula had some affinity with people who, in her estimation, were a bit different, not 'boring and ordinary'.

"I don't suppose you've been back there?" Paula asked.

Ruth hesitated as if the question was some sort of trap. When she spoke it was softly. "Only once. Five years ago when my father died."

Paula digested that without comment. When she continued her tone was now brusque again. "Can you cook?"

"Family meals. Nothing exotic."

"You've got family then?"

"Two daughters."

Paula scowled. "Not little I hope; always ill and wanting their mother."

"Teenagers. Never wanting their mother."

Luke laughed at this flash of humour which caused Paula to look at him as if surprised he was still there. She turned her attention back to Ruth. "Not politically correct to ask this, so don't answer if you don't want to, but do you have any support at home should the kids need it and you have to work?"

Ruth hesitated as if unsure of her response. "I have a partner."

Paula nodded and then moved on. "It's not very exciting work here. Washing up, waiting on tables, serving teas and coffees." Then she allowed herself a smile, "And putting up with me."

Luke looked at Paula with astonishment. He had never known her be self-critical in any way before. Paula caught his look. She coughed and then turned back to Ruth. "You've met my colleague here," she said pointing at Luke.

Ruth nodded. "Yes. Briefly."

"He will show you how everything works. He's more patient than me." She made a show of whispering to Ruth. "Just don't tell him any of your secrets. He's a journalist."

Ruth looked at a loss. "A journalist? But I thought—"

Paula laughed. "As I said, to survive in Cornwall you need two jobs. It's just that he doesn't get paid for this one. Do you?"

Luke shrugged helplessly. Ruth now looked seriously confused.

Paula stood up. The interview was clearly over, "You know the hours and the wages, you can start on Monday. A month's trial." She paused and stared at Ruth. "That is if you want the job."

Ruth still seemed dazed but made an effort to focus. "Yes. Thank you. I'll see you on Monday then."

FIVE

"Surely you two have got homework?" Ruth's was a rhetorical question and her daughters did not favour her with a reply. Esther managed the put-upon scowl characteristic of sixteen year olds and struggled to her feet as if all the problems of the world were upon her shoulders. Reluctantly she put away her phone, with which she had been urgently communicating with friends she had left barely an hour ago, gathered together her school books and began to head out of the kitchen.

"Plate!" Ruth reminded her.

Wearily, Esther retraced her steps and with a martyr's sigh of resignation carried her supper plate from the table to the sink. Ruth tried not to smile. "Thank you."

Esther favoured her mother with a disbelieving shake of her head and stamped off upstairs. Once she had gone Ruth allowed herself to laugh. Had she been like that when she was sixteen? She hoped not, but life had been so much simpler then. No social media, no smart phones, no pressure on which trainers to wear; no preoccupation with gender identity and other sexuality issues. Ruth felt sorry for Esther and her friends; they were burdened too soon with concerns even adults struggled with. How innocent now her time with

Ben exploring the Bush seemed. Her mother had needed only to express her persistent concern that they would be eaten by lions. She thought of Ben now. He had phoned her a few weeks ago. The move to Australia had worked out well for him. He said they were all enjoying the new freedom and the boys were well into surfing and the laid-back 'no worries' culture. He said Ruth must bring out the girls to visit: he would pay their air fares. It was a kind thought but Ruth knew it would be a pipe dream. She made no comment at the time but, as ever, Ben had made no mention of Simon.

Ben had not taken to Simon when they met on his first visit to England. They had been living in a poky rented flat in South London and Ruth had been pregnant with Esther. Ben clearly felt his sister deserved better and that Simon should provide it. Ruth tried to explain that Simon was an artist with a precarious income; that he was not materialistic; that he was a spiritual person. Ben had not been impressed: his view of the world was so different from Simon's. Ruth accepted that her brother had inherited their father's genes. He saw husbands as protectors and providers. Not that Simon was her husband. They had agreed from the first – or at least Ruth had not argued – that the chains of matrimony were not for them. Simon chafed at formality, at restraint and regulation. He stated frequently that his was a free spirit and that as an artist he would not be confined and blinkered by petty bourgeois conventions.

It was that casual disdain for the ordinary which Ruth found so compelling when their relationship began. They had met at a Jazz club, after her first few months in London, where Simon with his tangled dreadlocks and craggy good looks seemed a magnet for several young women in the crowd so it was a surprise to Ruth when he shrugged off their attentions and came to join her, standing at the bar.

He bought her a drink in spite of her protestations and they chatted easily about the music. Time seemed to pass quickly and when the club closed Simon offered to walk her the short distance home: to the Earl's Court collective, as she described it. On the walk through London drizzle she found it surprisingly easy to tell Simon about herself. How she was taking the typical colonial year off to travel. When he asked her if she was going back to Zimbabwe she told him she was unsure. He had views on the situation there; blaming years of white oppression for the mess. Ruth neither agreed nor disagreed with him but changed the subject by asking him about himself. He was happy to talk about that. His parents, he claimed, were old hippies who still smoked pot and lived on a self-sustaining small holding in Mid Wales. He told Ruth he had never really fitted in at school but had found his true calling at Art College. He was in his last year now and when Ruth asked him what he was going to do afterwards he laughed and said, "Paint; what else?"

In fact it was not quite as easy as that. Simon decided after graduation that he would take a few months off to travel around Europe: ostensibly to visit the great galleries; the Prado, the Louvre, the Uffizi and so on. He told Ruth she should come with him. By this time they had become more than friends. Simon was an easy and intelligent companion. He took Ruth to numerous gallery opening shows; to small off beat music venues and plays staged in rooms above pubs. There were frequent parties with his Art College friends: with cannabis, which only seemed to make Ruth fall asleep and on one miserable occasion, coaxed on by Simon, she dropped some acid which made her violently sick. Simon had laughed at that and at Ruth's obvious unease in the bohemian world he introduced her to. He said he found it endearing and joked she was a beacon of purity in a sea of depravity.

Ruth went with him on the Europe trip. She worked double shifts in the pub to save up for it but Simon seemed to fund it from his student loan. They were away for nearly six months: until the money ran out and they had to sell their blood in Athens to pay for the flight home. It was a memorable time. Ruth marvelled at everything and Simon took pleasure in her obvious excitement. The sun seemed to shine throughout and they pitched their small tent under the stars wherever Simon decided was a suitable spot; whether camping was allowed or not. They drank cheap red wine and made love most nights. Ruth could not believe she would ever be so happy again.

She was right of course. The return to London was depressing. Winter was setting in and they had no money. Ruth got her job back at the pub to tide them over and Simon was forced to take on some part time evening class teaching: 'painting by numbers for spinsters' was his uncharitable verdict. He managed to rent a shared studio for his own work but that didn't leave much over to pay for the damp and cramped one bedroom flat in Balham. Ruth realised she would need to find more work. One of the regulars at the pub was a successful Fitness Instructor who would come in with some of her class members after their gym session. She and Ruth struck up a casual friendship and when Ruth admitted she was looking to earn more money she was surprised to be asked to step out from behind the bar. When she did the Instructor appraised her visually. "You look pretty fit," was the verdict. Ruth admitted that at school she had been a keen athlete and that was enough to be told she should qualify as a Fitness Teacher. It was a growth area apparently. The Jane Fonda Feel the Burn trend of the 80s was gone perhaps but a new generation was avid for work outs, and new equipment and techniques and lifestyle philosophies beckoned them in.

Ruth was told to get in on the act and given details of courses she could go on to qualify.

For a year Ruth sweated blood. Even more pub hours paid for the course; the online theory study; the workshops and weekend seminars. Ruth was naturally strong and supple which helped and her musical sense it turned out was an asset in choreographing routines. She passed with distinction and with the help and encouragement of her pub friend advertised her first classes. The response was slow but gradually picked up as word of mouth brought in more punters. She was able to cut down on pub hours and concentrate on her classes. Simon was pleased for her and for the extra money. He looked forward to the time when he could give up the evening classes and concentrate on his painting.

That time never came. Hard though Ruth worked there was never enough money. This became a source of friction between them. Ruth was looking for a life beyond scraping by in a depressing flat and insisted on putting some of her money aside so that one day there might be enough to put down a deposit on a house of their own. Simon was dismissive of her plans: to him they were narrow minded and middle class. Why did they need to buy a house? What was the point of becoming a property owner? Surely that had gone out with Mrs. Thatcher.

When Sarah was born, life in the Balham flat became impossible. It had been hard enough with one baby. Ruth had gone on working well into her pregnancy and resumed her classes as soon as possible after Esther's birth. This had been difficult for Simon, she acknowledged. He had needed to stay at home to babysit and to give up renting his studio. They had arranged their times so that he could carry on with his evening classes because they needed the money but that was of little consolation to him. He clearly loved his new daughter but the restrictions that came with parenthood bore heavily on him. His life was becoming far removed from the idealised vision he had of himself as an unfettered spirit free to follow his creative inner self wherever it would take him.

Ruth felt both guilty and resentful and reproved herself for both. Guilty that she had to accept that Sarah had not been planned; they could barely afford one child, but resentful that she should have to even think of her beautiful child like that because of their poverty. She told Simon they could not carry on as they were. They needed a bigger house but there was no way they could afford London rents. Simon was depressed at the prospect of leaving the city which he claimed charged his artistic soul but when it was clear Ruth was insistent he despondently accepted the situation. He went online and looked for rental properties in areas which he hoped offered some nourishment for Art. He suspected that Cornwall might fit the bill. Its light and its dramatic seascapes had attracted painters and potters and sculptors for many years since the railway had opened access to England's rocky western outcrop. Art galleries proliferated in one-time humble fishing villages and Simon soon found Facebook assurance that painters were a vocal and active part of the local scene. So he and Ruth looked at the details of potential rental properties sent by local estate agents. Prices were not low but they were cheaper than London; particularly if you steered away from picturesque seaside locations and concentrated your search on the post-industrial inland towns which never appeared in the glossy tourist brochures. They hired a car for the weekend and with Sarah in her cot and Esther strapped into her car seat they drove the long miles to West Cornwall and inspected several properties. The weather was, they were told, typical. Typically windy and drizzly. The Estate Agent called it mizzle. If the weather was depressing the houses they looked at were even more so; most with obvious damp patches within and bleak granite without. Ruth tried to be positive. She told herself the sun must shine sometimes and when they grabbed lunch at a greasy spoon she was encouraged to see advertisements for fitness classes on the café notice board. Simon had bought a local paper and whilst they sipped their medicinal tasting coffee and tried to stop Sarah from crying, he became quite animated when he pointed out to Ruth details of upcoming openings at various galleries and even a couple of reviews of recent ones.

In the end they settled on a rambling former vicarage. It had more rooms than they needed and it would be difficult to heat and keep dry but Simon could use one room as his studio and they would no longer need to share a bedroom with their daughters. It was, like most places in Cornwall, only a few miles from the sea and Ruth could believe that the sun must shine sometimes and there might be days on the beach for the children away from the drab surroundings of the decaying town. They would need to buy a car of course but a quick inspection at a local garage showed plenty of old bangers on offer. So they gave their landlord in London a month's notice and Simon did the same for his evening classes. Ruth raided her house deposit savings to tide them over the first few weeks and with fingers crossed they headed west.

"Is Dad coming home tonight?"

Ruth stopped rinsing the dirty plates and looked at Sarah. "I don't know, darling. You never know with Dad do you?"

"I want to show him some of the artwork I did at school today."

"He'll want to see that I'm sure." Ruth smiled at her

younger daughter. Unlike her sister she was in some ways still part child, if nearly a teenager in others, but at least to her Ruth could still pretend they were a normal family.

"He must be painting a lot. He doesn't come home much does he?" Sarah could not keep some uncertainty out of her voice.

Ruth fought an impulse to blurt out the truth. To shout that of course he doesn't come home; that God knows what he was up to with his arty friends whose company he obviously prefers to that of his family. She restrained herself. "I expect he's got something important to finish off."

"Won't he be cold sleeping in his studio?"

Ruth was relieved at the banality of the question. "He'll be fine. He's got that little heater." She managed a laugh. "And that woolly hat you knitted him for Christmas."

Sarah smiled at that. She got to her feet and packed school books into her satchel. Before moving out of the kitchen she came to her mother, put her arms around her waist and gave her a quick hug. Ruth softly kissed the top of her daughter's head and then with forced briskness ruffled her hair and turned her round and propelled her gently towards the door. "Homework."

Sarah grinned at her mother and trailed off with her satchel over her shoulder. Ruth stood for a moment without moving and then sat at the table with a deep sigh. She held her head in her hands and tried to fight back the welling tears. She allowed herself a few seconds of indulgent sadness and then sniffed noisily and stood up. She dabbed her eyes with the edge of her apron and chastised herself. "For God's sake pull yourself together, woman." She went back to the sink and tried to concentrate on the washing up but unanswered questions broke through her defences. How much longer could she keep up this game of Happy Families? How long before Sarah saw through the pretence? Esther, she was sure, had worked out some time ago that whatever she and Simon had once had was over but, like all her feelings, kept them to herself in adolescent privacy.

Simon hated confrontation; hated to face reality. She had tried to talk to him on many recent occasions about their relationship. Ruth accepted that she was a less complex person. She remembered her father's advice and example: 'Don't agonise, just play the hand you are dealt; don't ask too much from life'. Was it asking too much to want your partner to share his life with you? Should she just get on with it? Work every hour in the day to pay the bills? She asked herself more and more why they were still together? Did she still love Simon? She didn't really know what love was anymore; or had she ever? She wondered about those months in the tent? Surely that had been love or had it just been the red wine, the sun, and rampant hormones? She had never slept with another man and never been tempted to do so. But Simon? He had always been attractive to women and she was too naive to think he might not have strayed and, if he had, no doubt he would shrug it off and say it didn't mean anything. Why then did they stay together? Ben had asked her that and Ruth could still find only one answer. She had needed Simon to give her a sense of identity, a sense of belonging. She had no extended family in England or anywhere else for that matter apart from Ben; no close friends. Simon had helped her to be English: to navigate for her this alien land so different from her birthplace. He had helped her make sense of a society far more complex and bewildering than the simple certainties of a pampered white elite. Without Simon she would have been lost; would perhaps have been forced to go home. She knew she had many reasons to be grateful to him but was that enough? Enough to compensate for all the rest?

Ruth put the last of the plates in the draining board and stretched to her full height. She massaged the small of her back with both hands. She had been working at the café for three weeks now and carrying on with her classes and her body sometimes protested at the end of the day. She looked resignedly at the pile of ironing waiting for her and wearily assembled the ironing board. As she sat and waited for the iron to heat up she tried not to listen to the voices in her head asking her how much longer she thought she could sustain punishing herself like this? She strained to quieten these traitorous whispers and began to iron one of Esther's school shirts but as she worked her way mechanically through the stack her mind again demanded answers to unwelcome questions. Why had Simon taken to spending longer and longer away from home? Why did he not bother to offer any explanations for his absences other than some vague mention of work he had to finish? Was that true? God knows he had not sold any paintings for months as far as she knew and there had certainly been no contributions to the mortgage payments or any of the household bills. She had tried not to nag him about it but when she had risked raising the subject he had shouted at her, which he rarely did, and stormed out protesting that she should trust him: he would find the money.

Of course he hadn't and maybe that was why he was staying away. Perhaps he was ashamed? Ruth considered that as a possibility but found it unlikely. Simon had never seen himself as a traditional provider. As long as he had enough money to rent his studio and buy his art materials he was content. If he did manage to sell a painting he would pass money over to Ruth but keep some back to take the girls out for a treat; a pizza or the cinema. Naturally they loved that and Ruth tried not to feel resentful that her role seemed to be that of the bad cop; the one who imposed discipline and order whilst Simon came up with the goodies. Of course, and Ruth confronted this thought more and more, Simon could well have found a lover. Someone who did not pester him for money; who valued his Art; who welcomed him to her bed without preconditions. Ruth had to face the facts that this was the most likely explanation for Simon's disengagement from her life. She could barely remember the last time they had made love. If they did share a bed now it was back to back and any embrace was perfunctory and mechanical. It had come to that.

Ruth finished the last of the ironing and folded away the board. She looked at the wall clock; too early to go to bed much as she wanted to. She really ought to work on new routines for her aerobic class but lacked the energy. Instead she made herself a cup of coffee and slumped with it at the kitchen table. As she drank she looked around her and found some consolation in what she saw. Her house might not be chic or stylish but at least it was hers and hers alone. Simon had not wanted his name on any property deeds. He had contributed to the mortgage when he could but that, he argued, was by way of rent. The arrangement had more or less worked for a while. Simon had reluctantly taken on some part time teaching at the Sixth Form College when they first moved down to the vicarage whilst Ruth had built up her classes. Then she went to Zimbabwe and came back with enough money to pay most of the asking price for a small terraced house in the back streets of Penzance. Simon decided her decision to use the money to buy a house freed him from the obligation of regular employment and he gave up his teaching to concentrate full time on his painting. He had some initial success which pleased them both and enabled him to rent a well-appointed studio on the edge of

Newlyn. But sales diminished and Simon railed against the fickle treachery of gallery owners who, weeping crocodile tears, blamed changing trends in the market. Trends which Simon refused to accommodate in his work for fear it would compromise his integrity.

The price of Simon's integrity was paid by Ruth. His contributions to household expenditure had virtually dried up. Giving up any hope of the situation changing she had taken on the café job. It was hard work but she was surprised to have to admit that she did not actively dislike it. Paula could be tiresome of course but she was never dull. Ruth simply ignored her outbursts and just quietly got on with her job. She smiled now, recalling an incident a few days ago which seemed to have been a defining moment in her relationship with her new employer. Paula had been in full cry in the kitchen, ranting about the latest Council Tax demand which she was waving expansively in one hand whilst trying to manoeuvre a glass of cider in the other. Predictably, her wind-milling arms dislodged a saucepan of soup from the stove which spattered its contents over the kitchen floor. For once Paula was speechless. Ruth instinctively got on her hands and knees and began to mop up the mess. She was aware of Paula staring down at her, and without thinking about a suitable form of words she just said, "Why don't you just go outside and have a proper smoke while I clean this up?" Paula had gaped at her as if to say something but had thought better of it and simply gone outside as instructed. Luke, who had been a silent spectator to the pantomime, offered Ruth a mimed handclap of approval. Ruth thought about Luke now. She couldn't really work him out. He was pleasant enough but guarded. He never asked her about her life and said nothing about his. She didn't really understand his relationship with Paula; why it appeared he worked without payment. It was not her business of course and she certainly didn't intend to ask. There was enough trauma in her own life without getting involved with anyone else's. But, she reflected, as she finished her coffee, Luke came across as an unthreatening and friendly presence and with her life as it was at the moment there was something to be said for that.

SIX

"Dolphins, you say?" Peter Rawlings looked at Luke as if he had misheard.

"Dolphin. Singular. George by name."

"Oh, George." Peter now seemed to understand. "Surely they're not interested in that? He comes every year. We did a piece on it last week."

Luke nodded. "I know. It was picked up by local television and someone in London must have got wind of it, so they want a story. Probably a filler for the inside pages."

Peter laughed. "They must be desperate."

Luke shrugged. "Indeed. But who am I to argue?"

Peter shook his head in disbelief. "You used to go after bigger fish than dolphins, Luke." He laughed at his own joke.

"Mammals I think. Not fish."

"Well done. Always check your facts." Peter pushed a slip of paper across the desk.

Luke picked it up and glanced at it. "Just the one exhibition then?"

"A quiet week for daubers. But you can make up the excitement at the Arts Centre."

Luke looked again at the note. "Another tribute band?"

"To a group no one had heard of in the first place."

Luke shrugged and tucked the note away in the breast pocket of his jacket. "Perhaps the dolphin will be more fun."

"When are you doing that?"

Luke glanced out of the office window. "This afternoon. It's not raining so I can take a few pictures and if I'm lucky talk to someone who might have swum with George."

"Vox pop. Heady stuff, Luke." Peter laughed again as some witticism came to mind. "Hopefully the story will make a big splash. Boom boom!."

Luke managed a tired smile. "Hopefully."

Peter was serious now, "Not that it will have your name on it."

"No by-lines. Stringer anonymity for me."

"Part of the deal, was it?"

Luke stood. That conversation was clearly over as far as he was concerned. "Better get on before the weather changes." He raised a hand in farewell and made for the door.

The weather had stayed fine and Luke could reflect on a successful assignment. The tide had been in at St. Ives and George was actually doing his stuff in the harbour. Luke was pleased with the pictures he had taken and the quotes he had no difficulty in extracting from a couple who had managed to swim alongside this sociable dolphin. They were quite excited that their names might appear in tomorrow's paper.

On the drive back to Penzance Luke opted for the coastal road and he pulled over into a layby to complete his piece and to use his phone to send it off. He did not drive away immediately. The sun was beginning its westward descent into the sea and the spectacle was breathtaking. There was little passing traffic and Luke was content simply to absorb the moment. Then his phone chirped into life to confirm the safe arrival of the article. The distraction reminded

Luke of the times in the past when the knowledge that his work was due for publication would have fuelled a surge of adrenalin; an expectation that his words would move mountains or at least cause the mighty to tremble. Now he was reduced to reporting on a friendly dolphin. It was the sort of stuff which had been his introduction to journalism; a necessary apprenticeship his first editor had told him and he had accepted that, even though from the start he had a fierce ambition to seek out the truth; to expose deceit and corruption. That is what had been his motivation: the consequence of his epiphany on his Damascus Road. It was not just the broken arm but what he saw as the lies of the establishment which impelled him into a career where he believed he could campaign for honesty and transparency. The years of acquiescence to his father's bigoted view of the world had made him feel ashamed of his cowardice and his conversion the more absolute.

For the first year or two he had to rein back on his idealistic crusade. He was told he needed to learn his craft. On a run-of-the-mill South London newspaper that meant, amongst other duties, court reporting on the transgressions of petty criminals; interviewing centenarians on their tips for longevity; looking for 'human interest' angles behind the bare facts of death and divorce and bankruptcies and, most wearisome of all, sitting in on tedious council meetings. But it was the last chore which turned out to be the most productive. Luke became suspicious that a prominent local councillor, Harry Kingdon, supposedly in his public persona a staunch Socialist and friend of the poor, was enriching himself by directing Council building projects to a favoured contractor. It was only because Luke was required to sit in on all council meetings that he became aware of the pattern and he would probably not have thought anything of it had he not recognised the name of one of the directors of the favoured company, Bill Fenwick, as someone who had recently filed for bankruptcy. He checked further and discovered the company had been re-registered in the name of the bankrupt's wife. It seemed that was common practice but his further digging showed a record of complaints and pending civil claims for compensation and breaches of contract in the company's recent history. Luke pondered why the Council would have dealings with such people and why Harry Kingdon in particular was so keen on them? He confided his suspicions to his editor who was initially nervous of any involvement but when Luke offered to follow the story in his own time he reluctantly agreed to consider anything he came up with.

Luke put in long hours in pursuit of Harry Kingdon. He had to admit to himself that he was excited by the chase which sometimes seemed to overshadow the altruism of his cause. His preoccupation with the hunt kept him out until late at night. Natalie called his involvement an obsession. Their relationship was already under strain. They had agreed to rent a flat together after University and Natalie had found a job with a publishing company. She kept regular hours but when Luke took to late nights she sometimes spent her evenings socialising with her work colleagues. Luke did not resent this and that was probably another cause of their disengagement. Natalie began to accept that Simon would never see her as the centre of his life. Their flat sharing was a consequence of habit more than anything else. There had been no talk of marriage and although they got on well enough what occasional sex they shared was dutiful at best. Luke's pre-occupation with Harry Kingdon was the tipping point. Natalie became close to someone at work and decided to move in with him. Luke accepted her decision calmly. They parted on amicable terms and agreed to revert to being just the good friends they had once been. Natalie promised to send him a Christmas card.

Luke learned his investigative journalist skills in chasing Harry Kingdon. The internet and social media were not then the channels of disclosure they have become. It was easier to keep secrets. Luke had to rely on what his editor called 'leg work.' He discovered the pub where Harry liked to hold court and feigning casual interest chatted to some of those who drank with him. He discovered the man was much admired; there was praise for how he had got on in the world; risen from humble beginnings. Luke pretended to be impressed too and without being seemingly overtly curious wondered how Harry had managed to do so well to afford the 'flash cars' and the 'posh gaff' he lived in. No one really had an answer for that. Apart from his work on the council Harry didn't seem to have a job that they could recall. He had started off in life as a builder's labourer but after that nothing much was known. That didn't seem to bother anyone. He was their man on the Council and that was all they cared about.

Luke, self-consciously, checked out Harry's house. It was in one of the leafier avenues off Streatham Common. A convenient bus stop gave him the excuse to loiter and watch. It was certainly a desirable residence. A new-looking BMW stood on the gravelled drive and whilst Luke nervously stood back and allowed a bus to pass he saw another car, smaller but equally new, drive in and park. A bottle-blonde middle-aged lady showed too much leg as she struggled out of it. Smoothing down her skirt she stared across the road at Luke before turning to walk to the front door which she opened with a key from a bunch in her hand. Aware of her scrutiny Luke decided to hail the next passing bus, irrespective of its destination.

Luke was now convinced Harry Kingdon was a fraud and

a crook but how could he prove it? All he could unearth from the published details of Councillors' personal information was that Harry described himself as a businessman: unspecified. It was trawling through the archives of his newspaper that Luke found what he thought was the smoking gun. There were plenty of references to Harry and his Council activities but one item caught Luke's eye; the wedding of Councillor Kingdon. The paper had a policy of covering such events if well-known local personalities were involved. Luke studied the twenty-year-old story. Harry was described as a new energetic force on the council. He certainly looked a slimmer and fitter figure than his recent manifestation and clinging to his arm in the wedding photograph was a less blonde and considerably less bulky version of the woman Luke had recently watched getting out of her car. But what gripped Luke's attention was not the bridal pair but one of the other celebrants in the picture. The best man in top hat and tails was identified as one Bill Fenwick/

"But it's all there," Luke had pleaded with his Editor. "Fenwick was his close friend. His company, in spite of being rubbish, gets all the big contracts from the Council which is dominated by Harry, and Harry gets to live like a lord in spite of having no discernible job and in spite of posing as the People's Friend. All you have to do is join up the dots."

Luke was stunned when his Editor said there was no chance of running the piece. He advised Luke to have a close look at the laws of libel. His story relied entirely on supposition and coincidence. Harry would deny it and sue the paper for millions. Without substantial third party corroboration there was not a shred of hard evidence to nail the man. The editor was not insensitive to Luke's disappointment. He congratulated him on his hard work and commitment and told him he had the makings of a fine investigative journalist and he would be happy to help him up the career ladder. Good to his word, two years later he brought Luke's name to the attention of the editor of a national newspaper and a new world opened up to him.

The sun had nearly given up its struggle with the devouring sea and it was getting cold in the car. Luke regathered his thoughts. He must stop dwelling in the past he told himself, not for the first time. How many more years would need to go by before the present had more to offer than the past? He forced himself to smile at the old adage he sometimes quoted to himself; 'my future is all behind me'. He glanced at his watch and was shocked to see how much time had passed. He must get on. He had the next podcast to write. Dave always protested he needed a day with the script to get into character even though his character was always the same: the dim-witted good old Cornish boy. Luke had a new target in sight this week and the prospect of going for it made him feel positively cheerful as he drove for home.

If Luke had not driven off so briskly he might, had he taken one last look out at the darkling sea, have glimpsed far offshore a fishing boat; its lights just piercing the encroaching gloom. Nothing unusual in that of course. It was a busy shipping lane out there and boats of all shapes and sizes would be plying their trade. What was not usual was that this particular vessel, if anyone had seen it, was neither fishing nor under power but just pitching gently in the lapping sea.

SEVEN

Paula tilted the cider bottle and drank noisily before turning to Ruth who was loading the dishwasher. "Your month is up, you know."

Ruth straightened up. "Sorry?"

"We agreed a month's trial. Four weeks ago."

Ruth remembered and looked warily at Paula. "So we did."

"Well then? Are you staying?" Paula asked in a tone which suggested it was a matter of complete indifference to her whether Ruth stayed or not.

"Yes. If you're happy with me."

Paula laughed. "Happy? I'm seldom happy with anyone or anything, as no doubt you will have observed."

"Well, I can see that it's not easy running a business. Not these days."

Paula glugged down more cider. "Tact. That's one of your good points. You don't talk too much or too little. You are more Holmes than Watson."

Ruth was lost now. "Is that good?"

"Holmes always complained that Watson saw but he did not observe."

"Really?"

"But I think you do both." Paula put down her glass and fumbled in her apron pocket for her packet of cigarettes.

Ruth waited politely for more from Paula but when nothing was forthcoming she bent again to tend to the dishwasher. When she looked up from that Paula was in her customary position; half in and half out of the yard, drawing on her cigarette and leaning against the open door frame. She lazily exhaled and then flicked ash away before turning her head to address Ruth. "The customers seem to like you. Some of the creepier men a little too much perhaps."

Ruth smiled. "Not a problem."

"Well if anyone gets too out of order you can always tip hot coffee over them." She broke off and pointed. "He's good at that."

"Good at what?" Luke had just entered the kitchen carrying a pile of plates.

"Never mind." Paula dropped her half smoked cigarette onto the concrete and ground it underfoot. She re-entered the kitchen. "She's staying. Decided she can put up with us."

Luke looked confused for an instant and then understood. He turned to Ruth. "Great. That's really good news."

Ruth smiled at him a little awkwardly. "Thank you. That's kind of you."

There were a few seconds of silence which Paula brusquely interrupted. "If you two have finished your mutual admiration moment we have lunch to clear."

Ruth took the plates from Luke and turned back to the machine; grateful to be able to hide the blush she could not suppress.

Luke went back to collect more plates. Paula had not finished with Ruth, "If you're going to carry on here you might as well have a free lunch too."

Ruth closed the dishwasher and turned to face Paula. "That's very kind of you but are you sure?"

Paula shrugged. "It's only leftovers." She drained the last of the cider bottle.

Leftover or not Ruth enjoyed the tuna bake. It meant she didn't have to dash home and make herself a hurried snack before her next class, and she told Paula that in gratitude. Paula had not joined them for lunch: her eating habits were as unpredictable as her moods but she eventually collapsed wearily at their table with a coffee. The caffeine seemed to enliven her sufficiently to respond to Ruth's thanks. "So how are they going? These strange classes of yours?"

Ruth shrugged. "I could always do with more people. Particularly the Shades of Grey."

"Who the hell are they?" Paula demanded.

Ruth apologised. "Sorry. I know it's corny but that's what I call my class for older people."

"Like me, you mean?" Paula asked challengingly.

"Not a bit like you, Paula," Ruth said tactfully.

"So why aren't they flocking to you in numbers, these sprightly Grannies?"

"It's the usual problem. Letting people know about it. I put up flyers all over the place but these are a group who are not so mobile: don't get out much. My online stuff, Facebook and all that is, not much use. They're not often computer savvy." Ruth was serious now. "It's a problem; how to reach out to them, and they are the ones who need to get involved. Not just from the fitness point of view, which is important enough, but to meet with others; escape social isolation. Of course the money would be welcome but it's about more than money with these people, it really is." Ruth broke off: surprised and embarrassed in equal measure at her speech.

"Sorry. I was banging on a bit." She looked apologetically at Paula and at Luke who simply smiled back at her.

Paula put down her coffee and looked thoughtfully at Ruth. "So you need to get the word out there. Is that it?"

"I suppose it is."

Paula jabbed a finger across the table at Luke. "There's your answer."

Ruth looked in confusion at Luke who also looked puzzled.

Paula went on. "There's nothing in that ghastly local paper of yours that is ever worth reading. You could make a story out of this. A new initiative to improve the morale and well-being of the overlooked. It would be a damn sight more interesting than most of the rubbish they print."

Ruth was mortified at Paula's intervention. She turned to Luke. "No. I couldn't possibly expect you to—"

"Why not?" Paula bellowed. "Be a whole lot more useful than scribbling about bloody dolphins."

Ruth was confused further with talk of dolphins and looked in helpless apology at Luke who, to her surprise, did not seem in the least offended by Paula's outburst. He took a few moments to consider what had been said and then stood up. "I'll run it past Peter. He might go for it."

Dave was giving it his full range now as Luke held up a finger, warning of the minute countdown. "So what you've been telling me, Prof, is that this here development you're going on about, won't do nothing for us locals."

"That's not at all what I'm saying Pasco."

"But," Dave protested as the script required, "you just told me none of us down here could pay those fancy prices."

"True. Those houses will be holiday homes or second homes. Or retirement homes for people selling up in London. There was a commitment to provide a percentage of affordable homes but that was scaled down after a profitability review. But that is not to say you will get nothing out of it."

"Now you've gone and lost me again, Prof."

"What you will get is more pressure on schools and Doctors surgeries which are overstretched already; more traffic congestion and more pollution."

"That's not good is it?"

"Not good, Pasco."

"So why have the Council allowed it?"

"Money, Pasco, it's always money."

"How do they get any money? They're not selling the houses."

"Maybe not. But think of all the additional Council Tax from all those houses. Now we're out of Europe, Cornwall has lost all that funding for our status as an area of economic deprivation. The Council is desperate for cash. From whatever source."

"So where does that leave us, Prof?"

"As always, Pasco, up the creek without a paddle."

Luke gave Dave the thumbs up and ended the recording. He was happy that with a bit of editing it would be ready for transmission.

Dave massaged his temples to ease the stress of performing. "Well, we should have upset a few people with that Luke."

"I hope so. Two birds with one stone; the Council and the Developers."

"I get a bit nervous we might be putting ourselves at risk a bit."

Luke frowned at him. "At risk of what, Dave?"

"You know: being sued or something."

Luke laughed. "Relax, Dave. If there is one thing I do know something about it's the law of Libel and Slander."

Dave nodded. "Good. I don't want someone coming after me for all my worldly goods." He smiled at the thought. "Even if I had any." He got to his feet. "You got time for a beer this week?"

Luke looked at his watch. "Sorry, Dave. I have to go and photograph some ladies." Leaving Dave open-mouthed at that he collected the scripts and left.

EIGHT

Helen handed over the last of the money. "There's a waiting list now, Ruth. Can you fit in a new class?"

"Possibly. I'll have to juggle things around a bit."

"Maybe you can give up the cafe job?"

Ruth smiled at that. "I don't think so."

"It's OK is it?" Without waiting for an answer Helen moved to the sink and filled the electric kettle.

Ruth watched as Helen plugged in the kettle. Could she admit to Helen it was more than OK; that she positively looked forward to her time with Paula and, of course, Luke? He had written the article for the Clarion. His visit to the class had gone well as he chatted and joked with the ladies and asked their permission to photograph their workout. They were clearly flattered by his interest and delighted to see themselves in the paper the following week. One of the class asked Ruth where she had found such a lovely man? Ruth had laughed that off, explaining that Luke was just a reporter and not her man at all; which, of course, was true. She had her man. Or did she? Simon's visits to his home were becoming more and more sporadic. He rarely stayed more than one impersonal night. He claimed he needed to concentrate on finishing off new work. He certainly seemed pre-occupied and tense. He did manage to ask the girls how they were getting on but even that was clearly an effort. Ruth knew it would be pointless to ask Simon about the future; to tell him she could not carry on much longer not knowing whether they even had any meaningful future. She said nothing but Simon appeared to interpret her silence as a reproach. On his last visit his departing words had been, as ever, to promise that he would sort out the money. Ruth wanted in despair to tell him it wasn't about money, that they had managed to scrape by in the past and they would manage somehow. She could put up with that if they could be a proper family again. That is what she had wanted to say but she had spoken similar words too many times recently to believe they would now serve any purpose.

"I mean not too boring?" Helen was carrying a cup of coffee over to Ruth.

"Sorry." Ruth refocussed. "I was miles away." She took the proffered cup. "No; not boring at all really. Not with Paula; never boring." She sipped the coffee.

"And the journalist guy? He works there too doesn't he?"

Ruth laughed. "In a funny sort of way."

"Funny?"

"It's complicated." Ruth drank more coffee to preclude the need to expand further.

"Whatever. But he certainly did you a favour with that piece in the paper; really boosted your numbers."

"He did." Ruth drained the last of her coffee. "Better dash. I need to get out of these," she pointed at her track suit, "and into my café gear."

Helen shook her head in disbelief. "I don't know where you get the energy from Ruth. What's your secret?"

Ruth carried her cup over to the sink and smiled back at Helen. "Poverty," she said.

There was definitely someone in the house. Ruth could hear footsteps upstairs. It must be Esther come home in the lunch break to retrieve some forgotten school book.

"Esther?" She stood at the foot of the stairs to shout up to her daughter.

The footsteps stopped for a moment and then someone began to descend the stairs.

"Simon." Ruth could not keep the surprise out of her voice.

She stood away from the stairs to allow Simon to walk past her. He was carrying a large rucksack which he swung down onto the kitchen table. He looked at Ruth nervously. She said nothing. He pointed to the rucksack. "I just came to pick up a few things. I'm going away for a bit."

"Away?"

"Yes. I was going to leave you a note."

"A note?" Ruth muttered.

"London. Just for a few days."

Ruth stood still at the foot of the stairs. She was trying not to lose it. Why the hell was Simon going to London? Was he going alone? Would he really have left her a note if she hadn't surprised him in the house? These thoughts raced through her mind but she knew better than to voice them.

Simon plucked uneasily at the strap of the rucksack. Then he looked at Ruth. "I'm taking up some of the new pictures. A couple of galleries there might be interested."

"I see."

"I thought it might be worth a shot."

Ruth looked at her watch. She must get on. This reminder of the routine helped clear her mind. "Well, good luck." She made to move upstairs to change. Simon had picked up his rucksack. He looked weary and uneasy. Ruth reproached herself for her insensitivity. After all he was trying to be positive; make things happen. She should try to be supportive; show some interest. "Where will you stay?"

Simon hesitated, perhaps surprised by her concern. "Er, Johnny Peters. We still keep in touch."

Ruth remembered Johnny. He had been one of Simon's art school crowd and the one who had gone on to enjoy success. She had even seen him on television a couple of times.

"Good. Give him my regards."

"I will."

"I must get on," Ruth said. "Work."

"Of course." Simon swung his rucksack onto his back. He stood looking at Ruth for a moment as if to say something but then moved slowly towards the front door.

"How long will you be gone?" Ruth called to him.

Simon turned back with one hand on the door. "Not sure. You know how it is." He opened the door and walked away.

NINE

Luke had heard enough. In truth, he had heard more than enough of the blaring Heavy Metal wall of sound after about five minutes but had forced himself to endure another half an hour. He gathered together the scribbled notes he had dutifully made, before slipping quietly out of the exit and making his way downstairs to the empty bar where Dave sat in front of the counter thumbing through a newspaper. He looked up as Luke entered. "Looks as if you could use a drink," and without waiting for a response he walked behind the bar and pulled them both pints. Carrying the two glasses carefully he pulled a bar stool alongside Luke's.

Luke put some money down on the counter. "This is on me."

They raised their glasses in silent affirmation and drank deeply. "That's better." Luke put down his glass. The noise of the band above was now sufficiently muffled to be no more than mildly irritating.

Dave pushed the paper he had been reading across to Luke. He jabbed his finger at an article. "Read that?"

Luke glanced down and then nodded. "Fluttering in the dovecots."

"We made the Western Morning News. Fame indeed.

And they tell me the Radio Cornwall phone lines have been buzzing with it. Some poor sod of a Councillor was given a right roasting they tell me."

Luke smiled. "My heart bleeds for him."

Dave pulled the newspaper back and read from it. "'The developers will be issuing a statement through their solicitors.' Should I be worried, Luke?"

"No worries, Dave."

Dave did not look convinced. "Look Luke, I was pleased when you asked me to do the podcast with you. I enjoy it. But I have to take you on trust; that you know what we can get away with."

Luke frowned. "'Get away with'. Is that how you see it Dave?"

"You know what I mean," Dave said uneasily.

"What we are doing Dave, in our small way, is telling people the truth. That isn't always popular."

Dave now looked intently at Luke. "Is that what got you sacked?"

Luke put down his glass. The question had clearly surprised him.

Dave pressed on. "You can tell me it's none of my business, if you like, but we're sort of partners now. Aren't we? So I've been digging around online; since you tell me bugger all."

Luke was silent for a few moments as if uncertain how to reply. When he spoke it was softly. "I wasn't sacked, Dave."

"That's what it implies. 'Left under a cloud' and all that sort of stuff."

"And I didn't quit just because I was trying to tell people the truth. I could have lived with that."

Dave shrugged and folded the paper. "Your call, mate. If you don't want to tell me that's down to you." He picked up his glass and drank but kept his eyes focussed on Luke.

Luke sighed. "It's not such a wonderful story. No heroes: plenty of villains."

"I know some of it from Google. Your name crops up in the Iraq war stuff."

"That." Luke shrugged. "Those were the good days. We knew the Government was lying about weapons of mass destruction. I spoke to a few insiders who were brave enough to question the so called facts. But the frustration was we could never prove it. My sources would only speak off the record." He leaned forward and looked at Dave intently. "Can you imagine how that feels? Knowing what was really going on and not being able to stop it. I know the world sees journalists as an adrenalin-fuelled bunch of cynical boozers but I like to think some of us had what they now call a moral compass. Anyway, I think I had." He paused and sat back, "Or at least I started off with one."

"So what happened to your compass, Luke?"

"Headed due South; like my career."

Dave smiled. "Join the club."

"It all started off so well. They put me with a Consumer Watchdog team. Exposing frauds; protecting pensioners from losing their savings to some evil scammers. You could really believe you were on the side of the angels."

There was a brief pause in the din from upstairs and then a smattering of applause. Dave looked up and both men waited expectantly. Then the band struck up their racket again. Dave looked back at Luke. "And then?"

Luke was now resigned to completing his narrative. "And then in due course I was promoted, if that is the word, to politics and current affairs. That was trickier territory. The lawyers were on your back all the time but we had some success: exposed some shyster MPs who would do anyone favours for cash. I helped set up a few stings. Can't say I felt too happy with that but I consoled myself it was a good cause. Then the Iraq war came along. We had the gut feeling we were being suckered into this nightmare to please the Americans. We tried to get at the truth but the Government PR guys were too smart for us and the Editor was warned off from on high. I still tell myself if we could have proved it the Government would have had to back off. How many lives would that have saved, Dave?"

"That must be a hard one, Luke."

"Very. I kept beating myself up about it. Could we have done more? Could we have found hard evidence?"

"Could you?"

"Only by crossing the red line. I couldn't do that. Not then anyway."

"Red line?" Dave queried.

"Hacking. Phone taps. Private Investigators."

"But later?"

Luke looked away. "It became common practice. All the papers were at it. We used crooked coppers, IT experts, ex-cons even. They could bring us hard evidence to nail a story down, and we didn't care too much how they got it; by then the story was everything. I tried to convince myself the ends justified the means; that the innocent had nothing to fear." Luke looked back at Dave. "I was a coward, Dave. I pretended to myself that it was in the public interest." He paused. "Until I couldn't pretend anymore."

"What changed?" Dave almost barked the question.

"The Milly Dowler case. That poor kid who was murdered and her mother's mobile phone was hacked. Not by anyone we used but that turned out to be the tip of the iceberg; celebrities, minor royals, footballers. Gossip and sleaze: how could that be in the public interest?"

"Even if it was interesting to the public," Dave said.

Luke managed a half smile. "No excuse. It was unforgivable and I had buried my head in the sand."

"So you resigned?"

"I didn't even have the courage to do that. I thought about it; told my editor what I felt about the whole sordid business."

"And then?"

"It was taken out of my hands. The whole industry was panicking. Skeletons were falling out of cupboards in numbers. The News of the World suddenly closed down and a Public Inquiry was trawling through the dirt; everyone was running scared."

"I remember that."

"The Proprietors were leaning on Editors; telling them to drain the swamp."

"So you got drained?" Dave asked.

"I was seen as a liability: that I would cave in if I was leaned on."

"Would you have done?"

"Who knows, Dave? I hope I would have had the guts not to give away my sources; even though I could have faced a prison sentence for contempt of court."

"That's serious stuff."

Luke sighed wearily. "Very. Probably just as well I was never put to the test."

"Because you got out?"

"Made an offer I couldn't refuse. Isn't that what people say?"

"A golden handshake?"

"More like a golden kick up the arse."

Dave laughed, "Nicely put."

"A lump sum: a generous pension."

"Sounds good to me."

"But you know what they say about a free lunch, Dave."

"Never been offered one."

"Well, the price of my lunch was that I could never write for them, or any national newspaper, with my by-line. As a small act of charity I would be retained as an anonymous Stringer."

"And you agreed to all that?"

Luke shrugged. "What was the alternative? My name was toxic in the industry: they saw me as a potential whistle blower. So I took my twenty pieces of silver and signed the NDA."

"The what?"

"Non Disclosure Agreement." Luke drained the last of his beer. "I probably shouldn't even be telling you this."

"Don't worry, mate. Sealed lips. But thanks for telling me anyway; I think I get it now."

"Get what?"

"The podcast. The flame still burns."

Luke laughed ironically. "Flickers briefly."

There was more applause from above and the sound of moving feet. Luke stood. "I'll leave you to it."

Dave retreated behind the bar with the two empty glasses amidst sounds of approaching customers. "I'd better get on."

Luke held up his notes and made for the door. He smiled at Dave. "They're holding the front page!"

Ruth hesitated for a moment as if debating her decision but then flicked through the old address book. She had found it in a cardboard box stacked away with other forgotten junk in the loft. Stuff she had squirreled away after their move from the vicarage with a vague plan that she would sort through it all later; which of course she never had. Many of the names in the book meant nothing to her now: old London contacts she had not seen in years. Most of them anyway were friends of Simon: his mates from art college in particular. Johnny Peter's landline number was amongst them. Ruth had no idea whether he would still be at the same address but she would try it. Simon had been gone for over a week now and Ruth was anxious about him. His mood when he left had been strange; almost tormented.

Ruth reproached herself for not showing more interest in his trip to London. He was after all doing it for them. She felt guilty that her constant preoccupation with money had perhaps driven him to London in desperation. Perhaps he would not welcome her making contact: would think she was checking up on him but she would risk that. She would try to reassure him that if he was unsuccessful in trying to sell the paintings then it didn't matter: they would manage. Surely, Ruth asked herself, that was the right thing to do? She almost convinced herself that her phone call was for the best possible motive. Almost. She could not entirely silence the small whisper of doubt that murmured to her in unguarded moments. Was Simon really selling paintings? Was he even in London? Was he alone? She tried to ignore those disloyal voices. Tried to tell herself not to be melodramatic. Surely that was not in her nature? After all in their early years together when they had still joked and bantered like a normal couple Simon had teased her that she had no imagination and she had defended herself, only half-jokingly, by asking him what could he expect from a simple colonial girl from the Bush? Remembering those playful exchanges now Ruth felt she was watching a film of someone else's life.

Taking a deep breath and rehearsing what she would say Ruth dialled Johnny's number. It rang and after a beat was picked up.

"Johnny speaking."

Ruth recognised that voice which had lost none of its confidence over the years. "Hello Johnny. Look I'm sorry to bother you—" Ruth broke off embarrassed by the triteness of her remark.

Johnny laughed. "No bother. But to whom do I have the pleasure of speaking, as they say?"

Ruth tried again. "You probably won't remember me. It was a long time ago. But it's Ruth. Ruth Kreutz."

There was only a brief pause. "Good Lord! Of course I remember you. Ruth from Out of Africa."

Ruth relaxed a little. "That's me, Johnny."

"Fantastic. How are you Ruth?"

"I'm fine, Johnny."

"And your two lovely daughters?"

"They're fine too." Ruth paused and then tried to keep her tone casual as she continued. "If it's not a problem I wondered if I could speak with Simon or at least get a message to him."

There was a lengthy pause. "Simon?"

Ruth was quick to sense the confusion at the other end of the line and adapted her thinking quickly. "I thought he might be staying with you. He's in London to visit a couple of galleries; trying to sell some paintings."

"Not with us, Ruth. Sorry. We speak on the phone from time to time – art stuff – I keep telling him to stay over when he's in town but I haven't seen him for years."

Ruth managed to keep her voice even. "Oh, I see, Johnny. I must have got my wires crossed."

"Not a problem. Lovely to talk to you again. We really should catch up some time."

"Yes. That would be good." Ruth tried to sound positive. "I must let you get on Johnny and sorry again for disturbing you."

"My pleasure, Ruth." He did not hang up immediately. "Did Simon say what galleries?"

Ruth was surprised by the question. "Not that I recall."

"Hm. Well, I wish him luck but the market for his stuff is pretty dead at the moment. I told him that when we spoke on the phone last. Just a few months ago."

"Oh. Well I guess he thought it worth a try. Ever hopeful."

Johnny laughed. "Or ever desperate. You know how it is Ruth."

"Yes, Johnny, I know how it is." She put down the phone and stood unmoving by it.

"You all right, Mum?"

Ruth refocussed her attention. Esther had come quietly down into the kitchen and was rummaging amongst the pile of ironed clothes.

"Yes. I'm good." She moved across the kitchen. "What are you looking for?"

"P.E. kit."

"Here. Let me, before you jumble the whole lot up." Ruth ushered her daughter aside and found the items Esther needed. "Here you are."

Esther took the proffered clothing. "Thanks." She made no move to leave the kitchen but stood looking at her mother. "Are you sure you're OK?"

Ruth turned away and began tidying the disturbed laundry. "Of course. Why wouldn't I be?"

"Only when I came in you were standing there as if you'd seen a ghost."

Ruth straightened up slowly. "No ghost, Esther." She sat wearily down at the table.

Esther put down her laundry. "I'll make you a cup of coffee. You look as if you could do with one." She walked over to the sink, filled the kettle and plugged it in.

Ruth stared at her in astonishment. "You are making me a coffee, Esther?"

Esther pulled a face at her. "I can, you know. It's just that you always do everything."

Ruth smiled. Some of the tension was ebbing away. "Well, I'm honoured."

Esther began filling two mugs with coffee powder. She fetched a carton of milk from the fridge and, waiting for the kettle to boil, turned back to face her mother. "It's Dad isn't it?"

Ruth was not expecting the question and had no time to compose an answer.

Esther said nothing but poured the hot water and carried the mugs back to the kitchen table. She sat opposite her mother and pushed one of the mugs across to her. Ruth took it and cupped both hands around it as if the warmth might be balm to her disordered thoughts. Esther drank some of her coffee. "Do you think I don't notice?"

Ruth shook her head and looked almost nervously at her daughter. "I don't really know what you notice, Esther. We don't talk much do we? Not about anything that matters. I guess that's my fault."

Esther shrugged. "No one's fault: just the way it is. You pretend everything is normal and I pretend not to notice that it isn't."

Ruth was silent. She looked at Esther as if there was a stranger sitting opposite her; not the bolshie teenager she squabbled with over an untidy bedroom or neglected homework but someone who had the maturity to recognise her anxieties. "What do you notice, Esther?"

Esther put down her coffee. When she spoke it was briskly; she showed no more emotion than reciting a shopping list. "Well, Dad's hardly ever here for a start; when he does come he never stays; the two of you look as if you're trying to avoid each other; you don't seem to ever hold hands or hug like you did when we were little and when you do talk it's always about money." Esther sat back almost defiantly; daring her mother to deny the truth of her words.

Ruth could think of nothing to say that would soften the stark reality of Esther's assessment of her relationship with Simon. She sought refuge in the mundane. "How long have you felt like this?"

Esther shrugged. "It's been getting worse for the last few months I suppose." She suddenly laughed. "Must have been if I noticed."

Ruth managed to smile at that but reflected on how little she appeared to know her own daughter. She had been so pre-occupied with the everyday business of just keeping going that she had found no time to stop and recognise that Esther was no longer a child; that she had matured into someone who hid a sharp sensitivity behind the façade of a truculent teenager. "Does Sarah know? Has she noticed?"

Esther considered the question. "A bit I think. But she's still a kid really."

Ruth laughed openly and felt she was regaining some control of the situation. "Not a wise old woman like you."

Esther was unabashed. "I'm old enough to know what's going on, Mum."

"I sometimes wish I did."

"Why don't you do something about it?" Esther insisted.

"Like what, Esther?" Ruth demanded challengingly. "What would you have me do?"

Esther was not taken aback by the question. "Split up. Call it a day. You have more or less anyway. I reckon you'd be happier on your own."

"And your father?"

"Well he is mostly on his own these days." Esther waited for a response and when none came she plunged on. "Isn't he?"

"You make it sound so simple, Esther."

"Well it is. Well at least I think it is. You agree to do your own thing."

Ruth sighed. "Do our own thing. What thing am I supposed to do?"

"Just carry on like normal but without worrying what Dad's up to all the time. And he can do his painting and stuff without having to try to be something he isn't."

"Just like that," Ruth muttered.

"He can't be what you want him to be, Mum; not anymore."

"Is that the problem? Me wanting him to be something he isn't?"

Esther saw no irony in the question and paused to consider her response. "That's part of it I think."

Ruth could not restrain her anger, "I only want him to be a normal father; a normal partner; to love his children." She broke off close to tears. "To love me."

"But he does, Mum. He does love us but he can't do all the rest of it; not now. He never has been much good at that has he?"

Ruth could not evade Esther's question. "I think he tried."

"Sure. But there's no point anymore. It's just making you both miserable. Let it go."

"And you and Sarah? Where does that leave you?"

Esther seemed surprised by the question. "Us? Here of course with you. Like now."

"But you would—"

Esther seemed to know where this was going. "Look,

Mum. In my class at school there are plenty of kids whose parents have split. But they get to see their Dads at weekends and stuff. It's no big deal."

Ruth said nothing. Esther reached for her empty mug and carried both to the sink. She rinsed them and put them on the draining board before looking back at her mother.

"Sorry. Mum."

Ruth looked up. "Sorry for what?"

"If I upset you."

"No: you haven't upset me." She managed a crooked smile. "Shocked me perhaps."

"How?"

"I suddenly realise you are wiser than your years, Esther," Ruth said quietly.

Esther tried to laugh that off. "Can I have that in writing?"

Ruth smiled and stood up. She picked up the ironed P.E. kit off the table and held it out to Esther. "You'd better get to bed and try not to get this all creased before the morning."

TEN

The café was empty now. Luke had left early to check out an Art exhibition and Ruth had cleared the tables and was now wiping them down. It was hard to concentrate. Her conversation with Esther was replaying in her mind. Was it just as simple as her daughter had suggested? Was it time to tell Simon it was finished? In her preoccupied state she managed to knock over one of the table flower vases. She swore under her breath and knelt to retrieve the flowers beached on the café floor.

"What the hell's the matter with you today?"

Ruth looked up from her kneeling position. Paula was standing at the serving counter and glaring at her.

"I'm sorry." Ruth mumbled her apology and stood with the limp bunch of flowers in her hand. She looked around vaguely, uncertain of how to dispose of them.

"Oh, for God's sake!" Paula marched over and snatched the flowers away from Ruth and threw them roughly into a wastepaper basket.

Ruth stood in awkward silence.

"Are you ill or something?"

"No. I'm not ill," Ruth said.

"Well you've been acting as if you are all morning. Mooning about the place: distracted."

"I'm sorry."

"Hm. Well it's not like you. You're usually buzzing around like a blue-arsed fly."

Ruth felt, in spite of herself, she should try to offer Paula some explanation. "It's just something going on at home. I know that's not an excuse but..." She faltered for a moment fearing that she had probably said too much already.

"One of the girls is it?" Paula asked.

"No. Not one of them."

"Well, what, then?" Paula demanded.

Ruth hesitated. She knew she should probably invent some minor domestic crisis to satisfy Paula's curiosity but she had never been very good at lying; probably lacked the imagination, as Simon would have said.

"Don't just stand there gawping like a goldfish." Paula pointed to the table they used at lunchtime. "Sit down and have a drink: you look as if you need one." Without waiting for a response Paula held up the bottle of cider in invitation.

Ruth shook her head and found a smile from somewhere. "No thanks. I have classes to teach later," she said, as she sat.

Paula seemed unimpressed by that but shrugged in acceptance. She poured herself a glass of cider and walked to the café door and reversed the open sign. Then she came back to the table and slumped heavily down facing Ruth, who looked at her nervously.

"Right. This is my caring employer mode. I might not show it but I appreciate what you're doing here. So if you think it would be any use you can tell me what the problem is and if I can help I will." She drank from her glass of cider. "Or you can tell me to bugger off."

Ruth was too surprised to make any immediate reply. To her embarrassment she felt tears pricking at her eyes.

"Well?" Paula prompted.

Ruth let out a deep breath. "My life is such a mess, Paula."

Ruth could not remember when, if ever, she had spoken at such length about her personal life to anyone. She felt an almost physical release of tension as she confided to Paula all her worries and anxieties about Simon and what the future might hold for them and their daughters. Paula had listened without interruption, taking only occasional sips. When, at last, Ruth sat back and fell silent Paula drained the last of her drink and put the glass down firmly on the table.

"Out of the mouths of babes and sucklings, Ruth."

"What?" Ruth asked.

"You might not believe it but I won the Scripture prize at school. 'Out of the mouths of babes and sucklings cometh wisdom'; or something like that."

Ruth was now totally lost but the thought of Paula winning a Scripture prize made her laugh; lightened her mood.

"The point is that your teenage daughter got it absolutely right as far as I can see. Decision time. You can't go on as you are. In fact from what you've told me I'm surprised you've stuck it as long as you have."

"I wonder that sometimes," Ruth admitted.

"And what do you conclude?"

Ruth took time to respond. "It's hard to explain to people who belong."

"Belong? What do you mean, 'belong'?"

"I came to this country when I was barely out of school. I had no family here; no relatives or anything like that. That didn't matter when I was just doing my year away travelling bit but then..."

"Then you met Simon. Right?"

"Yes. He was like a guide as well as a boyfriend to start with."

"A 'guide' for Christ's sake?"

"I know it sounds pathetic but he made me feel I could cope with England; all its complications and social layers and stuff."

"Was it that complicated?"

Ruth smiled wryly. "After Zimbabwe!? I grew up in a privileged bubble. I was a complete innocent. I was like Alice in Wonderland when I came to England."

"But that was years ago? You don't still need a guide."

"Perhaps not. When we had kids, we were a family: of sorts. I thought that was enough."

"And was it?"

"I knew it wasn't great but it was what it was. You make the best of it. My Dad taught me that. Play the hand you're dealt. Be thankful for what you have. Remember you're lucky to be given a life to live." Ruth could almost hear her father telling her that.

"You can do better than that Ruth; just putting up with things."

"So what must I do, Paula?"

"If you're asking me the first thing to do is to find out what's going on with Simon. What is he up to? When you do that then you can decide if you have any sort of future together but this not knowing is hopeless." Paula got to her feet abruptly and looked at Ruth. "God knows what qualifies me to give anyone advice about how to lead their lives."

Ruth stood too. "Thank you Paula. It was good of you to listen. It helped."

Paula turned back to the kitchen speaking as she went. "I'm glad to hear it. I can't have you knocking vases of flowers over all the time."

Luke had stayed no longer than was polite at the exhibition.

The artist was hovering hopefully in attendance and took it upon himself to talk Luke through his paintings. Luke listened respectfully and took the odd note whilst thinking to himself that needing to explain a painting was rather missing the point. However, he would try to find some words of encouragement for his piece in the Clarion. He knew most of the local artists and what a struggle it was for them to get by, so he was not going to rubbish their work just to pull a few literary tricks. Anyway, what did he know about Art? Until Peter had been kind enough to offer him what he joking called the weekly 'culture corner' he could not recall ever visiting an art gallery voluntarily, although Peter did not seem to think that was a problem! At school there had been the obligatory visit to the National Gallery and in his working life in London he had sometimes taken coffee at the Tate Modern but that was more to enjoy the views over the Thames than to immerse himself in the Surreal and the Abstract. He could not recall any paintings hanging on the walls at home when he was growing up. His father did not put great store by Art. There were a few family photographs and Luke seemed to remember a Country Life calendar his father received every Christmas from one of the firms he dealt with but he would no more have bought a painting than fly to the moon.

As Luke left the gallery the memory of his father stayed with him. He had been dead now for nearly twenty years; carried off, perhaps not so surprisingly, by a sudden massive heart attack. Luke's mother had been lost without him; unfamiliar with the most basic formalities of maintaining a household. Luke and his sister had persuaded her to sell their family home and move into sheltered accommodation. Surprisingly she had been quite happy there; enjoying the company of the other residents and when Luke made his regular Sunday visits he found her seemingly more relaxed without her husband's forceful looming presence. She was free to knit in peace, to watch whatever television programmes she wanted without acerbic interruptions and even to participate enthusiastically in regular bingo sessions. Mary had married and soon his mother had a grandson to fuss over and to knit for. She had survived long enough to be present at the boy's fifth birthday party. Luke had collected her and driven her to Mary's house where she had sat beaming amidst the rampaging small children and put on a funny hat on and tucked into the jelly. On the drive home she told Luke she had never felt so happy. Two weeks later she was dead: a severe bout of pneumonia. At her funeral Luke held Mary's hand as she cried softly but he could find no tears of his own and felt ashamed of his lack of feeling. What was wrong with him? Was he emotionally dead? He was reminded that Nicola had tired of his apparent indifference and after her there had been no other serious relationships; only a few meaningless short-lived liaisons in which neither party pretended there was more at stake than scratching a lustful itch.

The sun was still shining brightly and Luke didn't feel like going straight home after he left the gallery. Instead he walked along the footpath above the beach which separated Penzance from Marazion. Ahead of him St Michael's Mount rose dramatically out of the sea and he could just make out the trail of visitors walking across the causeway, now exposed by the low tide, to take the tour of the castle and its gardens. It was a reminder to Luke that soon Cornwall would be as submerged as the causeway by a flood of holidaymakers. But that was still a few weeks away. At the moment the long beach was sparsely populated: too cold for all but the most fanatical of swimmers, and the few dog walkers had plenty of space to throw balls for their pets to chase in joyous pursuit.

Luke scrambled down off the path and sat with his back against the sea wall; enjoying the warmth of the sun on his face. He could almost have allowed his drowsiness to succumb to sleep but the thoughts which had surfaced at the art gallery would not fade quietly away. Why was he so afraid of emotion? Had he ever felt really deeply about anyone? He did his best to observe the niceties of social interaction. He was, he hoped, a responsible and decent citizen but he had to accept that he was always an observer of life rather than a participant. No doubt he could attribute that to his choice of career. Perhaps he had spent too many years questioning and doubting; too many years confronting some of the less attractive manifestations of human behaviour. That made you wary, cynical even. Then, of course, his relationship with his father had no doubt stunted his emotional development. When he was growing up he had been too timid, he now accepted, to show his true feelings. He had settled for presenting to the world the bland face of inoffensive compliance. It seemed as if the years of counterfeited conformity had left him a stranger to spontaneous emotion; capable of neither joy nor rage. Perhaps he needed another life-changing walk along the Damascus Road.

Suddenly an exuberant Cocker Spaniel pursued an ill-directed ball to within inches of Luke's feet and scratched up a shower of sand in attempting to retrieve it. The distant owner called out an apology and Luke waved a tolerant hand in response. He watched as the frantic dog raced back to its master with the soggy ball in its mouth. Luke smiled as he recollected his recent train of thought. If he had the capacity of spontaneously giving free rein to his feelings he would no doubt not have waved a hand in mild acceptance but bellowed out in anger 'can't you keep your bloody dog under control?' Maybe restraint was the glue that held society together.

A thin layer of cloud was now shielding the sun. Luke stood and brushed obstinate sand off his clothing. He would need to think about supper. The thought was not inspiring. He doubted he could whip up much enthusiasm for cooking himself a solitary meal and would no doubt yield to the soft option of a takeaway. Normally in the evenings he settled for a sandwich because he took lunch with Paula but today his gallery visit had put the lid on that. As he walked back along the footpath towards town Luke thought back to the morning at the cafe. In particular he thought of Ruth. She had definitely been out of sorts. Normally she was bright and cheerful; although he guessed she sometimes had to make an effort to appear so. He had come to look forward to seeing her he had to admit; not just because she was good to look at – he hoped he was not that shallow – but because she gave off a positive energy which even Paula found infectious. Today he had almost found the nerve to ask her what the problem was and if he could help, but his besetting caution restrained him. The voice of cold reason had asked him what was it to do with him? He knew very little about her private life and if there was a problem who was he to offer a solution? He was hardly Counsellor material. So he had said nothing but he hoped she would soon be back to her normal self. It surprised him to accept that he felt that quite strongly. Musing over this perception Luke trudged the last stretch of the path into town and tried to concentrate on the ideas he was turning over for the next podcast. He would work on it over his fish and chips.

ELEVEN

"I'm not sure I really know what a podcast is, Luke."

Paula swept in from the kitchen, glass in hand, in time to catch Ruth's comment to Luke who was smiling at Ruth's confession. She joined them at the table where they had just finished eating. "Don't worry about it: you're not missing anything. In his case," and here she jabbed a finger at Luke, "it's just him and his tame Barman rabbiting on about our wicked Council or whatever."

Luke did not seem to object to this verdict. He laughed. "A poor thing but mine own."

"I don't know why you bother. Not after what you—" Then she broke off and made a point of picking up a newspaper a regular customer always left behind for them. She rummaged through the pages.

Ruth was curious. "Not after what, Paula?"

Paula did not look up from the paper. "Nothing."

Ruth looked at Luke for explanation but he merely shrugged as if he had no idea what Paula had been about to say.

Paula looked up from what she was reading and glared at Ruth. "I see your Godforsaken country is in the news again."

Ruth took a moment to comprehend. "Zimbabwe?"

Paula read from the paper. "'Rumours are circulating

in Harare that junior officers are plotting a coup to oust the President as the economic crisis worsens and food supplies are running out'." She pushed the paper across the table towards Ruth. "That lot don't look as if they're starving do they?"

Ruth looked at the photograph. It showed a group of high-ranking military officers flanked by menacing-looking men in dark suits and dark glasses, who were presumably their bodyguards, standing on a platform. The caption explained they were celebrating forty years of Independence but identified some of the officers who might have Presidential ambitions. She was about to return the paper to Paula when a flash of memory jolted her; she looked at the article again and picked up the paper to study the photograph more closely. She felt the shock of recognition; now she recalled that hot morning outside Bulawayo airport and the man who had stood by the car. She lowered the paper slowly and was aware of Luke and Paula looking at her. "It's him. The scar is the same."

Neither Paula nor Luke spoke. They were clearly waiting for Ruth to explain. "It's Mobil. That one." She pointed at one of the dark-suited bodyguards.

Luke took the paper from Ruth and studied the picture.

"Who the bloody hell is Mobil?" Paula demanded impatiently.

Luke had an opinion on that. "Well, if you look at the way he's positioned in the group I would guess he's the bodyguard for this guy." Luke read from the caption. "Who seems to be Air Vice Marshall Ovanga."

"Ovanga! Yes, of course. That would be it." Ruth was fitting the pieces together in her mind.

"Would you please tell me what the hell this is all about?" Paula was insistent now.

Ruth took a deep breath to compose herself. "It's complicated. But Mobil was the fixer and—"

"Fixer? Fixing what?" Paula interrupted.

Luke was brave enough to hold up a restraining hand. "Give her a chance, Paula."

Ruth offered him a grateful smile and then started again. "A few years ago I sold my Dad's house in Bulawayo. Ovanga bought it."

"That sounds straightforward enough." Paula sounded disappointed.

Luke guessed it was not that simple. "How did he pay for it? Not in Zim Dollars I would hope."

"No. American dollars," Ruth admitted; even now nervous of the admission.

Luke was keenly alert now. "How did you manage that?"

"Mobil and my brother fixed it."

"You have a brother?" Paula inquired.

Ruth welcomed this diversion, "Yes. Ben. He's younger than me. He lives in Australia now."

Luke was quick to pick up on that. "But not then, presumably?"

"No. He had a business in South Africa."

"What sort of business?" Luke's tone was almost interrogatory. Perhaps he sensed it and he continued more casually. "Just out of interest."

"Engineering."

Luke digested this without comment.

Ruth stood and made a show of looking at her watch. "I must get on. I'll be late for my class." She picked up her plate and carried it quickly to the kitchen and then hurried to the door and called back to Luke and Paula who were still sitting at the table looking at her.

"Bye. See you tomorrow," she called out with a forced cheeriness as she left.

Neither Luke nor Paula moved from the table. Luke

seemed preoccupied with what Ruth had told them, unaware that Paula was staring accusingly at him. "Don't even think about it, Luke," she rasped.

Luke looked at her in surprise. "Sorry. Think about what?"

"I could see the cogs turning."

Luke laughed half-heartedly. "I'm not following you Paula."

Paula hesitated as if debating whether to continue but then stared almost accusingly at Luke. "Look. Do you really think I go along with your charade?"

Luke frowned. "What charade would that be?"

"That you are just a moth-eaten hack scraping a living writing a few pieces for the local rag."

Luke was silent. The he smiled. "Nicely put, Paula."

"I did pretend to go along with it of course. I thought if that's the face you want to present to the world that's fine by me. I can understand that." She looked at Luke wryly. "It was my game too."

Luke leant forward intently, "Now you've really lost me, Paula."

"Have I? Then let me give you a clue." She held Luke's stare. "Hartmanns."

Luke sat back in seeming confusion for a few seconds before some flicker of memory stirred. "The merchant bank?"

"The former merchant bank. Now defunct; largely thanks to you."

"You flatter me."

"Do I? It was your investigation that did for them."

"It was the truth. I don't regret it."

"No reason why you should. The banks were all guilty as hell. Directors paying themselves huge bonuses on the backs of selling suicide mortgages to people whose lives they ruined."

"You seem well informed, Paula."

"I should be." She hesitated for a moment. "I was the P.A. to the Chief Executive at Hartmanns."

Luke was too stunned by this admission to speak.

Paula, with no customers to offend, sat back in her chair and lit a cigarette; she drew deeply on it and blew a lazy smoke ring into the air. "So I know all about you, Luke. I recognised you the moment you stepped into the café nearly ten years ago."

"You recognised me? How?" Luke still seemed to be disorientated.

"The shareholders' meeting. You remember that?"

Luke was now more focussed. "Not easy to forget."

"You managed to wangle your way in somehow and to ask a question before they rumbled you: about the bonuses the Directors were paying themselves. Caused quite a stir." She laughed. "You were still demanding an answer when they threw you out."

Luke smiled ruefully. "None too gently I remember."

Paula drew deeply on her cigarette. "Not that it mattered. You had enough to crucify them with. A week later, your article appeared and the shit hit the fan."

"I suppose I should say I'm sorry."

Paula laughed at the notion. "Sorry? What for? They were no better than crooked market traders, barrow boys. Profit was everything no matter who got trampled in the rush to cash in."

"Maybe; but I'm sorry you were a casualty."

Paula shrugged. "Maybe you did me a favour."

"How?"

"Living the high life with that lot couldn't last. The partying; sneaky affairs with married men. And of course; the drinking." As if to underline that point she picked up her glass of cider and held it up as an exhibit. "I stick to this now; not perfect but you should have seen me in my prime." She put the glass down without drinking. "It was killing me."

"So what did you do?"

"Took a long hard look at myself and decided to run as far away as possible."

Luke nodded. "I can understand that."

Paula smiled at him briefly. "I thought you might."

Luke looked around the empty café. "So you bought this place?"

"Yes. I sold up my smart flat in London."

"Why a café?"

"I had to earn a living; no pension and no golden handshake." She pointed accusingly but without malice at Luke. "You put the kybosh on that."

Luke held up both hands in mock surrender. "Mea culpa."

"At least I knew I could cook. My mother had great hopes for me in Society. My father died when I was a baby but left us well provided for, so it was Cheltenham Ladies' College for me, and after that my mother lashed out on a Cordon Bleu cookery course, as one of the necessary accomplishments she thought were required to snare some sprig of the aristocracy." She shook her head in in disbelief and sipped reflectively from her glass.

"No sprig?" Luke prompted.

"I ran off with a Jamaican rock guitarist."

"Ah," was all Luke could manage.

"Nearly killed my mother of course. We haven't spoken since."

"And the guitarist?"

"I had a great two years; following the band around Europe. I suppose I was what they call a groupie."

Luke's eyes opened wide at that. "Hard to imagine, Paula."

Paula grimaced. "It couldn't last of course. Too much temptation for him. He kept promising it would never happen again but even through the clouds of ganja I could see it was time to bail out. I left the band in Hamburg and flew home; got myself a lowly office job and did well enough to climb the ladder; a career girl. No time for proper relationships; I think the band tour had put me off those." Whilst she had been talking her cigarette had burned down to a stub. She got up and carried it through to the kitchen and flicked it into the back yard. When she came back to the table and sat down again her mood had changed. She spoke briskly to Luke. "So there you: an exclusive. But not for publication."

Luke held up a hand in reassurance. "Of course." He smiled at her. "Thank you for telling me."

Paula drained what was left in her glass. "When you walked into the café for the first time I thought of Casablanca."

"What?" Luke asked in confusion.

"The movie. The famous line; 'of all the bars in all the world, et cetera'."

Luke understood now. "Coincidence."

"I nearly accosted you; reminded you of the shareholders' meeting."

"Why didn't you?"

"There was something about you that deflected questions. You had changed."

Luke sighed, "The passage of time, Paula."

"It was more than that." She chose her words carefully now. "You looked as if the fire had gone out."

Luke could find no words to deny it.

"So," Paula continued, "I thought he obviously doesn't want to be who he was any more." She looked intently at Luke. "I was right there wasn't I?"

"I suppose you were," Luke agreed.

"Then it wasn't hard to work out what had happened. The news was full of stories of disgraced journalists and collapsing newspapers."

"So you knew all the time?" Luke could not hide his surprise.

"I guessed. But it didn't bother me." She softened her voice now. "In fact I think it brought us closer: a common bond . Both refugees from a shattered past." She sat back and smiled at Luke.

"Hence the free lunches?"

"I think it suits us both."

Paula stood and made to move away but Luke called after her. "Why now Paula? After all these years."

Paula walked back to the table but did not sit. She stood with her hands braced on the back of her chair and glared at Luke. "Because I saw that look in your eye; a rekindling of the fire."

TWELVE

Abba blared from the CD player and Ruth cut them off full flow in the midst of 'Mamma Mia'. She picked up her notepad from the kitchen table and scribbled down a few possible moves. Choreographing new routines for her classes had to be fitted in when she was not teaching or working at the café or doing an endless round of household chores. She chewed on the end of her pencil and tried on focus on the next set of exercises.

Sarah appeared at the foot of the stairs. She was in her pyjamas and looked as if she was still half asleep. Ruth was instantly contrite. "Oh, I'm sorry darling. Did my music wake you up?"

"A bit," Sarah yawned.

Ruth looked at the kitchen clock. Half past ten; really far too late to be playing loud music. "I'll finish now. You can go back to bed."

"Can I have a biscuit? One of the chocolates ones."

Ruth smiled. "I suppose so. The least I can do for waking you up." She opened a cupboard door and found the tin and handed Sarah a biscuit.

"Thanks, Mum." Sarah sat at the table and nibbled on her biscuit.

Ruth put away the tin. "What about Esther? Did I wake her up as well?"

"No. She's still finishing off her Geography project." Sarah took another bite. "She told me to come down."

Ruth laughed. "I see."

"She said if she heard any more Abba she would scream."

Ruth laughed again. "Not a fan then. You can tell her she can relax. I promise no more Abba tonight."

Sarah finished her biscuit. "I'll tell her." Sarah did not move off but stood at the table with her eyes fixed on Ruth.

Ruth became conscious of the silence. "What is it, Sarah?"

Sarah spoke hesitantly. "Dad. When is he coming home?"

Ruth took a breath and tried not to let any anxiety show on her face. "I'm not sure darling. Soon I expect."

Sarah did not look convinced. She looked down at the table and when she spoke it was barely a whisper. "Esther says he might not come back; not here; not ever."

Ruth's immediate intention was to rush out a denial; to scold Esther for talking nonsense and to reassure Sarah everything was fine, but the words would not come. Instead she walked to her daughter and put her arm in reassurance around her shoulder. "I don't know what Esther has been telling you but it is true that your father and I haven't been too happy together for some time now. I don't know how it will work out. That's the truth Sarah and I know you are grown up enough now to understand that."

Sarah did not reply but Ruth could feel the tremor in her daughter's body. She hugged her closer. "Whatever happens you know that we both love you and always will."

Ruth fought to hold back her own tears now. She held Sarah tightly for a few seconds more and then from somewhere conjured up a brightness that was entirely counterfeit. "Better get back to bed now. School tomorrow."

Sarah sniffed away her tears and tried a brave smile for her mother. She trailed off towards the stairs and Ruth watched her go barely able to retain her composure. After a few seconds she let out a deep sigh and slumped at the table. In repressed fury she clenched a fist and slammed it down within an inch of the table. "Simon," she mouthed silently, "what are you doing to us?"

"Luke? This is a blast from the past. How are you doing my old friend?"

Luke could visualise Rick Davies at the other end of the phone, in his crumpled alpaca jacket which he wore as a defiant gesture of disdain to his fashionably dressed younger colleagues. "Surviving, Rick. And you? I keep thinking you must have retired by now but then I catch your name toplining some big exclusive story."

"Not quite ready for the golf course and the allotment yet."

Luke smiled at that. "Glad to hear it, Rick." It was hard to imagine someone of Rick's restless energy placidly tending runner beans or planting carrots. He had worked with Rick on a number of high-profile stories and had formed as close a friendship with him as their frenetic world allowed. Rick had survived the cull but only by accepting a sideways move to the less controversial foreign affairs desk.

"How are you coping with life in the fast lane in deepest Cornwall?" Rick teased.

"Hardly time to catch my breath."

"Bit of a dolphin watcher they tell me."

Luke groaned. "Mine not to reason why. I go where I am sent."

Rick's tone now changed. "But I guess you're not ringing me after all these years to talk about dolphins?"

"No." Luke paused. "What do you know of Air Vice Marshall Ovanga, Rick?"

There was no instant reply. Rick had clearly been surprised by the question. "Ovanga?" he asked. "The guy in Zimbabwe?"

"Yes. Him."

Rick took time to gather his thoughts. "Some see him as the coming man." He laughed dryly. "He's got the qualifications."

"Which are?"

"He's smart; comparatively young when you look at the dinosaurs at the top of the party."

"Sounds promising."

"He's also ambitious and ruthless. Not a man to mess with they tell me."

"So he could make it all the way?"

"Possibly. If the old guard let him."

"Would that be a good thing, Rick?"

Rick scoffed at the question. "He's no liberal democrat, Luke. He's got more energy than his rivals. More energy to crush any hint of dissent. Hard to believe I know but I reckon if Ovanga makes it to the top job all the lights will go out in Zimbabwe."

Luke digested this for a moment. "Suppose I could stop him, Rick?"

There was a moment's silence and then a snort of disbelief. "Sorry! What am I hearing, Luke?"

"Just hang on a second, Rick. I know it sounds crazy but let me explain."

"Be my guest."

Luke spoke slowly now. "I've got to know this Zimbabwean ex-pat in the past few weeks and quite by chance the connection to Ovanga came up; shows him up as a crook; probably misusing public funds."

"I'm sure they all do that; but they usually manage to conceal it."

"Exactly. But if Ovanga can be fingered as a petty fraudster it might dent his credibility."

"It might," Rick accepted. "It could spike his guns."

"It would at least let people know the true character of the guy."

Rick sighed. "I remember that was always your thing, Luke. Let the truth be out."

"I'm not ashamed of that." Luke paused. "Sorry, that sounds a bit preachy."

"Idealism, Luke. That's what did for you and why an old cynic like me plods on and you are left with the dolphins."

"Never mind the bloody dolphins, Rick. What about Ovanga? Are you interested?"

"I could be." Rick's manner was now brisk and business-like. "This Zimbabwean mate of yours. Is he a reliable source?"

Luke hesitated before answering. "It's not a him."

Rick was quick to pick up on the hesitation. "I see. A lady friend." He emphasised the description suggestively.

Luke managed to suppress an unexpected irritation. "Just a work colleague."

"Work? I didn't know—"

Luke cut him off quickly. "Never mind about that. The point is that five years ago Ovanga bought her house in Bulawayo in what I am sure was an illegal deal moving American dollars out of the country in some scam involving her brother."

Rick considered that information. "I agree if that came out it might dent his ambitions."

"So you would be interested in picking this up?"

"For sure. But we'd need hard evidence; dates, names, documents and so on."

"I know," Luke said softly.

"Can you get all that from," Rick now spoke with emphasis, "your lady friend?"

"To be frank I don't know. But I wanted to check that you were interested before asking her."

"Very interested, Luke. This could be really big," Rick said forcefully.

"OK. I'll talk to her and get back to you."

"Fine," Rick cleared his throat. "Forgive me mentioning it Luke, but you do realise that if we ever get to run this it can't have your name anywhere near it."

"I know that, Rick. Don't worry about it."

"So, again excuse my curiosity. Why?"

"Why what?"

"Why are you bothering?"

Luke had asked himself that question too and now he tried to explain his reasoning to Rick. "Midlife crisis, I expect."

"Sorry?"

"For the last few years I've been pottering about kidding myself I'm still a journalist. Dropped a few crumbs as a Stringer for which I know I should be grateful and churning out a weekly column of drivel which no one reads."

"Sounds depressing, I admit."

"I know I shouldn't complain; it's what I signed up for. I thought I had come to terms with it; stopped fretting about the past."

"So what changed?"

"I don't know. Maybe one last hurrah."

"To prove you could still do it?"

"Who knows? But when Ruth—"

"Is that her name? Your lady friend?"

Luke ignored the question. "When she told me about Ovanga the old reflexes kicked in. I couldn't let it go. I thought this is a chance to exit with a flourish."

"The adrenalin rush: the chance of a big story. Not quite out of your system by the sound of it."

"It's not just that, Rick. It's a chance to let people see behind the lies for once. That's what I joined up for."

"So to stay with the military metaphor this could be Custer's last stand for you."

"I hope with a happier outcome."

"Right. Get me the evidence and we might still move mountains, Luke."

"Will do. Thanks for your time, Rick."

Luke put the phone down and thought with unease about what lay ahead.

THIRTEEN

Paula was staring at the list in her hand. She did not seem pleased by what she was reading. "Sod it! I can't get all of this in town." She scowled at Luke who was shutting down the coffee machine. "Are you sure we're out of napkins?"

Luke nodded. "Down to the last packet." As if to add emphasis to his remark he twisted a knob on the machine to release an expiring jet of steam.

"I'll have to get a taxi back from the cash and carry with all this lot." She waved the list accusingly.

Ruth looked up from the table where she had just started eating her lunch. "Do you want me to come with you to help you with all that stuff?"

"I dare say I can manage," Paula said with an air of martyrdom. "You two enjoy your lunch."

"If you're sure?" Ruth asked.

"The burdens of command," Paula muttered as she folded the list and stuffed it into the bag slung over her shoulder. She marched to the café door and pushed it open, "Make sure you lock up properly, Luke. You'll be long gone by the time I get done with all this." She refrained from slamming the door for fear of breaking the glass panels but she shut it behind her as firmly as prudence would allow.

Luke smiled at Ruth. "Not a happy bunny."

Ruth sighed. "I probably should have gone with her."

Luke gave the coffee machine a final wipe before collecting his lunch from the kitchen. "I thought you had a class this afternoon," he said as he joined Ruth at the table.

"Cancelled. Boiler failure at the leisure centre."

"Oh." Luke concentrated on his food for a few moments but then put down his knife and fork and looked warily at Ruth. "So you don't have to rush of for once." Ruth finished eating and pushed her plate to one side. She drank from her glass of water but became aware of Luke's stare. She held his gaze for a moment. "Was there something, Luke?"

Luke abandoned his lunch and pushed his plate away too. He took a deep breath. "There is, actually." He paused; uncertain of how to continue.

Ruth sat back in her chair. She smiled wryly. "Let me guess. Ovanga."

Luke groaned. "Was it that obvious?"

"Paula warned me."

Luke could not hide his shock. "Paula did?"

Ruth nodded. "She told me yesterday."

"Told you what exactly?"

"That you had once been a big shot journalist."

Luke frowned. "What else did she tell you about me?"

"Nothing," Ruth reassured him. "Just that. She said if I wanted to know more it would have to come from you."

"Why did she even tell you?"

Ruth thought about the question. "I don't know for sure but I expect, like me, she picked up on how interested you seemed to be in what happened in Bulawayo."

Luke sighed. "It was that obvious?"

"So I expect she was sort of warning me off; that you might chase a story."

Luke looked steadily at Ruth. "Do you need to be warned about me, Ruth?"

Ruth shook her head. "I don't think so." She held his gaze. "Not that I really know anything about you, Luke."

"No more than I know anything about you, Ruth." He looked away and fiddled fretfully with his discarded fork. "I wanted to ask but somehow never plucked up the courage."

Ruth smiled at that. "There really isn't much to know, Luke. Nothing exciting I'm afraid."

"Snap!" Luke said and they both laughed. "Until Ovanga."

Ruth was serious again now. "You're really not going to give up on that, are you?"

Luke was equally serious when he replied, "Paula was right when she said I was once a serious journalist. Years ago. Then it all went pear-shaped; a long story I won't bore you with. I can't write for any national newspaper any more so I have just pottered about doing what I do down here, so if there is a story about Ovanga it won't be about me. It will be about him: what he is. The truth."

"And that matters to you?" Ruth asked warily.

"It does."

"Is that what made you become a journalist?"

Luke smiled reflectively. "With the help of a policeman's truncheon." He sensed Ruth's bewilderment. "Another story for another time."

"Why is Ovanga suddenly so important? Now?"

"Somebody else asked me that. I passed it off as a midlife crisis; raging against the dying of the light."

"Sounds a bit melodramatic."

Luke laughed. "Thank you, Ruth."

"What for?"

"Recognising bullshit when you hear it."

Ruth shrugged. "I've often been told I have no imagination."

"Really. By whom?"

Ruth hesitated. "Simon," she replied awkwardly.

"Simon? Is he your partner?"

"Yes," Ruth muttered. "At least I think so." She said no more for a moment and then registered the concern on Luke's face. She sat up straight and forced a smile. "So if not midlife crisis, what?"

"Don't take this the wrong way, Ruth."

"Take what the wrong way?"

"Well, of course it sounded like it could be a big story," Luke hesitated and looked away nervously, "but what made it different was you."

"Me?"

"If I'm honest, and I know this sounds really pathetic, I think it was because it would have given me a chance to get closer to you; perhaps even impress you." He broke off and shook his head in despair. "You must think I'm a complete weirdo."

Ruth said nothing for a moment and then she leaned forward and put her hand on Luke's. "Not a weirdo at all, Luke. And thank you for being so honest. That must have been hard." She pulled her hand away and sat back.

"You're not upset then?"

"Not at all. Now it's my turn to be honest." She spoke quietly but emphatically. "I like you, Luke; a lot. You're a good friend." She smiled wistfully and looked directly at Luke. "Perhaps, if things were different." She let the thought hang in the air for a moment and then turned her head away.

Luke said nothing, whilst trying to process what Ruth had just said.

Ruth sighed. "So I wish I could help you with your story but I'm sorry, I can't."

Luke pulled himself together. "Is it your brother?"

"Yes. He put himself in danger for me. I couldn't possibly involve him."

Luke was quiet for a moment. "I understand," he said with a slight sigh.

"So I'm sorry Luke, but that means no story for you I'm afraid."

"True." Luke accepted the inevitable. "So Ovanga is off the hook."

"I know that matters to you, Luke, but would it really make a difference?"

"Well, he is, it seems, a ruthless and vicious criminal and he could be the next President of your country."

"My country? Do I have a country?" Ruth asked defiantly. "I still feel a stranger here. I have a German passport and soon I will have to apply for permission to stay in England. My father was a Jew; my mother a Rhodesian. What does that make me?"

Luke seemed to consider the question before replying. "I can see there is a lot I don't know about you, Ruth."

Ruth persisted. "And this Ovanga. If you stop him what difference will it make? There are dozens just like him waiting to take his place. My brother, I know, is a good man. How could I risk harming him for the sake of getting at Ovanga?" She had raised her voice to make her case and when she fell silent she did so with an embarrassed shake of her head. "Sorry Luke. Was I shouting?"

"Just a bit." He smiled. "But I don't blame you."

Ruth relaxed at that. Again she reached across the table and took Luke's hand. "I'm sorry Luke, really sorry. About your story. I know it was important to you."

Luke did not let go of her hand immediately. "Not that important, now." He then released her hand and stood up awkwardly. "Better get this place tidied up before the Dragon returns."

FOURTEEN

Luke delayed contacting Rick for a couple of days. It gave him the time to be reconciled to the fact that there would be no big story; to accept that his brief dream of shaping major events again had been no more than that: a dream that had faded away with Ruth's unwillingness to get involved. He reflected that in his zealous past he would not have accepted defeat so easily. He would have pestered and harried her to get at least enough to make a headline. He had briefly flirted with the idea that he could still cobble something together for Rick with such weasel words as: his source 'wished to remain anonymous', or something like 'the alleged involvement of a Zimbabwean businessman now living in Australia.' He knew from experience that such flimsy evidence had not stopped newspapers in the past from splashing front page exposés, checked by lawyers to ensure the lack of specifics was protection from litigation. But he could not be party to that. Not now. Not with Ruth. They were no longer just work colleagues he told himself. But what were they? Friends certainly; good friends who had shared confidences and even allowed moments of something more. Perhaps he was reading too much into it. He could not deny he found her attractive; not just her looks but also her personality. And he was more or less certain she felt the same about him: she had as good as admitted it and implied if her circumstances were different they might have moved to a deeper relationship. But, Luke reproved himself, her circumstances were not different. She had a partner and two children. Paula had occasionally let slip inadvertently that all was not well between Ruth and this Simon guy but offered no details and Luke could certainly not pry into that. He would just have to settle for the role of a good friend; but somehow the prospect was less than fulfilling.

Sighing in resignation, Luke tapped Rick's number on his phone. This was not a call he was looking forward to. Rick would almost certainly scoff at his failure to secure the co-operation of his 'lady friend' as he would no doubt describe her. He would also be understandably niggled that Luke had offered an exclusive headline-grabbing story which he could now not deliver. Luke braced himself for the onslaught.

"Luke," Rick sounded cheerful enough. "Yes. I was expecting you to call."

Luke tried to sound nonchalant but it was an effort. "Sorry, Rick, been a bit tied up. You know how—"

Rick did not wait for Luke to elaborate. "Sod's Law isn't it?"

Luke tried to make sense of that. "Well. I suppose—"

"Like my first editor used to say, 'Life is like a cucumber'."

Luke was seriously lost now. "Cucumber?"

"Yes. One minute it's in your hand and the next minute it's up your arse."

Rick was so busy chortling at his own bizarre analogy that Luke had a moment to gather his thoughts. He had no idea where Rick was coming from but it would be wise to let him do the talking. "I see what you mean, Rick."

Rick had now composed himself. "I don't know whether you've had a chance yet to look at the details?"

Luke feared that the time had now come to admit failure but he still played for time. "Not completely Rick."

"They say it was a car crash of course. They always do. Never a good idea to get behind the wheel of your car if you're an ambitious politician in Zimbabwe."

Luke was beginning to detect a glimmer of sense in what Rick was saying. "It seems not," he muttered cautiously.

"They'll give him a hero's funeral of course. All the old comrades wiping tears from their eyes in public and celebrating in private that they've seen off another threat."

Luke now understood. "No point in my stuff now, of course."

Rick laughed. "Mustn't speak ill of the dead, Luke."

"Oh, well. There you go."

"Sorry about it, Luke. All your hard work come to nothing. You'll have to buy your lady friend a glass or two of bubbly for her efforts; wasted as they are."

Luke gritted his teeth. "I'll do that Rick."

"And if anything else crops up feel free to call me."

"Very doubtful, I think."

"I dare say." Rick laughed and Luke could guess what was coming next. "Never mind. There are always the dolphins." The phone went dead.

"So there is no story anyway?" Ruth wrapped another knife and fork in a napkin and laid them on the table she was setting. The café was empty at the moment as they prepared for the lunchtime trade.

"No," Luke admitted as he chalked the day's specials on the café blackboard.

"And you say it was a car crash?"

"That's what they say. They always do."

Ruth paused from her table-laying and stood in silent

reflection for a moment. She sighed despairingly. "Dreadful." She slowly resumed laying the table.

"What's dreadful?" Paula had emerged from the kitchen and caught Ruth's comment.

"Ovanga. You remember? The one who bought my house."

"Yes. What about him?"

"He's dead."

"Oh." The news did not seem to trouble Paula.

"A car crash; probably set up," Luke offered.

Paula digested this for a moment. "Wasn't he the one you were getting all of a quiver about?" She stared at Luke challengingly.

Luke managed a smile. "Momentarily, but it soon passed."

"Glad to hear it." She looked at Ruth who was standing awkwardly listening to the conversation. "He didn't badger you about it then?" She pointed accusingly at Luke.

Ruth glanced nervously at Luke who responded with a relaxed shrug. "We talked about it a bit."

Paula frowned at Luke. "I'm sure you did."

Ruth hurried on; almost gabbling. "It really wasn't a problem. I couldn't really tell Luke anything useful. I just..."

Luke interrupted. "Ruth didn't want to involve her brother. End of story."

Paula looked sceptical. "And you accepted that?"

Ruth answered for him. "Yes. He understood." She smiled at Luke.

Paula still seemed doubtful but decided to give them the benefit of her doubt. "Age must have mellowed you, Luke." She paused and fixed them both with a stare, "Or something has." She left it at that.

Luke was the first to break a difficult silence. He turned back to the board. "Are there two T's in frittata, Paula?"

"Three, to be pedantic," Paula snapped as she strode

back to the kitchen. Luke finished writing on the board and walked over to the table Ruth was setting. From the kitchen they could hear some muttered curse and a clatter of pots. Luke jerked his head towards the source of the noise. He whispered conspiratorially to Ruth, "She would have been a great asset to the Gestapo."

Ruth stifled a laugh. At least it was good to laugh: she had not had many opportunities for that recently. She held a warning finger to her lips to shush Luke but they were still giggling when the bell announced the first lunchtime customer.

FIFTEEN

The text had been brief but at least it gave Ruth a chance to prepare herself. Simon had sent it from the train. He was on his way back from London. He would not be in Penzance until late; there were delays on the line but he should be home before midnight. Ruth pondered the word 'home'. Did Simon really think of her house as home? Was he coming back to stay? In his text he had told her not to bother about making food as he would get something to eat on the train, but she had made some soup. As she stirred the pot she could almost believe that a return to some sort of domestic normality was not impossible. Perhaps it was not too late. But she would need to screw up her courage to demand that Simon must be honest about their future. Did they have one together? Perhaps it was a risk to present Simon with an ultimatum but enough was enough. Esther and Paula were right: it was no longer possible for her to live in a fog of pretence.

The soup began to bubble and Ruth moved the pan off the heat. She turned off the gas burner but as she watched the flame flicker out her thoughts were elsewhere. Their focus of late had been almost exclusively on rescuing her relationship with Simon but she could not ignore that there were other questions now which could not be entirely stilled. Was she even certain that she wanted to stay with Simon? Even if he came home and stayed home, was there a strong enough bond between them any more to make that work? She felt huge guilt for admitting those doubts to herself. She thought again of her father and his advice not to expect too much from life: to make the best of things; to be content with what was possible and not bay for the moon. No doubt if he was alive now he would tell her she should not risk losing what she had in pursuit of some fantasy. She had two beautiful and talented daughters and a roof over her head. Wasn't that enough? Ruth found herself answering the imagined question out loud. "No Dad," she muttered, "nowhere near enough."

Embarrassed that she was reduced to talking to herself, Ruth sought preoccupation in a mindless domestic chore. With the girls asleep upstairs she settled quietly at the kitchen table and attempted to patch a tear in Sarah's school blazer. She had never learnt to sew as a child, there had always been maids to do that, but, when her children were small, financial necessity had forced her to take to needle and thread because there was no money for new clothes, if the old ones could be darned back to life. She would be the first to admit that she had never really mastered the craft and now as she looked at her handiwork on the blazer she tried to convince herself the patch was symmetrical, although it clearly wasn't. In exasperation she attempted to unpick it but only managed to jab the needle into her thumb. Swearing under her breath she surveyed the bead of blood forming on the pad of her thumb, and with a sigh of reluctance put down the blazer and walked across to the sink to rinse the blood away. She let the tap run for a moment and then dabbed her thumb dry. She wondered whether she should bother with a plaster. She thought she had a packet in the cupboard under the sink somewhere and she knelt to rummage amongst its contents. Still on her knees in search she was distracted by the sound of the front door opening. Instantly she forgot about the plaster and stood and turned in nervous anticipation.

Simon entered the kitchen and waited hesitantly in the open doorway. He looked at Ruth still standing by the sink. "Hello," he said, and put his rucksack down on the floor and closed the door behind him.

Ruth walked across to him and kissed him tentatively on the cheek and stepped back. For a moment neither spoke nor moved towards the other.

Simon broke the silence. "Sorry I'm so late. The train."

Ruth found refuge in the ordinary. "Doesn't matter." She walked over to the stove. "I've made some soup. You must be hungry."

"I had a sandwich, but..."

Ruth was already ladling soup into a couple of bowls. Simon walked over to the table and sat down wearily. Ruth carried the soup over and cleared Sarah's blazer off the table and found some cutlery for them both. She sat opposite Simon and gestured to him to eat. He was clearly hungry but Ruth had no appetite and merely sipped the odd spoonful as she watched Simon. He looked worn out; drawn and tense; dark shadows like bruises under his eyes; his thick hair matted and unkempt. For a moment Ruth wondered if he had been sleeping rough. He looked up from eating and caught her gaze; sensed her scrutiny. He put his spoon down. "That was nice; thank you."

Ruth was no good at evasion. "You look washed out, Simon. Are you OK?"

"Yes. Fine."

"Are you sure?"

Simon fiddled with his spoon and looked down at the empty bowl. "It's been a hectic few days."

"Over a week," Ruth reminded him.

"Has it? Sorry. I should have called you, but there never seemed to be time."

Ruth decided not to press the point. She nodded in pretend understanding. Anyway, she had no heart to argue with Simon now. He looked broken; defeated. What had happened to him to strip him of his usual careless self-confidence? There was part of her that wanted to reach out and hold him, comfort him, tell him everything would be all right, but there was another part of her which resented his deceit; his refusal to be honest with her. Torn by these conflicting emotions she said nothing. She stood and carried the bowls across to the sink. She opened a tap and held the bowls under the stream of hot water for a few seconds before shaking them dry and inverting them on the draining board. Wiping her hands on a kitchen towel she turned back to the table. Simon had lifted his rucksack off the floor and placed it on the empty chair next to him. He searched in an inside compartment and produced a thick brown envelope which he put down in front of him. He looked up and saw Ruth watching him. He pushed the envelope across the table towards her. "For you," he said.

Ruth looked in puzzlement at the envelope.

"Open it," Simon instructed.

Ruth picked up the bulging envelope and slid her finger under the flap to open it. She took a step back in astonishment and looked questioningly at Simon.

"Two thousand pounds," he said.

Ruth waited for him to explain but he was now fastening his rucksack and did not meet her stare of confusion. She guessed at the explanation. "The paintings. A gallery took your paintings?"

Simon set the rucksack aside and met her gaze. "I got lucky."

Ruth looked more closely at the contents of the envelope. She saw that the packed notes seemed to be a mix of denominations and some seemed well handled and some new. She looked back at Simon. "Are you sure?"

"Sure of what?" Simon's tone was sharp.

"I mean are you sure you can afford this?"

Simon relaxed. "I told you didn't I? That I would get money."

"You did, Simon." Ruth moved to sit down on the chair facing him. She stretched out her hand to take his. "I'm sorry if I doubted you."

Simon shrugged and moved his hand away. "I can't say I blame you." He stood up. "I could use a shower and a good night's sleep."

Ruth stood too. "There are clean towels in the airing cupboard."

Simon moved towards the stairs. "Thanks." He stopped at the foot of the stars and looked back at Ruth. "Then I'll turn in if that's all right with you?"

Ruth had no time to reply before he was climbing the stairs. She looked again at the envelope she was still holding and tried to ignore the questions it raised.

"Dad is here! Really here?" Sarah asked for Ruth's assurance yet again.

"Yes. But eat your cornflakes or you'll be late."

Sarah had no appetite for her cornflakes. "Why can't I go and wake him up?"

"He's very tired." Ruth could vouch for that. Simon had been in a deep sleep when she had climbed into bed beside him and they had lain back to back all night. Ruth had not slept well; her mind refusing to be still as she tried to make sense of what Simon had told her; which was next to nothing. Of course the money was welcome but why did she have doubts about how it was acquired? Perhaps it was the knowledge that he had not stayed with Johnny Peters which triggered all her uncertainties but it was possible there was an innocent explanation for that. If only they could have a normal conversation. Once or twice in the night Simon had stirred in his sleep and, seemingly troubled, mumbled and muttered inarticulate words. Ruth instinctively wished she could turn and hold him but cold reason held her back. There were too many uncertainties that could not simply be wished away.

Esther had said little when Ruth had told her daughters their father was home beyond raising her eyebrows quizzically at her mother. Now she sat ignoring the food on the table frowning in concentration over paperwork scattered around her. As Ruth moved to clear used plates she could make out that Esther was scrutinising pages of figures and numerical tables and graphs. Ruth felt immediately guilty that she had not shown sufficient interest in the project Esther had been working on for months now. She had been too tied up with her own concerns. She tried to make amends. "How's it coming on? Your Geography project?"

Ruth expected at best a non-committal grunt in reply and was surprised when Esther seemed to take the question seriously. She put down the papers she had been examining and looked up at her mother. "We've come up with some amazing stuff." She sighed, "But how do we get anyone to take any notice?"

The question remained unanswered as Simon appeared at the foot of the stairs. Sarah was the first to see him and rushed from the table to hug him. "You're home."

Simon held Sarah close. Ruth could see his eyes were tearful. Sarah clutched his hand and tugged him over to the table. Before he sat he stopped at Esther's chair and she looked up at him and he kissed her on the cheek. Then she resumed studying her papers.

Sarah jabbered away excitedly to her father as Ruth poured him a cup of coffee and put toast in front of him. Simon listened patiently to his younger daughter as she told him rapidly of her school exploits and her adventures with her friends. As Ruth watched them she remembered how things used to be; when they all functioned as a family. It was perhaps no more than a year ago but it seemed an eternity. She looked at the kitchen clock and reminded the girls it was time to get ready. Sarah looked anguished at that. "Can't I have the day off, to be with Dad?"

Ruth hesitated, but Simon spoke first. "That would be lovely, darling, but I have too much to get done today. Perhaps some other time."

Sarah made no attempt to hide her disappointment as she stood up. Simon must have sensed her sadness. "I'm sorry, Sarah, but I tell you what."

Sarah brightened at this. "Yes?"

"I've left some money with Mum so that you can buy yourself something nice; go shopping in Truro, perhaps on Saturday." As he spoke Simon looked at Ruth in confirmation of his suggestion and she nodded an acknowledgement.

"Thank you. I'll think about what to get." She looked happily at Simon. "You can help me choose. There's this shop in Truro with lots of art materials—"

Simon interrupted her. "I'm sorry, sweet, but I can't come with you this Saturday."

Sarah could not hide her dismay. "But why?"

Simon sighed. "I have to go back to London."

Ruth shared her daughter's dismay; compounded by frustration and anger but she said nothing.

Esther, perhaps sensing her mother's mood, flashed her

an empathetic glance. She rapidly put her notes back into a folder and left the table to collect her school bag from the foot of the stairs. "Get moving," she called out to Sarah, "you don't want a detention do you?"

That threat was enough to get Sarah moving. She hugged Simon briefly and swung her satchel over her shoulder and hurried off after Esther who was already out of the front door.

In the silence that followed, Simon concentrated on drinking his coffee. He seemed wary of catching Ruth's eye. She waited for him to say more: to explain his need to return to London but when he said nothing she forced the issue; trying not to let her irritation show. "So you have to go back to London, do you?"

Simon sipped at his coffee. "Afraid so."

"More paintings is it?" Ruth tried to keep doubt out of her tone.

Simon began to butter a piece of toast; a task which gave him an excuse not to look directly at Ruth. This evasion forced her into an unworthy approach. "Will you stay with Johnny Peters again?"

This time Simon did look directly at her. "More than likely," he said.

SIXTEEN

"You seen the picture in the Clarion, then? Right handsome." Dave was in full Cornish voice. "Bout time they smartened the place up I reckon."

Luke affected the patient weariness he adopted in these exchanges, as if humouring a small exuberant child. "Not a photograph, Pasco, an artist's impression."

"Same difference, Prof."

"Not at all. One reflects reality, the other is simply an expression of wishful thinking on the Council's part; designed to suggest they are actively engaged in regenerating the town centre."

"Aren't they?"

"What signs do you see of it, Pasco?"

"Well um... they put flower boxes about the place."

"Most of which have been vandalised."

"And they made the road traffic-free; you can walk about."

"Between 11 a.m. and 3 p.m. and you still risk being run over by buses, taxis, delivery lorries, motorbikes, cyclists and all those car owners who choose to ignore the restrictions which are not enforced."

"Fair point, Prof. Tamsin nearly got knocked down by one of them electric scooter jobs."

"It's just tinkering, Pasco. The Council say they want to breathe new life into the high street and yet they are actually engaged in choking it to death."

"How come?"

"Consider this, Pasco. How many shops are there on our main street?"

"That's a tricky one, Prof. Never counted them."

"Approximately eighty."

"As many as that? Fair old number."

"You might think so but I have to tell you, Pasco, that as of now, more than a dozen are boarded up; about the same number are charity shops and most of the rest are outposts of national chain stores or phone companies. Small, independent traders are a vanishing minority."

"So why is that?"

"A number of reasons. Landlords demanding unrealistic rents; business rates unreasonably high—"

"And Amazon. They got a lot to answer for I reckon."

"Well spotted, Pasco. Very perceptive of you."

"Thanks, Prof. But I know Tamsin gets all them cardboard boxes delivered."

"Quite. And why not? Far more convenient than having to find somewhere to park and then have to pay a small fortune to leave your car there while you lug your shopping back to it. So people choose the out-of-town supermarkets with free parking or go online. Can you blame them?"

"Suppose not. No-brainer really."

"Exactly. To get people to shop in town you need to offer free parking and sensible rents and business rates to encourage independent traders who can provide specialist products you can't get online or at the supermarkets, and you need to ban all traffic for most of the day if you want the sort of café society in your artist's impression."

"Big ask, Prof."

"Too big for our Council, I fear, Pasco. I doubt they will get beyond the artist's impression."

"Needs thinking about."

"Indeed. As does this question, Pasco. How do you make a small fortune opening a business in Penzance?"

"You got me there, Prof."

"Start with a large one!"

Paula had heard the joke before but she was still laughing as she switched off the podcast as the café doorbell rang and she turned, expecting to greet her first customer of the day.

"Oh, you're early. I thought you were a punter."

Ruth closed the door behind her. "Sorry. I wanted to catch you before we started. If that's OK?"

Paula stood up from the table where she had been listening on her phone. She frowned as she looked at Ruth. "Are you not well? You look ghastly if I may say so."

"Do I?" Ruth looked nervously at Paula. "I'm sorry. I didn't sleep very well."

"Oh, for Christ's sake, stop apologising and come and sit down." Paula gestured to a chair at her table. "The machine is on if you want a coffee."

"No. Thank you." Ruth sat wearily down on the proffered chair. "I just need to talk to someone before I go mad. Someone who can tell me if I'm being paranoid or not." She looked at Ruth. "And apart from you, Paula, and maybe Luke, there is no one I'm close to; no one I can really confide in." She looked almost tearfully at Paula. "I'm sorry."

"There you go again." Paula sat and glared at Ruth. "If you say you're sorry one more time I swear I won't be answerable for the consequences."

Ruth managed to smile at that and sat back in her chair;

her tense shoulders relaxing slightly. Paula softened her glare into an answering smile but that quickly turned into a scowl as the café bell rang again. She stood and muttered to Ruth, "Hang in there until we close and we'll talk then: you, me and Luke."

Ruth just about managed to stay focussed on her café chores; forcing a smile to greet the regulars and occasionally managing a dutiful laugh in response to some quip or other. That just about carried through the morning but when Luke arrived for his lunchtime stint he seemed to sense her suppressed tension. She was conscious of him casting her concerned looks and at one point he raised his eyebrows quizzically in invitation for some explanation of her state of mind, but she responded with a small shake of the head and busied herself with some cutlery wrapping. This mechanical task helped to damp down her restless thoughts but not quench them entirely. Had she been too impulsive in confiding in Paula? Was she being disloyal to Simon? Was her imagination distorting a mundane reality? These questions spawned a sense of guilt but then that was countered by other questions. Why was Simon really going back to London? Why had he lied about staying with Johnny Peters? Was the money really from a sale of his paintings and, if not, where was it from? The questions churned around in her head in bewildering counter-point. That's why she needed to ask for help. She had no close family at hand to confide in: she could not possibly involve her children in her doubts about their father. She had to accept the only two people she could look to for advice were Paula and Luke. She had barely known them more than a few weeks and yet her instinct was to trust them. She was sure Paula would give her opinion, bluntly but honestly, and Luke might be more measured in his response but since the Ovanga business she could not ignore that there was a feeling of mutual affection between them which was barely expressed but difficult to ignore. As she considered this, Ruth could not help but wonder if this might colour Luke's judgement of Simon but then she reproached herself for the thought; for daring to presume in her vanity that Luke would behave like a jealous suitor. She told herself to grow up and reinforced the rebuke by polishing an already clean fork with painful vigour.

"But why should he lie about where he was staying in London? I don't see the point of that?" Paula seemed to demand an answer from Ruth.

The afternoon was well advanced now. After the café had emptied the three of them had sat at their lunch table but no one seemed interested in eating, although Paula sipped at her glass of cider and had kept a cigarette on the go but, in a concession to the others, remembering to blow the smoke away towards the kitchen where the open doors might permit it to be wafted into the fresh air. It was Paula who had asked most of the questions after Ruth had explained her anxiety over Simon's reappearance with the money. Luke had said little and Ruth felt uneasily that perhaps he was embarrassed to be involved in this dissection of her relationship with Simon. She knew enough about Luke now to accept that he kept his emotions under close control; whatever life had done to him had made him wary. To be a successful journalist perhaps you needed a suspicious carapace; question everything and believe nothing you can't prove. So why should he place any credence in her misgivings about Simon and the money? She only had doubts to offer: not certainties.

"I don't know, Paula," Ruth said, addressing the question. "I've asked myself that a hundred times."

Paula frowned. "It's clear he didn't want you to know what he was up to." She turned and glared at Luke. "Isn't that obvious?" Luke said nothing so Paula repeated the question more forcefully. "Isn't it? Or am I missing something here?"

Luke took time to respond. "There are a number of possible explanations," he said quietly.

"Oh for Christ's sake." Paula shook her head in exasperation. "Go on then. Tell us mere mortals."

Luke would not be hurried. He looked at Ruth. "You said when Simon came back he looked exhausted, dishevelled."

"Well he had spent eight hours on Great Western Railway!"

Paula's joke did not deflect Luke. "Isn't that what you said, Ruth?"

"Yes. Really worn out."

"Do you think it's possible he was sleeping rough in London and was ashamed, or at least too embarrassed, to admit it?"

Ruth considered the suggestion. "It did cross my mind. He would have found it hard to admit to me that he had no money; too demeaning."

"So that might explain his appearance?"

"Hang on a minute." Paula jabbed her finger-held cigarette towards Luke. "Why would he sleep rough? This Johnny guy told Ruth there was an open invitation for Simon to stay any time. So, I ask you again, why would he need to sleep rough?"

Luke shrugged and turned questioningly to Ruth. "What do you think, Ruth?" he asked quietly.

Ruth shook her head despairingly. "I keep wanting to believe there is some simple and innocent explanation for it all. I feel so disloyal to have doubt; and guilt too."

"Rubbish! What have you got to feel guilty about? This is a man who never comes near you or his children and then lies to you about what he is up to." Paula was at full volume now. "And you feel guilty!"

Ruth made as if to protest on Simon's behalf but Paula's fierce outburst did not invite contradiction. She noticed Luke casting her a concerned glance and she realised that until Paula's declamation he had probably not been aware of the full extent of her collapsing relationship with Simon.

No one spoke for a few seconds Then Paula, perhaps aware that her outburst had been a little too forceful, moved them on in a more moderate tone. "Then there's the money. What's your worry there, Ruth?"

Ruth sighed. "It doesn't feel right. I don't know about these things but if he had sold paintings to a gallery would they pay him in cash?"

"Well?" Paula addressed her question to Simon. "You know about galleries don't you?"

Luke shrugged. "I guess it would be unusual. They only pay on a sale and never in cash."

Ruth remembered something Johnny Peters had told her, "And there didn't seem to be any demand for Simon's sort of stuff."

"Perhaps he had a private buyer," Luke offered.

"Then why did he tell me he sold at a gallery? Perhaps he thought I was stupid enough to believe him." Ruth spoke in frustration, turning to Paula and Luke in turn in hope of some explanation which had eluded her.

Paula dragged on her cigarette and stared at Luke as if challenging him to provide an answer. He did his best. "I suppose if the gallery had paid him with a cheque he could have cashed it at a bank and then given you the money."

Ruth shook her head. "I had thought of that but the bank wouldn't have given him a mixture of old used notes would they?" She addressed her question to Luke.

"I suppose not," Luke said, almost apologetically.

Paula got impatiently to her feet and stubbed out her cigarette on a saucer. She strode towards the kitchen. "New packet," she explained.

Whilst Paula rummaged in the kitchen Ruth looked helplessly at Luke. "I'm sorry," she said quietly.

Luke looked surprised. "For what?"

"For involving you in all this but I didn't know what else—"

Luke reached across the table and took her hand. He smiled at her. "It's an old cliché but that's what friends are for."

Ruth squeezed his hand in thanks and then released it quickly as Paula emerged from the kitchen who, if she had observed this moment of intimacy, chose to ignore it. The cigarette break – a new one was already alight – had clearly galvanised her into proposing a new line of action.

"This is hopeless," she declared, "we can sit here all day wondering whether Simon sold his paintings or not but we can't ignore the elephant in the room." She sat down heavily and drew vigorously on her cigarette.

"What elephant are we talking about Paula?" Luke asked innocently.

"Let's not pussyfoot about," Paula snapped back. "It seems clear to me there were no paintings sold. So the question is how did Simon get hold of the money and should Ruth care?"

"Of course I should care!" Ruth could not hide her anger. "What if he's mixed up in something criminal, even dangerous? I need to know, Paula." She hesitated; embarrassed by her show of emotion. "Sorry. I just."

Paula laughed and Ruth looked at her in astonishment. "There you go Ruth: apologising again. Of course you want to know what Simon's been up to and where the money came from. I just wanted to be sure you cared enough to risk finding out."

Ruth looked at Paula for clarification but her attention had now switched to Luke. "Investigative journalist. Isn't that what you were?"

Luke looked confused by the question. "What?"

"Don't play the innocent. We all know it, and you were bloody good at it. The best."

"I don't see what—"

Paula raised her hand to silence Luke's protest, oblivious to the ash falling on the tablecloth. "If you could uncover government secrets it shouldn't be too difficult to find out what, if anything, Simon has been up to."

Ruth made to speak to rescue Luke from any such involvement but Paula quelled her, with a steely glare and a downward flap of her non-smoking hand, before turning back to Luke. "You don't have to do anything too desperate. You know all the artists in Newlyn and you know how they all love to gossip about each other." She paused for confirmation. "Don't you?"

Luke nodded reluctantly. "I suppose."

Paula took that as confirmation. "Just sniff around. See if Simon has been painting anything saleable." She looked challengingly at Ruth. "Or even if he has been painting at all."

Ruth shook her head. "Look, Paula, I don't feel comfortable with this; spying on Simon."

Paula sighed in exasperation. "Well, make up your mind. Do you want help or not?"

Ruth felt close to tears again but she blinked them back; told herself to think clearly. It was true that she had little idea in recent months of how Simon spent his time except that it was not with her. She also knew that whatever had kept them together over the years was now gone but did that give her the right to pry and probe into his behaviour?

"Well?" Paula demanded a response.

Luke broke the tension. "I could just ask around I suppose." He looked at Ruth. "If it would put your mind at rest: stop you worrying about Simon."

Ruth managed a small smile of thanks but her mind was still conflicted. "Thank you; but I don't know. I really don't."

Paula threw up her hands in despair. "It's quite simple. You have to make up your mind. Do you carry on as if nothing had happened and just keep the money and shut up, because if you do then we can all stop banging on about it and get on with life; such as it is. Or do you want to try to find the truth? Even if that turns out to be uncomfortable?" Paula kept her eyes firmly on Ruth; demanding a decision.

Ruth made one. "Well, perhaps if Luke could just ask around."

SEVENTEEN

Simon Wilson. Luke had felt embarrassed to have to ask Ruth her partner's surname and more embarrassed to tell her that he remembered writing a review of Simon's work a few years ago when he had first arrived in Newlyn and held an exhibition. He had dug that article out of the Clarion archives and reminded himself that he had genuinely been impressed by the paintings; by their vivid colours and challenging abstract imagery. They were not the comfortable wall hangings the tourists would buy so it was clear that Simon was looking at a more sophisticated market; one, which, Luke had been told, was dormant of late.

This had been the view of the artists he had spoken with over the last few days. He had, with an uneasy conscience, cloaked his inquiry about Simon with the deception he was updating his files on the current work of artists he had featured in past reviews in the Clarion. He had listened patiently to the familiar tirades against the avarice of gallery owners and the fickle shifts of the art market and the depressing need to pander to the philistine taste of holidaymakers in order to make a living. He had nodded in sympathy at the appropriate moments when there were pauses for breath and, only as an apparent afterthought, made casual inquiry about the current output of one of the artists on his list: Simon Wilson. He had a readymade excuse for asking. He had checked that Simon's studio was locked and empty; presumably because he was away in London as Ruth had told them. He had risked peering in through the studio windows but saw little sign of recent activity or work in progress. Dust sheets covered a couple of easels and brushes stood in jars of cleaning fluids on disordered benches. Skulking outside the empty studio took him back to his early foray into role of investigator; doing the 'leg work' by lurking at a bus stop near Streatham Common to check on the lifestyle of Harry Kingdon. All that effort had come to nothing but it had given him an appetite for finding what lay beneath the surface. An appetite fuelled later by the world of electronic surveillance and telephone tapping and shake outs; an appetite which could never be sated and which in the end had poisoned him. So, he asked himself, why was he now lying and snooping to try to discover what lay beneath the surface in the life of Simon Wilson? The answer disturbed him. He had to accept that he had only become involved because of his feelings for Ruth; feelings, he warily acknowledged, which were more complex than simple friendship. But recognising that presented its own dilemma. Was his decision to delve into Simon's life an act of journalistic objective investigation or was it a way of getting closer to Ruth? And if what he discovered about Simon was suspicious: could he really pass that on to Ruth without seeming to be trying to insinuate himself into her life? Struggling with these conflicting emotions, Luke knew there was one last line of inquiry he needed to pursue before having to make difficult decisions.

It was quiet in the Arts Club bar. The evening performance was an hour away and Dave was not expecting much of a crowd anyway. Apart from family and friends he did not anticipate many turning out for a solo performance by a local singer songwriter who, in his opinion, was deservedly unknown. So he looked up in some surprise when Luke entered the bar. "Didn't know you were covering this."

Luke slumped down on a bar stool. "I'm not, thank God!" He pushed a ten pound note across the counter. "And one for yourself."

"So to what do I owe the pleasure? Got a new script for me?"

Luke shook his head. "Not ready yet. I've been tied up with other stuff."

Dave laughed. "Big news story breaking is there? 'Penzance man bites dog.'" He pulled two pints for them and pushed one in front of Luke.

Luke managed a weary smile. "Nothing so exciting." He took a sip of his beer and then put the glass down on the counter and leaned in towards Dave and lowered his voice when he spoke. "I've come to pick your brain, Dave."

Dave laughed at that. "Pick away. Tell me if you find anything."

"I think you know most people around here, Dave. Not just your customers of course but the gossip they pass on."

Dave raised his hands in mock outrage. "Are you suggesting I listen to gossip?"

Luke smiled. "I certainly am. That's why I'm here."

Dave drunk some of his beer, then spoke with theatrical solemnity. "If I can help the cause of truth and justice in any way, sir, then—"

Luke cut him short, and although the bar was empty spoke almost in a whisper. "What can you tell me about the Trebenten family?"

Dave was suddenly serious "Are we talking about the Newlyn Trebentens?"

"We are."

Dave frowned at Luke. "You don't want to get mixed up with them."

"Is that so?"

Dave, too, now spoke softly. "Some of the brothers have been in here. Hard as nails. Everyone watches themselves when they're around."

Luke nodded. "And the sister?"

Dave raised his eyebrows. "Now there's a piece of work."

"So what have you heard?"

"I gather old man Jack Trebenten built the business up; bought himself a fleet of boats from those who couldn't hack it and now the family have got themselves quite an operation. Made a bomb when the fishing was good but might be struggling a bit post Brexit, from what I hear."

Luke thought that over. "So they might be diversifying, you might say."

Dave looked cautiously again around his empty bar. He seems almost nervous. "Possibly, but don't quote me on any of this, Luke. I value my kneecaps."

"Don't worry, Dave, this is not for publication. Just a private inquiry."

Dave seemed reassured. "Well you know how it is in Newlyn. If you know the right people you can lay your hands on any substance known to man. Not just fish that some boats catch."

"And the Trebenten boats?"

"Just gossip, Luke."

"Do you believe it?"

Dave pondered that. "I wouldn't put it past the brothers."

"How many are there?"

"Three of them. They run the business."

"And the sister?"

"Elowen Trebenten. She's really the power behind the throne they say. Lovely looking too; long blonde hair. You must have seen her about the place."

Luke shrugged. "Not that I recall."

"Maybe not." He frowned in recollection. "Come to think of it I suppose she's only been back just over a year."

"Back from where?"

"London. She went to Uni there. Got a good degree it seems. Don't know where she gets her brains from. Lots of gossip about that too." He smiled reflectively. "Then she got a good job up there they tell me; imports and exports or such."

"But she came back here?" Luke prompted.

"Yes. That was a bit of a mystery too."

"Why?"

"Well, she had this boyfriend, or partner, in tow. Smooth city type. He came in here with her once; wanted some fancy cocktail." He laughed at the memory.

"Is he still around?"

"No. Lasted a few months. I don't think he saw eye to eye with the brothers. Wanted to tell them how to run the business and she wasn't having that I guess. She could sort them out and she didn't need him putting his oar in."

Luke looked quizzically at Dave. "How do you know all this?"

Dave tapped the side of his nose. "I keep my ears open. We get all sorts drink in here: not for the culture but because it's the cheapest booze in town."

"I see. Including fishermen."

"Correct."

"So he left? This fancy boyfriend."

"I suppose he must have."

"Suppose?"

"Well, let's just say he just wasn't around anymore."

Luke frowned. "What are you telling me, Dave?"

"Look, Luke, this is just gossip and rumour; make of it what you will." He paused to consider his words, "But some wondered if he had pushed the brothers too far."

Luke did not speak for a moment. When he did it was with incredulity. "I can't believe what I'm hearing."

Dave spread his arms resignedly. "You asked for the gossip."

"But even so."

"There was an argument on the quayside; a lot of shouting and swearing. Several of the guys on other boats saw it."

"Maybe—"

"And the next day he was gone."

"Got fed up no doubt."

"Or fed to the fishes."

Luke stared at Dave in disbelief. "Are you saying what I think you're saying?"

"No, Luke. I'm just repeating what some people were saying, or rather whispering, at the time."

"Did anyone speak to the police?"

Dave laughed without much humour. "And upset the Trebenten brothers? I don't think so!"

Luke shook his head. "No. It's ridiculous. I can't believe it."

"Your choice. I'm just passing on gossip and rumour."

"I expect he just went back to London."

Dave nodded half-heartedly. "Probably." He looked at Luke, who was frowning in concentration. "Anyway, why are you so interested in the Trebentens?"

Luke was spared having to answer as the bar doors swung open to admit the singer songwriter, struggling with a large guitar. Luke got to his feet. "Some other time, Dave," he called in farewell.

EIGHTEEN

Ruth saw the cyclists coming. Two young men in colourful singlets and black Lycra; their heads down over the handlebars and their helmets reflecting the bright afternoon sun. She stood to the side of the path as they powered past; one of them lifted his head sufficiently to mouth 'thank you' and then they were gone. Ruth watched them race away. She supposed they were really going too fast on the path shared with walkers and family groups, who were simply ambling along enjoying the warmth of early Summer, but it was hard to be angry with them; young and fit and confident. Jealous possibly, but not too critical.

Ruth resumed her walk; trying to recall when she had last felt the carefree optimism the cyclists seemed to epitomise. Exploring in the Bush with Ben probably. She tried not to dwell on the memory but accepted that then she really didn't have a care in the world: but now? She stopped herself from this dangerous introspection. She tried to lift her mood by registering the activities on the beach. From the elevation of the cycle path she had a good view of the families in their staked-out sandy enclaves; mothers proffering food to boisterous children just released from school; dogs yapping in frenzied excitement when a ball was thrown for them; toddlers digging earnestly in the sand; older brothers and sisters flirting with the small waves breaking at the water's edge and shrieking in pretend panic if the cold water splashed their legs. Ruth briefly felt her mood lighten. When the girls were small there had been days like this on the beach; she had joined in digging sandcastles and held their hands as they paddled; laughing and squealing as the waves butted against them. Just normal things; what normal families did. Simon had never really enjoyed those beach days. He tried; at least to start with. But he always seemed distracted; even bored. Gradually he found excuses not to participate. There was always work that needed finishing. Ruth had tried not to nag him about it. She had accepted that Simon was different from what her mother would have called a 'family man'. For all his liberal views he seemed to assume day-to-day childcare was women's work and Ruth, with only the experience of her African upbringing to draw on, could accept that, even if her mother's care had been exercised through surrogate black maids.

Simon had been gone a week now and had made no contact. Ruth tried to feel angry but all emotion seemed spent. In its place she perversely felt a sense of acceptance; not resignation but a growing awareness that whatever the future held for her, Simon would not be part of it. She would tell him when he eventually returned that it was over; that they would need to go their own ways. She doubted he would be too distressed. He would no longer have to feel any obligation. They would work out arrangements for him to see the girls. Sarah would be upset of course but Ruth would try to reassure her that her father would still be part of her life. Esther would understand. After all she had more or less told Ruth she should make the break.

Ruth ran all this through her mind as she walked. It all sounded quite clear cut and sensible. The right course of action, she told herself, one which two mature adults could handle without tearing themselves apart. But no matter how hard she tried to convince herself that she had made the right decision the doubts would not be entirely stilled. Would she be strong enough to cope on her own? Would she be able to make a new life undefined by Simon? He had been her anchor in the uncharted waters of English society when she first arrived and they had shared so much; good times at first and then a dogged resilience in the face of hardship. They had two children whom they both loved. As Ruth reminded herself of all this she could hear her father's voice again: 'what more do you want?' She wished she could articulate a detailed reply.

Luke saw Ruth coming and noticed she was frowning slightly; looking preoccupied. It made him feel uneasy. He was unsure what the outcome of this meeting might be. Ruth had told him she needed to talk; somewhere away from work. He had suggested the beach café. He had arrived a few minutes early and ordered himself a coffee. He had taken it to one of the outside tables overlooking the beach. Ruth saw him and raised her hand in greeting. He stood and pulled out a chair for her.

"Thanks. Am I late? Sorry."

Luke smiled. "No. I'm early. Neurosis. Always afraid of missing trains and buses; so end up hanging around for hours worrying about losing my ticket."

Ruth laughed at that. "I'm always rushing; seconds to spare." She sat and leaned back against the chair. She looked out at the activity on the beach for a few seconds and then turned back to Luke. "Everyone having fun," she said, flatly.

Luke stood. "What would you like? Tea? Coffee?"

"Coffee would be nice. Thank you."

Ruth watched as Luke made his way to the serving hatch.

She reflected that this was the first time they were meeting alone, away from work; away from Paula. She had been nervous about suggesting it; wondering what Luke might read into the request but he had gone along with it easily enough. He had not seemed surprised at the idea but she knew by now how hard it was to really know what Luke was thinking. She remembered the occasion, almost guiltily, when for a few moments they had briefly expressed feelings beyond friendship. But had that just been a fleeting aberration for both of them? Neither had visited those dangerous emotions again.

"There you go." Luke put the cup down on the table.

"Thanks." Ruth took a sip. She put her cup down and looked away; narrowing her eyes against the sun.

Neither of them spoke for a while; both nervous of what might come next.

It was Ruth who broke the silence. "I hope you didn't mind. Meeting me like this."

"What's to mind?" Luke raised he cup. "Good coffee; great view."

Ruth managed a smile. "It's just that I couldn't really talk in front of Paula. I know that sounds disloyal and she has been really good to me but..." She paused trying to find the words.

Luke helped out. "She can be a bit overpowering. Is that it?"

"Just a bit. It's hard to say no when she's in full flow."

"And do you wish you'd said no?"

Ruth looked at him. "The more I have had time to think about it the more I realise I was wrong."

Luke put down his cup and looked hard at her. "Wrong about what, Ruth?"

"Asking you to find out about Simon; what he's been

doing. It wasn't right. And it wasn't fair on you either." Ruth fiddled nervously with her cup and looked apologetically at Luke.

"No need to apologise Ruth. I only asked a few questions. I don't have any answers."

"Even if you had, I wouldn't want to hear them." Ruth broke off in embarrassment. "I'm so sorry, Luke. That must sound so ungrateful. What I mean is, that whatever is going on in Simon's life doesn't matter anymore. I have got to handle it and not expect anyone else to make decisions for me." She broke off and looked away towards the glinting sea. She breathed out deeply and when she turned back to Luke she spoke softly. "Does that make any sense, Luke?"

"Of course."

"So you see I had to tell you. To stop you wasting any more of your time."

Luke shrugged. "My time is not so precious."

Ruth shook her head in wonder. "How do you do it, Luke?"

"Do what?"

"Always stay so calm; so reasonable. Don't you ever get mad?"

Luke smiled at her. "I used to. Look where it got me."

"I don't think I could ever be so in control."

Luke stopped smiling and spoke with intensity. "I had a lot of practice, Ruth. Growing up as I did. I learnt not to betray emotion; not to say what I really thought about anything, just to keep the peace. And then when I got over that I let my emotions rip, in what I believed was the pursuit of truth, only for that to explode in my face." He sat back as if abashed by his admission and managed a rueful grin. "Makes one a bit wary."

Ruth looked at him in surprise. "I can see there is a lot I don't know about you, Luke."

Luke seemed keen to move on. "Probably just as well." He stood up. "Fancy another coffee?"

Ruth glanced at her watch, "That would be great. Just a quick one; but let me get these."

Luke waved away her offer and carried their empty cups off with him. She felt her spirits lifting. Luke had not pressed her on her change of mind or what she would do next nor did he seem to resent wasting his time chasing Simon. Or was it that he had just disciplined himself not to show his true feelings? She still felt she really did not know the real Luke – if such a being existed – but be that as it may she could not deny she was grateful for the company and friendship of the outward persona. She smiled warmly at him as he returned with the coffees. He returned her smile. "So what are we going to tell Paula?" he asked.

They had sat over their coffees far longer than Ruth had planned; until the air cooled and the sun began to sink. They had agreed that Ruth would tell Paula that she was grateful for the help offered but had resolved to take the initiative in bringing matters to a head with Simon. That agreed, they had chatted easily over other things. Ruth had pressed Luke for more details of his polarised childhood and she had told him of her family history and the escape from genocide. When Ruth realised she would be late for her class and dashed off, she felt they knew something more about each other; perhaps she could even glimpse the 'real' Luke she had pondered over.

Luke sat a while longer after Ruth's hasty departure and smiled to himself watching her almost sprinting back towards town. He felt contented. Contented that Ruth's decision to abandon the probing of Simon's activities had precluded the need for him to have to make the difficult decision about passing on what he had found out. It would have been challenging to have to tell Ruth that Simon had almost certainly not got the money from any sale of paintings and that he seemed to be involved with a Newlyn family of dubious morality and in particular with the striking blonde daughter of that family. If you joined the dots up there it made for worrying reading. He would now never have to choose between passing on that disturbing intelligence to Ruth or keeping it to himself, lest he appear to be discrediting Simon in order to worm his way into Ruth's affections. He hoped he could never be accused of that but he could not deny his feelings for Ruth were a little more complex than the outward show.

NINETEEN

Dave silently turned over a page of his script and composed his features into the required frowning bemusement he adopted to characterise Pasco. "I never know where that word comes from."

"Gig?" Luke queried.

"I know we likes our gig racing down here. Tamsin rowed in the Zennor boat back awhile."

"Splendid. But nothing to do with rowing Pasco."

"So, then?"

"A gig is a performance by a musician. A one-off event often paid for in cash."

"But I don't see..."

Luke adopted a slightly weary but patient tone. "In the gig economy work is handed out in individual bits and pieces; no contracts."

"And that's not good?"

"Not good for job security, state benefits, or a living wage."

"But it gives you work. That's OK isn't it?"

"Yes. And it gives you a county ranked with the most economically deprived in the whole of Europe, with a dreadful record on affordable housing, homelessness, child poverty, and mental health provision."

"You make it sound a bit grim, Prof."

"It is, Pasco."

"So why does everyone want to come here for holidays?"

"Because they are only on holiday. Here for a fortnight. Sun, sea, surf, pasties. What's not to like?"

"I don't know about that Prof. Loads of people want to live down here too, so it can't be as bad as you say. And they don't mind forking out silly money for a house. You can't buy nothing for under half a million in St Ives they tell me."

Luke sighed theatrically. "Indeed Pasco. And who are these people?"

"Well, I don't know any of them personally, like."

"No, I don't suppose you do Pasco. Clearly they have considerable disposable income; perhaps from selling up in London or running a successful business. And of course for many their purchase is an investment. They can get sky-high rents from summer holidaymakers so it doesn't matter if the property stands empty in the winter."

"Right enough, Prof. Mousehole is like a ghost town in winter they say. All them empty houses."

"Rows of empty houses and Cornish young couples forced to live with their parents."

"And with this gig business, and all the rest of it you've been on about, no hope of ever earning enough cash to buy a place of their own."

"You've got it in one Pasco."

"Can't the government do nothing?"

Luke affected a scornful laugh. "The government took us out of the EU which provided more cash for Cornwall than any other region of the UK."

"But they said they'd match it. I heard one of their blokes say it. On the telly."

Luke groaned. "Pasco, I sometimes think you are too good for this world."

"What?"

"Your trust and belief in our political masters is truly inspirational."

Dave affected a hurt tone. "Are you taking the piss, Prof?"

Luke put down his script. "I think we must let our listeners decide that, Pasco."

There was a pause whilst Luke shut down the recording equipment. Then he sat back in his chair and breathed out deeply in relaxation. "Thanks Dave. Another flawless performance."

Dave laughed. "I think the accent might have slipped once or twice."

"Surely not."

"'Mummersetshire'. That what they called it in radio drama when anything West Country was needed."

"Those were the days. Eh, Dave?"

"Gainful employment."

"Well, I might have to consider paying you if you get too accomplished."

"Only in used notes I hope."

They both laughed at that. "But for the moment," Luke said, "don't give up the day job."

"Day and night, if you don't mind. Spreading culture to the masses and listening to mindless chatter at the bar."

"I'm sure you have a sympathetic ear for the troubled."

"A fixed smile." Dave stood, and said, "Must get on." He made for the door.

Luke stood too. Dave paused by the door. "By the way are you still interested in the Trebenten gang?"

Luke hesitated. "Not really. Not anymore. But why do you ask?"

"Well, word has it they are doing very well for themselves. Just bought a new boat. That caused quite a stir at Newlyn."

"Is that so unusual?"

"In the current climate it is. Most of them are just about hanging on by their fingertips."

Luke nodded. "Well, the Trebentens must be doing something right."

Dave opened the door and then turned back to look at Luke. He gave him a crooked smile. "Or something wrong."

Paula stood in her characteristic pose; leaning against the frame of the open kitchen door and puffing smoke out into the back yard. At the stove, Ruth lowered the gas flame under a saucepan to simmer level.

"So you've called off the bloodhound?" Paula addressed the question to Ruth without turning her head.

Ruth paused before replying. She chose her words carefully. "I have had time to think about it. It didn't seem fair."

"Fair!" Paula snorted her disbelief and, flicking her cigarette stub into the yard, turned to glare at Ruth.

Ruth had anticipated how Paula would react to the news that she had asked Luke not to carry on checking up on Simon. She knew she owed Paula an explanation, even an apology, for backtracking on her original decision, but it was hard to find the words to express her muddled feelings. "I know you must think I'm a wimp but really I have to do this for myself. I realise that now."

Paula did not look convinced. "So what changed?"

"Luke, I suppose," Ruth muttered.

"Luke changed?" Paula demanded disbelievingly. "How?"

Ruth was floundering now. She was fighting an impulse to tell Paula to back off; to stop haranguing her, but she controlled that reaction because she understood that Paula was, in her own bullish way, trying to be helpful and supportive. So she composed herself and tried to explain. "Luke has been asking around; he told me that—"

"And?" Paula interrupted.

Ruth took a deep breath and continued. "And I asked him to stop." She was aware of the look of scepticism on Paula's face so pressed on quickly. "You see it wasn't just Simon who would come out of it badly if there was anything; I don't know," she paused to consider how to proceed, "if anything dishonest or whatever was going on."

Paula looked unconvinced. "Who else would be affected?"

Ruth struggled on. "Luke." She registered Paula's puzzlement. "If he found out stuff about Simon; stuff which would damage him; and damage us and what was left of our relationship, then to expect him to tell me that would be unfair." She looked nervously at Paula, "Do you understand what I'm trying to say? Does it make any sort of sense?" She was almost pleading with Paula for some sign of awareness.

Paula said nothing for a moment and in the silence found time to light another cigarette. She drew on it deeply and turned to the open door to blow out the smoke. She did not turn back to Ruth when she spoke. "I think I get it. It's Luke isn't it? You and Luke?"

Ruth protested to Paula's back. "No. Not like that. I don't really know him. We are..."

Paula turned to face Ruth. "Don't tell me; 'just good friends'. Is that what you were going to say?"

Ruth hesitated. "I suppose I was."

Paula flipped her newly lighted cigarette out into the yard and walked across to the stove and absently stirred the contents of the saucepan. After a few seconds she stopped stirring and looked hard at Ruth standing nervously close by, braced for some abrasive comment. To Ruth's relief and astonishment Paula smiled. "Did you think I hadn't noticed?"

"Noticed what?" Ruth's confusion was genuine.

Paula carried the stirring spoon across to the sink and tossed it onto the draining board. "The smiles, the shared jokes, the quiet conversations. How you both seem so easy in each other's company."

Ruth could feel herself blushing. "But it's nothing, we just—"

Paula shook her head. "Trust me Ruth. It's more than nothing. So perhaps I do get it. You don't want to put Luke in a position where you both might have doubts about his reasons for bearing ill tidings of Simon." She paused and looked directly at Ruth. "I'm right aren't I?"

Ruth hesitated. "But perhaps there are no ill tidings anyway."

Paula was not to be deflected. "Maybe. But I'm still right. You and Luke." She offered that as a statement not a question.

Ruth said nothing. For a moment Paula held her gaze challengingly. Then she turned back to the stove and when she spoke her mood seemed entirely changed. "Let's sort this bloody saucepan out before it boils over."

TWENTY

The text had been brief and recent. Ruth had picked it up as she was clearing away after her last session of the day at the leisure centre. She barely registered the chatter and laughter of the class as they made their way out and it was an effort to smile in response to their cheerful departure. She managed to tell them she would be looking forward to seeing them next time but as they drifted away she was left in anxious silence. There could be no going back now; no more fumbling along in tormenting indecision. She knew what had to be done but she was still fearful of doing it.

"What are you cooking?" Esther looked up from the kitchen table where she had been absorbed in sorting through the pages in her project file.

"Soup. It's always soup," Ruth said without looking at her daughter.

Esther snapped her ring-file shut. "For Dad?"

"He's on the train. I got a text." Ruth stirred the soup but still did not turn to look at Esther.

"Is he staying?" Esther's tone was sharp.

This time Ruth did turn, after pushing the saucepan away from the gas ring. "I don't know, Esther. Perhaps just for the night."

Esther frowned. "And then?"

"We'll see." Ruth sat wearily down at the end of the table. "I don't know, Esther, I just don't know." She shrugged nervously. "We'll have to talk."

Esther shook her head. "Bit late for that isn't it?"

Ruth stared at her in exasperation. "You make it sound so simple, Esther. You think I can just forget what your father and I have been through, shared, for nearly twenty years. You think I can just say 'it's over now, so off you go'?" Ruth had raised her voice to make her point.

Esther said nothing.

Ruth continued, making an effort to rein in her emotion. "Look, I know we have to come to a decision: about us. I know that." She stopped; unsure of how to procced.

Esther leaned forward and looked hard at her mother. "You don't hate Dad, do you?"

Ruth recoiled as if she had been slapped. "Of course I don't."

Esther persisted. "That's why you should finish it. Now. While you can still talk to each other. If you try to carry on you'll end up forgetting all the good times, all the good memories. You'll grind each other down." She paused and sat back. "That's what I think, anyway. I wouldn't like that."

Ruth found the logic inescapable. She accepted that what Esther was telling her was right, but that didn't make it easy. "I know," was all she could bring herself to say.

Neither spoke for a few moments. The only sound was the low hiss of the flickering gas burner. It was Ruth who sought to change the mood. She pointed at the ring-folder on the table in front of Esther. "How's the project coming along?"

Esther sighed. "It's really important, Mum. The stuff we've got together. Not just to pass an exam but to try to change things," she sighed. "But who's going to listen to a bunch of schoolkids?"

Ruth felt immediately guilty. "I'm sorry, Esther. I haven't really looked in detail at what you've been doing; I don't seem to have found the time."

Esther smiled ruefully, "I think you've probably had quite a bit of other stuff to think about recently; saving the planet will have to wait." She stood and tidied up her papers. "I'd better go to bed; can't think straight anymore tonight."

Ruth stood too. "And don't wake Sarah. She looked worn out after school."

Esther grinned, "Netball. She's very sporty: takes after you I suppose. I think I'm a bit more like Dad." She broke off abruptly. "Sorry: not very clever of me."

Ruth managed a half smile in acceptance of the apology and walked back to the stove to check on the soup. She moved the saucepan back over the flame. When she turned it was to see Esther still standing by the table. They held each other's gaze for a few seconds.

"Love you, Mum," Esther said, before she turned and walked away.

Ruth put the envelope down on the table in front of Simon. He looked at it and then raised his head to look in confusion at Ruth. She pointed. "It's all there. I've taken nothing."

Simon picked up the envelope and raised the flap. He looked briefly at the wad of notes inside and then back at Ruth standing at the end of the table. He pushed aside the half empty soup bowl. He had said he was not hungry but Ruth had insisted he eat something. She had been even more shocked by his appearance this time. Not so much by the lank hair and scruffy clothing but by his downcast and fretful demeanour. He had barely spoken as he had sipped half-heartedly at his soup. Now he seemed to be bemused. He held up the envelope. "It was for you; you and the girls."

Ruth sat and, putting both hands on the table in front of her, confronted Simon. When she spoke it was slowly and carefully; words she had clearly rehearsed in her mind. "I don't know where that money came from, Simon, and I don't want to know. You always said I had no imagination but I have enough to guess that however you got that," here she pointed at the envelope, "it looks to have taken a terrible toll on you. So please take it back and don't offer me anymore. I can manage; I always have. You don't have to do this: this charade. I can't pretend anymore. You're free, Simon, to lead the life you want. Free of me. Maybe there is someone else you want to be with; I don't know and it doesn't matter." She paused for a moment and gathered herself for her final words. "You see we're both free now, Simon. We can start again; but not together. We have the girls; we have some great memories. It was good before life wore us down. We needn't tear each other apart. Need we?" Ruth sat back, tearful now. She looked apprehensively at Simon who had sat motionless through her outpouring. He now looked away from her and absently fidgeted with the soup spoon. After a few moments he looked back at Ruth but said nothing. Then he picked up the envelope and with a brief shrug put it in the inside pocket of his jacket.

"If that's what you want, Ruth." His tone was neutral; it was hard to read the emotions behind it.

Ruth had been bracing herself for argument, recrimination, denial; anything but flat acceptance. "Yes, Simon, it is what I want. It's for the best."

Simon again displayed no reaction. "If you say so."

Ruth wondered if the comment was sarcastic but Simon was poker-faced. She filled in the silence. "We can sort out all the practical details. You'll want time to move your stuff out. Will you be able to live in the studio?" She found herself gabbling. "And of course you can see the girls whenever you want."

Simon nodded slowly. "And what will you tell them?"

"We can tell them together if you like."

"No. I think you're better at that sort of thing."

Ruth wondered for moment what sort of thing Simon might be alluding to but she pressed on. "I think Esther has seen this coming and I expect she has spoken to Sarah. I'll just tell them that we have decided we are better off living apart and—"

Simon interrupted her. "You have decided, would be more to the point."

Ruth controlled herself with difficulty. "OK, Simon; I have decided."

Simon looked for a moment as if he might contest the issue but then thought better of it. He stood and picked up the rucksack he had put down by his chair. He retrieved his anorak from the back of the chair and put it on.

Ruth watched this in silence for a moment before a reflex concern was triggered. "You don't have to go now. It's late. I can make up a bed down here."

Simon's smile was ironic. "I think not. A clean break is always recommended isn't it?" Simon hitched his rucksack over his shoulder and walked towards the door.

Ruth called after him. "You'll be in touch? To sort things out."

Simon looked back at her. For a moment Ruth anticipated a bitter retort but instead he managed to nod an agreement. "In due course." He shrugged. "You know me, Ruth."

The door closed and she heard Simon's footsteps walking away down the street. She stood unmoving for some time before slumping down in chair. She felt drained: even physically exhausted. She had been prepared for a furious row; for tears and shouting. Simon's passive acquiescence had not been expected and in some ways that was more disturbing than a stand up fight would have been. She was not sure what to read into it. It was probably wise not to speculate.

She sat for several minutes at the table; trying to calm her thoughts. She tried the deep breathing recommended to relieve tension and eventually had regained sufficient composure to carry Simon's discarded soup bowl across to the sink. She ran it under some hot water and placed it in the drying racks. These mundane domestic chores seemed to complete what the deep breathing had started. She leaned back against the sink and looked around her empty kitchen. She reflected now, without panic at last, that she had ended the only intimate relationship she had ever known. No longer could she be defined as Simon's partner; although she had to admit wryly to herself she could now be defined as Simon's ex-partner. The recognition of what she had just done made her both nervous and, at the same time, hopeful. In this emotional confusion she switched off the kitchen light and went to her bed.

TWENTY-ONE

"He's gone, then?" Paula had her back to Ruth as she chalked up the daily special on the board.

Ruth looked up from laying the café tables. She paused, before replying in a low voice. "Yes. Over a week now." She really didn't want this conversation but she and Paula were alone in the café; awaiting the first customers of the day.

Paula turned from the board. "And the money?"

"I gave it back," Ruth muttered and tried to avoid Paula's gaze as she continued to arrange the cutlery.

"Probably just as well." Paula walked over to the serving counter and put down her chalk.

Ruth said nothing and carried on at the tables.

Paula persisted. "So how did he take it?"

Ruth gave up trying to avoid the cross examination. She turned to face Paula. "It was weird. He just accepted it; no argument, no shouting." She smiled wearily, "And certainly no tears."

"Hm." Paula mulled this over. "Have you seen him since?"

"Yes. Once. He collected all his stuff; not that there was much of it." She shook her head in disbelief. "We were icily polite to each other: unreal."

"And the girls?"

"I told them. Sarah cried a bit but I think she felt it was expected of her. Esther had probably warned her what was going on."

"No great drama then?"

"No." Ruth frowned. "Everything seemed so matter of fact; so ordinary. He's even arranged to take them to the cinema this Saturday."

"And you are OK with that?"

"Yes. I suppose I am." She said, almost in disbelief at this humdrum course of events.

Paula had found a packet of cigarettes on the counter and was extracting one. "So where is he living now?"

"I didn't ask. In his studio I expect."

Paula put the unlit cigarette between her lips. "Do you, now?" She stared accusingly at Ruth.

"I don't know much about his—"

Paula removed the cigarette and moved a pace closer to Ruth. "You are an innocent, my love."

Ruth managed not to step back in retreat. "Am I?"

Paula planted herself firmly a few feet from Ruth. Her cigarette became an accusatory pointer as she made her case. "You say he was not distressed by you booting him out?" she demanded.

"I wouldn't put it like that," Ruth protested.

Paula was not to be deflected. "Put it how you like, but from what I can gather he went off without protest and looks to be getting on with life quite unperturbed. Am I not right?"

Ruth tried to halt the flow. "Paula, I don't really know what—"

Again she was not allowed to finish. "I doubt whether this really comes as a shock to you Ruth but all the indications are that your ex has another woman in his life." With a quick glance to make sure there was no customer about to enter,

Paula fished in her apron pocket to find her lighter and flicked on the flame. "I repeat; am I not right?" She drew a mouthful of nicotine down into her lungs and stood awaiting an answer.

Ruth avoided the basilisk stare by needlessly rearranging the knives and forks at the nearest table.

"Had it not occurred to you?"

Ruth gave up and turned back to Paula. "Yes. Of course it had occurred to me, but I suppose I did the ostrich thing. Stupid wasn't I?"

Paula took another intake of tobacco smoke. Then she smiled and spoke quietly. "You're not stupid, Ruth. Very far from it. You were brave and long suffering; trying to hold things together against all the odds. That's what women do they tell me." She laughed ironically. "Not that I ever did. But don't beat yourself up. It's over; you can start again." With that instruction she made for the kitchen door to give the cigarette her full attention.

Ruth watched her go in amazement. Paula had just paid her a compliment; of sorts. She felt her mood lighten in response.

Paula did not allow her long to enjoy the moment. She bellowed from the back yard. "Squirt some of that smelly stuff around. Otherwise they might think someone's been smoking in there!"

Esther sighed theatrically as she collected together the pages of her project which lay strewn across the kitchen table. "Why all the fuss?" she demanded of her mother.

"No fuss, Esther, I just don't want the place looking like a pig sty."

Sarah had already tidied away her homework as instructed and was standing by the stove peering into a simmering casserole dish. "Smells lovely, Mum. What is it?"

Esther answered for her mother. "Bobotie. Mum's signature dish; one of her tastes of Africa!"

Ruth managed a smile. "I never cooked in Africa; we had maids."

"Gross!" Esther grunted.

"Different times, Esther," Ruth said only slightly apologetically. "Anyway, I had to learn to cook when I came to England but people always expected me to do African food so I had to buy a cook book."

"That *Taste of Africa* one." Esther laughed.

"I know. Ridiculous really. But if we ever had people round for a meal, which was not often, your Dad always wanted me to cook something African." She paused a moment. "Perhaps he thought it made me seem a bit less ordinary."

Esther quashed any chance of self-pity. "Crap. You were never ordinary, Mum."

Ruth accepted the reproof. "Whatever."

"Anyway," Esther persisted. "It feels weird."

"What does?" Sarah asked.

Ruth ignored the question and shooed Sarah away from the stove before picking up a wooden spoon and taking an experimental sip from the saucepan. She frowned. "More salt, I think." She shook some in.

"Having this Luke guy round for dinner." Esther answered Sarah's ignored question.

Ruth put the spoon down and turned to face Esther. "There's nothing weird about it. As I've told you he's just a work colleague."

"Really?" Esther could not keep the scepticism out of her question.

"Yes really!" Ruth glared at her daughter. "He's been very supportive over this whole thing with your Dad."

"I'm sure," Esther agreed with a knowing smile.

Ruth felt exasperated and tried to explain. "Look. He's been a good friend. He's listened and tried to help, but—" She broke off awkwardly, reluctant to detail Luke's involvement.

"But what, Mum?" Esther persisted.

"Never mind." She turned and moved the pan off the gas. Then she addressed both her daughters. "Please; try to get this place tidied up. Sarah, you can lay the table and Esther put all those papers somewhere out of sight."

Sarah moved readily enough to comply but Esther allowed herself a weary sigh before making a dramatic production over carrying her project documents over to the nearest cleared surface. She piled them in a vaguely tidy stack before turning her attention back to her mother. "I hope he's worth all this bother," she grumbled.

It had not taken long for Luke to win Esther's approval. Ruth watched them now as they sat at the end of the cleared table. Sarah had gone, reluctantly, to bed but Esther was now showing Luke her project papers which had been retrieved from their hiding place. Luke had insisted on seeing them, after Esther had spoken so earnestly about the assignment her group were working on. He had seemed genuinely interested and not in the least patronising. Perhaps, Ruth reflected, that is what had made him a successful journalist. He listened, and that encouraged people to talk. Esther was certainly talking now; jabbing her finger at what looked like a page of statistics and Luke was nodding in understanding of her explanation of them.

Ruth smiled at the sight. The evening had gone better than she dared hope. In spite of her protestations to Esther that the occasion was of no special significance she had agonised over the decision to invite Luke for a meal. It was the first time, since she had been with Simon, that she had enjoyed what people might call a date, although she could not label it as such. It had been nearly a month now since she had been on her own and in that time she and Luke had enjoyed the occasional coffee sessions at the beach café. They had got to know each other better; had spoken, amongst other things, of their childhoods and the circumstances which had brought them both to Cornwall. There was less wariness in their relationship now but, whilst they spoke easily enough of such matters, there was no discussion of their feelings for each other; no concession to emotion. For all Ruth knew, perhaps Luke did not feel the same tug of emotion that sometimes unsettled her when they were together. Perhaps she was being too fanciful – although she had never been accused of that before – in wondering whether Luke's apparent composure was ever similarly ruffled.

"And you've been doing this for nearly a year?" Luke addressed the query to Esther. He was looking at a piece of paper she had given him.

"Yes every weekend. Even in the snow once."

"I'm impressed."

"On Saturdays we do Marazion and on Sundays we go over to St Ives. On the bus, unless Ellen can talk her Dad into giving us a lift."

"Ellen?" Luke asked.

"She and Tom. That's the team."

"So the three of you produced all this?" Luke gestured at the disordered piles of paper.

"Yes. Tom's really cool with online stuff. He's done all the graphs and statistics."

Luke re-examined the sheet of paper in his hand and studied it. "And these are the conclusions?"

"More or less. We'll have to tidy it up a bit before the deadline."

"I'm pleased to hear that!" Ruth gestured at the papers littering the table. She walked over from stacking the last of the dishes in the drying rack and sat wearily at the table.

Luke smiled at her and held up the paper he had been studying. "This is worth a bit of mess, Ruth. It's really good isn't it?"

Ruth shifted warily in her seat. "Is it? I haven't really been much involved." She looked at Esther. "Sorry. It was thoughtless of me."

Esther shrugged. "No worries, Mum. I think you had more important stuff to think about, didn't you?"

Her question went unanswered. Ruth glanced at Luke who held her gaze for a moment before breaking the silence. He turned to look at Esther. "This won't be popular in some quarters you know."

Esther nodded. "Yes I do know that. But who's going to see it apart from a teacher or two?"

"I suppose not," Luke agreed.

"Anyway, popular or not, it's the truth."

Ruth looked at them both. "I know it's my fault but what are you talking about exactly? Esther told me she was doing something on pollution and that's why she spent all her weekends on the beach but I didn't – I am ashamed to admit – really ask for any details." Once more she turned in apology to her daughter. "You must think I'm a rotten mother."

"An absolute monster!" Esther laughed.

"So if it's not too late, tell me now."

"Go on, Luke, you tell her." Esther pointed to the paper Luke was still holding.

Luke glanced at the details on the page. "Well, if I understand these figures correctly, Esther and her friends have evidence that nearly seventy five percent of the plastic litter deposited on local beaches comes from the three big supermarkets in town." He looked up from the paper and sought confirmation from Esther. "Have I got that right?"

"Yes."

"But how could you know that?" Ruth asked. "Surely all sorts of stuff gets washed in by the tide. It could have come from anywhere."

Esther shook her head. "No." She turned to Luke. "Tell her."

Luke offered Esther a mock salute. "Yes, sir!"

Esther had the grace to blush. "Sorry."

Ruth laughed. "She was always the bossy one. Do tell me Luke; but keep it simple. I have a very tiny brain, don't I Esther?"

Esther held up both hands in contrite surrender.

"Well," Luke began, "to put it in its simplest terms, Esther and her friends only recorded plastic waste at low tide and concentrated on items that showed no evidence of marine exposure."

"That hadn't been in the sea you mean?" Ruth asked.

"Well done, Mum, you're catching on quick," Esther joked.

"Correct," Luke continued, "this litter might be swept out to God knows where at the next high tide but it definitely started its polluting life on that beach." He looked at Esther. "Have I got that right?"

"You have."

"But how do you know it came from these supermarkets, Esther?" Ruth asked.

"The plastic bags with the logos on were obvious but all the rest-the crisp packets, the sandwich boxes – the drink cans and so on – we could identify which supermarkets they came from."

"That was clever of you," Luke observed.

"That was Tom, really. All to do with serial numbers or something, he said."

"I see. I really am impressed. Seriously," Ruth said.

"Thanks, Mum," Esther muttered awkwardly, looking at her mother.

Ruth smiled back.

Luke broke the silence. "If I have got this right, Esther, then your conclusion is that if the local beaches are typical of England's beaches in general, and why wouldn't they be, then more than three quarters of maritime plastic pollution is a consequence of the refusal of supermarkets to reduce the use of plastic."

"Yes," Esther agreed. She sighed. "But I guess we all knew that anyway."

"Maybe. But don't put yourself down, Esther. We may all suspect it but you have proved it. That's a big difference," Luke said emphatically, as he put the paper down firmly on the table.

Esther gave Luke a broad grin. "Thank you. That's good to hear."

Luke looked thoughtfully at the papers on the table and picked up one or two to glance at the contents. Esther and Ruth watched him in silence. After a few seconds he put the papers down and looked at Esther. "When do you have to submit this?"

Esther seemed surprised by the question. "In a couple of weeks."

"Would you trust me enough to take photocopies of some of it? I can do it in a day and let your Mum have the originals back, at work?"

"Yes. Fine. But why—"

Luke anticipated her query. "This is important work, Esther. People need to know about it."

Esther could not conceal her excitement. "You mean in your paper?"

Luke nodded. "I can't make any promises of course but I am pretty sure I might persuade the Editor to print something based on your research."

"That would be fantastic. Wouldn't it Mum?" Esther turned to beam at Ruth.

"Fantastic indeed," Ruth agreed. "If Luke can manage it."

"I'll do my best," Luke said, whilst concentrating on selecting the pages he wanted to take away.

Ruth stood up and glanced at the kitchen clock. "It's gone ten, Esther. You need to get to bed, and try not to wake Sarah up, please."

Esther raised her eyebrows at this intrusion of domestic routine into her recent euphoria. She barely suppressed an exasperated groan.

Luke recused the situation. "I'll take these, if that's OK, Esther?" He held up several selected pages.

Esther stood and walked behind Luke to look. "That's no problem. I don't need those at the moment."

"I'll do it tomorrow and give them back to your Mum at the café." He looked towards Ruth. "That OK with you?"

"Of course." Ruth suddenly laughed. "Paula will wonder what's going on."

Luke echoed her laugh. "We'll keep her in suspense. You know how she loves a bit of drama."

Esther stood in some confusion at this exchange and looked to her mother for enlightenment but none came. Instead Ruth pointed again at the clock. Esther reluctantly began to tidy the papers Luke had finished with. When she had gathered them together she turned and headed for the stairs but paused and turned back to look at Luke and Ruth. She seemed to be trying to find the right words. "Thanks,

Luke. And I'll try not to be disappointed if it doesn't get in the paper."

Luke smiled. "Fingers crossed."

Esther had not finished. "And Mum. Thanks for the Bobotie."

Ruth concealed her surprise at the compliment. "Glad you enjoyed it."

"And thanks for inviting Luke." Esther turned quickly and headed for the stairs.

No one spoke for a moment. Ruth looked in some embarrassment at Luke who held her gaze only briefly before absently tidying the pages he would be taking away with him. Ruth forced herself into brisk action. She held up the bottle of half-finished wine left from the meal. "There's some left," she said by way of invitation.

Luke hesitated only briefly. "I probably should be going but it seems a pity to leave any." He pushed his glass towards Ruth who filled it and then did the same with her own. She raised her glass to Luke who responded in kind. Ruth sat at the table facing Luke and they sipped the wine appreciatively.

"This is really nice wine you bought Luke," Ruth said. "Not that I know anything about wine."

Luke laughed. "Nor me really: not these days. I asked the guy in the off licence."

Ruth looked surprised. "I thought that in your high-flying career in London you would have dined and wined with all those smart and sophisticated trendsetters."

Again Luke laughed. "You forget Ruth I was an observer, not a participant."

"That lifestyle not for you then?"

"Only by proxy." Luke paused reflectively. "I learnt from an early age I was not cut out for high society."

"Really? How did you learn that?" Ruth did not often drink and she could feel the wine was making her less cautious, even slightly light-headed, but the sensation was not unpleasant; indeed it was quite liberating. She pressed Luke further. "Was there a particular moment?"

Luke put down his glass. He sighed. "There was actually, and I can still feel it now after all these years. The shame, and then the realisation."

Ruth was now fully attentive. "What realisation?"

"That you can only pretend so much before you are found out."

"What do you mean?"

Luke ordered his thoughts. "I must have been about twelve: first year at grammar school. I had a friend called Zack whose mother was an actress. She invited me to tea. There was an old actor fellow there too. I can still picture it. I was only there about an hour but in that time I knew this was a completely alien world to me. I had no idea what they were talking about. I might just as well have been on Mars. I knew that my family would never pass muster in comparison."

Ruth interrupted. "What was wrong with your family?"

Luke shook his head in disbelief. "Nothing. Absolutely nothing. My father was opinionated and narrow-minded but not unlike millions of others at that time. My mother was a housewife and content with that but I didn't have the courage to accept them for what they were. I was embarrassed by my family when I compared them with the likes of Zack's." Luke groaned. "What a pathetic creature I was."

"You were only twelve," Ruth protested. "And I'm sure most kids get embarrassed by their parents at times. You shouldn't beat yourself up over something like that."

"Maybe. But it stayed with me. I never really had an honest relationship with my father: never told him what I really thought about anything. Until I left home it was like playing charades."

"That's sad, Luke."

Luke sat up straight and forced a smile. "Sorry, Ruth, banging on like that. Must be the wine." But he still took another sip.

"And what happened to the sophisticated Zack? Did you keep in touch?"

"No. I realised he was out of my league."

"So you have no idea what became of him? Where he is now?"

Luke was suddenly smiling broadly. "Actually I do know where he is now."

"Where?"

"Prison."

Ruth spluttered on her wine. "What?"

"I saw it on the inside pages of one of the tabloids; a couple of years ago. I recognised the name at once: Zack Langton. And there was a picture. Same old Zack."

"Prison. But what for?"

"Fraud!" Luke could not contain his laughter now.

Ruth joined him. "There you go, Luke. That's where sophistication gets you."

TWENTY-TWO

Paula flung open the café door and marched in with a thunderous glower on her face. Ruth and Luke looked up in startled surprise from the table where they were eating their late lunch and looking over Esther's papers, which Luke was returning after photocopying them at the Clarion's office. Paula flounced through to the kitchen after the briefest of glances. "God! I'm dying for a fag," she shouted back at them and they could hear the click of the lighter and the first deep inhalation.

Luke leaned close to Ruth and whispered, "So much for keeping her in the dark."

Ruth smiled and quickly began to tidy the papers away but not quickly enough to prevent Paula, returning with a cigarette between her lips, from seeing what she was doing.

"So what's this?" Paula demanded. "Exchanging sweet nothings in my absence?"

Ruth felt herself blushing. "As if, Paula. It's just that Luke has been kind enough to take an interest in some of Esther's project findings."

"Has he now?" Paula loaded her question with such innuendo it was now Luke's turn to hide a blush.

Ruth tried to change the subject and asked with a perky brightness she did not feel, "So how was the seminar?"

The tactic worked. "Allergies! Three sodding hours on allergies. A complete waste of time. I told Nosey Nicholson that."

"Who?" Ruth asked.

Luke explained. "Bernard Nicholson. Environmental Health Inspector. Pays us unexpected visits from time to time."

"I'm sure he'd like to close us down," Paula growled.

"Why would he want to do that?" Ruth asked innocently.

"Because I refuse to be intimidated by him and all his paperwork and record keeping and temperature checking and all the mountains of bumph he expects me to wade through."

"I dare say it can be a bit tiresome," Luke said tactfully.

"Tiresome? It's a complete nightmare. And to make it worse the man knows bugger all about cooking. I doubt he can even boil an egg. I've told him on numerous occasions that I have cooked hundreds of meals in my time and never poisoned anyone." She drew deeply on her cigarette. "As far as I know."

Luke and Ruth both laughed.

"But that's not enough for him. Every year I have to attend one of his seminars; continuous professional development he calls it and threatens me that if I don't attend he could downgrade our hygiene rating."

"Oh, I see," Ruth said.

"And today it was allergies. I told him I never use peanuts in my cooking but he blathered on about dozens of other potential killers in the kitchen. Then we had a presentation on various intolerant reactions: lactose, gluten, caffeine and so on. It's an industry now this allergy business. Never heard anything about it when I was growing up; now having an allergy is like a fashion accessory."

"I hope you didn't tell him that," Luke laughed.

Paula seemed to have relaxed a little. She ground out her cigarette on a convenient saucer. "No, Luke. You would have been proud of me. I managed to restrain myself."

"I'm impressed."

Paula smiled at some remembered incident. "But as a parting shot I did tell him I was running a café and not a clinic."

"Ah."

Paula looked around her. "So how did you two manage for the first time without me? Were you busy?"

Luke looked at Ruth. "Not bad. It went off OK, I think."

"Fine, Paula," Ruth agreed, but then added hastily, "you'd left everything so well organised we couldn't go wrong."

"And of course," Luke added, "all the customers wondered where you were and asked after you."

"Hm," Paula muttered doubtfully. "Well you could have told them I was being professionally developed; learning not to poison them." She marched off to the kitchen and returned with a wad of pamphlets she had retrieved from her handbag. "Talking of which you can scatter these about the place. Allergy advice. Nosey was adamant I should stick them up somewhere." She laughed. "I nearly told him where."

Luke and Ruth stood and took the pamphlets. Paula watched them. "Fun working together was it?"

Luke and Ruth looked at each other nervously. Luke looked back at Paula. "Yes. It seemed to go alright," he said with affected diffidence. He turned again to look at Ruth. "Didn't it?"

Ruth simply nodded in agreement.

Paula allowed herself a brief smile. "I thought it might."

Luke and Ruth said nothing.

Peter Rawlings looked up as Luke entered his office. He

gestured to Luke to sit but continued to sift through papers on his desk. After a few moments he put them to one side and looked up. "We can definitely use this," he said. "In fact I think we can lead with it."

"Good. That will make one young lady very happy."

Peter was thinking out loud now. "Of course we will have to keep the school on side. I'll try to get a photographer up there. Four to five hundred words from you should be about right." He paused and then another thought prompted him. "You'll need to get on the supermarkets of course; to give them a right to reply, won't you?"

Luke leaned back in his chair and smiled at his Editor. "It had occurred to me."

Peter looked abashed for a moment but then allowed himself a wry smile. "I know; grandmothers and eggs and that sort of thing. Sorry."

"Not at all. You forget I haven't made the front page for years: not even your front page!"

Peter was silent for a moment. When he spoke he did not look directly at Luke. "You know it's possible the Nationals could pick up on this and—" he broke off awkwardly.

Luke helped him out. "And my name can't be anywhere near it. Don't worry, I know that." He gestured expansively at Peter. "It's all yours."

"That doesn't bother you?"

"Not any more. Different priorities."

Peter seemed puzzled by the response but quickly moved on. "How did you get hold of this stuff?"

Luke hesitated slightly, "Daughter of a friend showed it to me. I could see it was important."

Peter nodded in agreement. "She must be a clever girl."

Peter's approval suddenly seemed important to Luke. "She is. No question of that."

Ruth gnawed on the end of her Biro. She was wondering how much she could tell Ben. She tried to write to her brother regularly but not burden him with her problems. She kept her letters light and prosaic; padded out with talk of the weather and how the girls were doing at school. She preferred to write rather than telephone because it was more difficult to dissemble on a phone call. She knew Ben worried about her; offered to send her money which she always refused and told him she could manage. She knew also that he didn't really approve of Simon although he never said as much. She remembered how close she and her brother had been growing up; had no secrets from each other, but now, although he was the only person in the world she felt she could really trust, she hesitated to tell him about Simon. Not because he would shed tears or perhaps be surprised that they had broken up, but because he would feel more protective of her and worry that he was too far away to be supportive. That would not be fair, so Ruth was trying to think of a way to break the news without alarming him. Perhaps she would gradually drip in suggestions that she and Simon had together decided, as mature and sensible adults, that they might be happier leading independent lives. She knew that was a half-truth and an evasion but it might prepare the ground. Of Luke she would make no mention. After all, she told herself, there was nothing to say. It was true they were spending more time together; certainly enjoying each other's company, but she wouldn't want Ben reading too much into that. After all, she was trying not to. Having decided on her strategy Ruth began to write, but had not gone beyond the first sentence when the front door was banged open and Esther and Sarah burst into the kitchen.

"Mum! Guess what Esther..." Sarah gabbled excitedly but her elder sister shushed her.

"What has Esther—" Ruth began but got no further.

Esther took over. "I got called into Deano's office this afternoon."

Ruth groaned in anticipation of the worst. "Not again Esther. What was it this time?" Deano was Mr Dean, Esther's head teacher, with whom she did not always see eye to eye.

Esther looked affronted. "Nothing like that. He congratulated us; Ellen, Tom and me. Said we were a credit to the school."

"Really?" Ruth tried to hide her disbelief.

"And the paper is sending up a photographer tomorrow."

"Oh, I see." Ruth began to understand. "They are going to print something on your findings, then?"

"Yes. Isn't it great? Luke must have fixed it." Esther fumbled in her satchel for a piece of paper. "Deano gave us a consent form for you to sign." She held out the paper for Ruth to take. "It can be either you or Dad but I don't know where he is," Esther said this without particular concern.

Ruth glanced at the form and, with her Biro still in her hand, signed it. She handed it back to Esther and then stood up. "Well, if you are going to be photographed tomorrow we had better try to find a clean shirt."

"... and think about cucumbers," Luke persisted.

"Cucumbers?" Dave, sitting opposite Luke in the recording studio, queried in his best thick Cornish accent.

"Indeed. They are a prime example of the misuse of plastic."

"Because you get them all wrapped up in it from the supermarkets. Is that what you mean Prof?"

"Exactly."

"But it keeps them fresher for longer. I read that somewhere."

"Congratulations, Pasco. But for how much longer?"

"Dunno. A day or two I reckon."

Luke sighed theatrically. "Let us suppose that is correct. I will grant you that your fifty pence cucumber may well be edible for a little longer than if it was unwrapped."

"There you go then. A result."

Luke raised his voice in academic intensity. "But consider this, Pasco. Your cucumber will rot away in a few days, even with the wrapping, but the plastic will last for all eternity."

"As long as that?"

"It is virtually indestructible. That is why it has valid uses in specific situations. It has revolutionised medicine; made space travel possible; facilitated the provision of clean drinking water and so on."

"That's all good then, Prof."

"Of course. That is the discriminating use of plastic few sensible people would have a problem with. But—" here Luke paused dramatically, "—do we really need it to wrap cucumbers? Do we need virtually everything we buy in a supermarket to be encased in plastic?"

"I get what you're driving at Prof. I bought a couple of light bulbs the other day and it took me about half an hour to get the buggers out of their packet; cut myself with scissors doing it."

"And what did you do with all the plastic debris, Pasco?"

"Can't remember. Put it in the bin I suppose although Tamsin is always on at me to recycle all that stuff. She checks it out."

"Good for her. And what does it usually say?"

"Can't be done?"

"Correct. 'Not currently suitable for recycling.' So your plastic rubbish will end up down a mine shaft where it will leach into the soil for the next few thousand years. That is if it is not transported to some third world country for them to fail to sort out."

"Can't they just burn it, Prof?"

"If only it was that simple, Pasco. Unfortunately burning most plastics releases dioxin, a highly toxic environment pollutant. It is just too prohibitively expensive to build incinerating plants to burn plastics safely."

"So we can't do nothing, then?"

"But we can, Pasco. We can reduce our dependence on non-essential plastic. Educate ourselves; change our life styles. Put pressure on the supermarkets to stop unnecessary plastic packaging."

"Won't be easy."

"But it has to be done. It's a problem for all of us. Even on our own doorstep here."

"Here?"

"Yes, Pasco. A recent research study has found that the vast majority of plastic waste fouling our wonderful local beaches can be tracked to our supermarkets."

"Blimey!"

"And, Pasco," here Luke slowed to make his point, "this research was carried out by schoolkids." He paused before his final remarks. "Kids fearful of the sort of world we are creating for them."

Luke raised a restraining hand and counted a silent five seconds before closing down the recording.

Dave put down his script. "Bit different, that one Luke."

"In what way, Dave?"

"It sounded like it was personal."

"I suppose it was, in a way."

"How come?"

"I know one of the girls who did the research."

Dane looked surprised. "Who is she?"

Luke hesitated. "Daughter of a friend."

Dave seemed to be expecting more but Luke busied himself with packing up equipment. Dave stood. "By the way I saw the Trebenten girl last night."

"Who?" Luke looked up; puzzled.

"Elowen Trebenten. I told you about her."

Luke remembered. "Oh, yes. The blonde femme fatale."

Dave laughed. "I don't know about that. She's certainly a looker."

"So how did she cross your path?"

"We had a jazz group playing. Quite a well-known one: they were good. Had a big crowd."

"She there with her brothers?"

"No, thank God. She was with some bloke. Close they were: cheek to cheek dancing and all that."

Luke now gave Dave his full concentration. "Who was he? This dancing partner?"

"I didn't know him but I might have seen him around at some point. I asked some of my regulars."

"And who did they say he was?"

"Simon Wilson. Some sort of artist. Do you know him?"

Luke hesitated. "I may have heard the name." He quickly resumed tidying up.

"Well, let's hope he doesn't upset her," Dave said.

"What?" Luke asked distractedly.

"I told you what they said happened to the last boyfriend." Dave laughed as he gathered his script together and waved Luke a cheerful goodbye.

Luke sat in thought pondering what Dave had told him. It confirmed what his earlier inquiries about Simon had suggested; that he was involved with the Trebentens; or at least with Elowen. Fortunately, Ruth's decision to separate from Simon had spared him having to make the difficult decision as to whether or not he should pass on that information. Now, he told himself, he could let the matter drop completely. Simon was free to do what he wanted with whom he wanted. As he finished packing up the recording equipment Luke felt relieved that if Simon had clearly moved on, Ruth was free to do the same. That suddenly seemed important to him but unsettling as well. The doubts and uncertainties which, over recent years, had shaped his default outlook on life were likely to be challenged. His relationship with Ruth could not be frozen in perpetual bland caution. He knew that but hesitated from accepting the conclusion. Did she feel as strongly for him as he now accepted he felt for her? Was he misreading the signals? Or were there any signals? He wished he knew the answers in case he blundered ignorantly into the complexities of intimate personal relationships which he had avoided all his life. He thought now of Natalie's advice all those years ago, that events would make decisions for you. Perhaps, he told himself as he locked the studio door behind him, he would travel again along the Damascus Road.

TWENTY-THREE

"I saw your daughter last night," Paula announced from the back yard.

"Oh, you watched?" Ruth replied from the kitchen, where she was peeling onions for the bolognese sauce.

"Of course. I don't get to meet many celebrities. Not that I have met her yet." Paula flipped her cigarette butt into a convenient flower pot and came into the kitchen. "You should bring her in one day."

Ruth looked up tearfully from the onion chopping and dabbed her streaming eyes with a paper napkin. "She'd like that. I've told her all about you, Paula."

Paula smiled briefly, "Not everything about me, I hope."

Ruth laughed. "No, just the edited highlights."

They both laughed at that. Ruth reflected on how much more relaxed she was around Paula now. Maybe it was after the trauma of the break from Simon and maybe because Paula had become much more of a close friend than employer. She could still be volatile and abrasive but Ruth had learned to see through that carapace to someone who could be genuinely sympathetic and concerned; but would never admit it. She blinked away more tears and resumed chopping the onions.

"She and her friends came across very well. Didn't you think so?" Paula queried.

Ruth pushed the sliced onion to one side of the chopping board. "I suppose they did. I must say I had been nervous about how they would perform."

"No need to have been. They knew their stuff. And Esther was clearly the spokesperson."

Ruth smiled at that. "She's no shrinking violet. Ellen and Tom scarcely got a word in edgeways. Mind you, Luke had spent time prepping her. Running through the sorts of questions they were likely to ask."

"I suppose he felt responsible," Paula observed as she reached for a saucepan on a kitchen shelf.

"Responsible?" Ruth asked. "In what way?"

"Well, he got the paper to splash the story and then local TV must have picked it up from there."

"Oh, I see. Yes."

"And he tells me some of the national dailies carried it as well."

"Yes. He brought them home for us to see. Esther's making a scrapbook of the cuttings." Ruth laughed. "She's told Luke she has decided she wants to be a journalist."

Paula laughed too. "God forbid!" She put the saucepan on the cooker ring and tipped the onions into it. She did not immediately light the gas but turned to look quizzically at Ruth. "Luke comes round, does he?"

Ruth's instant reaction was to prevaricate; she certainly would have done if asked that question a few weeks ago, but after a pause she answered Paula without embarrassment. "A bit. Particularly with all this newspaper stuff, and then the television."

Paula considered this information. "And your girls? Are they OK with that?"

"I think so. Esther is a number one fan of course and Sarah is getting used to him."

"I expect she still misses her father?" Paula said as she lit the gas.

"I'm sure," Ruth sighed.

"But she still sees him, doesn't she?"

"She can of course. That's fine with me. But—"

"But what?" Paula demanded as she splashed some oil into the saucepan.

Ruth frowned. "He hasn't been to see them or take them out for the last week or two. There's always a text with some apology or other."

"Or excuse," Paula muttered as she stirred the onions.

"I texted him about Esther's television appearance," Ruth said. "I hope he watched it. He would have been proud of her."

Paula said nothing, as the onions began to spit in the hot oil.

Ruth seemed preoccupied as she washed her hands at the sink; absently checking that there was no lingering onion odour on them. She dried her hands and watched Paula working at the stove. When she spoke it was softly. "You know, Paula, when I was watching Esther I found it hard to believe she was my daughter."

Paula rounded on her in some surprise. "What on earth are you talking about?"

Ruth tied to explain. "She was so confident; so composed." She laughed wryly. "Everything I'm not."

"Don't be ridiculous," Paula snapped. "If your daughter has those qualities it's because of the way you brought her up." She wagged her serving spoon at Ruth, "You really have got to stop putting yourself down. Simon may have drained all the confidence out of you but now you can start again." She gave the onions a vigorous stir before offering Ruth a final verdict. "Time we saw the new Ruth."

Ruth stared at Paula in some bewilderment before regathering her thoughts. "I'll lay up the tables shall I?" She said tentatively, before leaving the kitchen where Paula was now energetically sharpening a knife with which to attack the minced beef.

Luke read the instructions on the wrapper carefully. A Marks & Spencer 'Meal for Two'. He felt guilty that he had needed to resort to microwave food but he had no confidence that he would have been able to create anything special by his own efforts. He had never really bothered much about food other than as necessary fuel. In his London days, irregular hours and adrenalin overload meant eating nourishing meals was low on his agenda and, since moving to Cornwall, Paula's lunches were more than enough to get him through the day. If he felt hungry in the evenings he usually just opened a tin of soup or occasionally lashed out on a takeaway. But tonight he needed to make an effort. Since the Bobotie dinner with Ruth he was determined he would return her hospitality. He had visited a few times since then but had never stayed long. After a coffee and a chat with Esther about her plans for her ongoing assignment and showing an interest in Sarah's drawings, he took himself off, in spite of Ruth assuring him he was welcome to stay as long as he liked. He still could not shake off the feeling that he was an interloper; intruding into the lives of a family of which he was not part. He had not, of course, expressed these doubts to Ruth. He feared she would be embarrassed by any assumption of his that he might see himself as anything other than a good friend. 'Friend'. A word of wide ambiguity, Luke accepted. It encompasses a range of relationships from casual acquaintance to lifelong companionship. And, of course, there are categories of friendship; school friends; work friends; fairweather friends and so on. He supposed, if asked to categorise his relationship with Ruth, it would be 'platonic friendship' which he understood to mean a close relationship between two people but one in which there is, to put it at its bluntest, no sex. Therefore, he should not regard his invitation to Ruth as a date and he assumed she did not see it as such either. So what was it then? he asked himself. Cold reason reproved him for seeing the evening as anything other than an opportunity to relax and enjoy each other's company with no expectations or assumptions beyond that. Of course, that was it, Luke told himself, and if he had made an effort to create a pleasant ambience that was simple politeness. Miles Davis was playing a soulful trumpet on the stereo and the lighting was subdued. An open bottle of half way decent rioja, another suggestion from the off licence proprietor, was ready on the dining table on which Luke had laid cutlery in a fashion of which Paula would have approved. He recognised that his surroundings were rather sterile. Books lined the walls but there were no paintings. His laptop and sound system were the only adornments. Luke contrasted his antiseptic home with the warm disorder of Ruth's kitchen. Apart from Miles Davis the only disturbance was the occasional muffled footsteps of someone walking about in one of the upstairs flats he had created when he had bought the house.

It had been on impulse that he had asked Ruth. She had told them in the café that Simon was taking both girls to the cinema on Saturday night and out for a pizza afterwards and she was looking forward to an evening when she didn't have to cook. Luke had, after restraining himself sufficiently to ensure Paula was out of earshot, blurted out his invitation. Ruth had hesitated, as if surprised, for a moment and then said it would be lovely. Looking again at the instructions on the ready meal, Luke hoped it would be lovely. Nervously he pricked the film covering on the coq au vin and placed it into the microwave to await the electromagnetic waves.

The technology had worked. Ruth had complimented him on his cooking and had laughed when he admitted his reliance on kitchen gadgetry. At least, he told her, he had assembled the strawberries himself to decorate the bought pavlova. They had finished it all and most of the wine and now coffee was percolating. Ruth had helped him clear the dishes to the kitchen but he had resisted her offer to do the washing up. He told her it could wait until the morning. As he fussed over the coffee he could see that she was browsing through his stack of CDs and some vinyl classics he had once collected. He carried two cups of coffee through to the sitting room.

"I see you're a jazz fan," Ruth said, pointing at his music collection.

Luke nodded. "It's like Marmite isn't it? You either love it or hate it."

"I love it. Or at least I used to." Ruth took one of the proffered cups of coffee and moved to the sofa where Luke had indicated they should sit.

"Used to?" Luke inquired.

Ruth sat and carefully sipped her coffee. She put the cup down on the small table Luke had placed in front of the sofa. "When I first came to London, Simon took me to loads of jazz clubs. Mind blowing. My dad had liked classical music and he had a few records we got to listen to, but jazz was something else."

Luke smiled. "A bit of a culture shock I suppose."

Ruth looked at him earnestly. "You have no idea, Luke. I was like a kid given the freedom of the sweet shop. Cinema, theatre, art galleries. I was an addict."

"Nothing like that at home, then?"

Ruth laughed ironically. "Perhaps once a year some fading English celebrity would perform in Bulawayo. That was it. Otherwise drinking to excess in white-only hotel bars was the main cultural activity. Not that we did any of that; not with my Dad."

"Teetotal, was he?" Luke asked.

"No. He sometimes took a small beer. It wasn't that. He just wasn't part of the social scene. He was different and he knew he was different."

"Because he was German?" Luke remembered what Ruth had told him about her father.

"Not that. A lot of Rhodesians were second generation Europeans."

"Then, what?" Luke asked.

Ruth took another sip from her coffee cup and remained quiet before replacing it on the table. She seemed to be gathering her thoughts before she spoke, quietly and slowly as if trying to make Luke understand; or perhaps finally to articulate her own interpretation of her father's take on life. "My dad never went near a synagogue: we never observed any of the Jewish festivals or practices. But his parents were, at least before they were driven out of Germany, practising Jews. As were his grandparents, aunts, uncles, cousins. He never met any of them of course but he had family photographs. Ben and I used to ask him about the people in them. He told us they were probably all dead; starved or incinerated in death camps." Ruth broke off and shook her head in disbelief at the remembered horror.

Luke could think of no words of comfort. "How do you live with something like that?"

Ruth managed a wry smile. "He never forgot what he was; what he came from and what he had escaped. But he had the strength not to wallow in self-pity. He worked hard;

raised a family. I never knew whether he was happy or not. He wouldn't have understood the question. You have been given a life: get on with it and don't expect more than you can attain."

"He sounds a strong character."

"For sure," Ruth said softly, then, perhaps aware the mood was too dark, she added more brightly, "but not one for jazz."

Luke picked up on her change of tone. "Neither was my Dad. I'm sure he would have disapproved of all the music I listened to had he known."

"You kept a lot of secrets from your father, Luke?"

"Separate lives, Ruth." Luke sighed. He noticed Ruth's cup was empty and picked it up. "Refill?"

Ruth nodded. "Thanks." She watched Luke walk through to the kitchen to pour more coffee. She called out to him. "You see, Luke, we're both misfits."

Luke stood holding the cups in the doorway and looked at her in surprise. "Misfits?"

"Neither of us really knows what we are, do we?"

Luke came and sat down and put the full cups on the table. "Don't we, Ruth?"

"Well I certainly don't feel English: never have; too many cross currents. Class, education, politics. I couldn't place myself. But I certainly don't feel German whatever it says on my passport of convenience. And Jewish? Hardly. But I think some part of me can identify with that terrible suffering." She stopped. "Sorry, Luke, this is all a bit too much naval gazing."

Luke shrugged. "Don't worry. Must be the rioja."

Ruth said nothing but picked up her coffee cup.

"So, Ruth. You said we are both misfits?"

"Sorry. That was rude of me." Ruth smiled apologetically at him.

"Not at all. Come on, out with it." Luke invited with a feigned authority.

Ruth put down her cup and composed herself. "Well, since you ask."

"I do," Luke insisted playfully.

"OK, then. Here you are masquerading as a third rate journalist when you were once a brilliant one; working for nothing in a café and never ever letting anyone really know how you feel about anything because from an early age you trained yourself to keep your emotions private." Ruth had raised her voice to finish her character assessment but when she broke off and registered the shocked look on Luke's face her tone was immediately contrite. "Oh, Luke. I'm so sorry. That was so hurtful but I didn't mean it to be; it just came out wrong."

Luke shook his head as if to clear his mind. "No, Ruth. It came out just right. A fair cop." He smiled at her.

Ruth relaxed. "You're not cross, then?"

"Of course not. Guilty as charged."

"Noting to be guilty about, Luke. We are what we are."

"We are indeed, Ruth," Luke said it softly and with his eyes on Ruth. He moved closer to her and she held his gaze and said nothing. Briefly they kissed and then more intensely but after a few seconds the embrace ended mutually and they looked at each other in surprise and shock.

Ruth was the first to speak. "Phew," she said.

The spell was broken. Neither of them seemed to know what to say. The silence was fractured by the sudden gurgle of the percolator. Luke stood. "Needs more water." He turned and walked back to the kitchen: that pragmatic action broke the intensity of the moment.

"Don't put any more on for me, Luke. I need to get moving. Simon will bring them home by ten."

"OK." Luke had now recovered his default mode of calm. "How is Simon?" he managed to ask politely.

Rut sighed. "I wish I knew. We barely exchanged a word when he picked the girls up. Although we have split up I can't help worrying about him. He looks so, I don't know, hunted; on edge."

Luke had views on that but offered no more than, "Oh, I see."

Ruth had now found her coat and was preparing to leave. She walked up to Luke still standing in the kitchen doorway. "Thanks so much, Luke. Great evening."

Luke nodded his thanks. "My pleasure." He walked Ruth along the hallway to the front door.

Ruth paused and then reached up and gave him a quick and chaste kiss on the cheek. "See you on Monday then."

"Yes, Monday." Luke opened the door.

Ruth turned and waved before setting off down the street.

Luke closed the door but turned and leant his back against it for a few reflective seconds. "Phew," he whispered to himself.

TWENTY-FOUR

Helen handed Ruth a glass of squash. "A bit too hot for coffee, I think."

Ruth nodded her agreement and gulped down most of the drink. "Thanks, I needed that. It was really sweltering in there."

Helen laughed. "I thought one or two of your ladies looked a bit flushed when they were leaving."

"I had to slow it right down. I was afraid someone might pass out on me." Ruth drained the last of the glass and put it down on the sink.

"It is August I suppose," Helen said. "High summer."

"I know; but down here that usually means wind and rain. Holidaymakers in plastic macs sheltering in bus shelters." They both laughed at that.

"Certainly plenty of them about. It took me ages to drive in this morning."

Ruth sighed. "Tell me about it. It's flat out at the café. Paula's tearing her hair out."

"Nothing new there from what you tell me, Ruth."

"True; but she barely has time for a cigarette now which is not good for her humour."

"I see."

"But it has its plus side; at least for me."

"How's that?" Helen asked, as she handed Ruth the class fees she had collected. Ruth put the money in her shoulder bag before she addressed Helen's question. "In August she keeps the café open later so that she can offer the visitors cream teas." Ruth smiled. "She says it's naff and hates doing it, but it's very profitable."

Helen frowned. "But how does that help you? Do you have to work longer hours?"

"I can't. I have my classes."

"So?"

"She has employed Esther. To wash up and serve the teas."

"I see. And is that working out OK?"

Ruth held up fingers crossed on both hands. "It seems to be. Paula suggested it. I was a bit doubtful. Esther is sixteen now but she's not exactly meek and mild and, knowing Paula, I had my doubts, but they seem to get along fine. Esther is delighted to be earning her own money for the first time and of course it keeps her occupied in the holidays."

"And what about Sarah, in the holidays?"

Ruth sighed. "That's a bit harder to sort out. It's not fair to leave her home on her own too much although she says she doesn't mind, so I've tried to organise stuff. This week she's gone pony trekking in Wales with a school group." Ruth shrugged. "Expensive, but worth it. And later her best friend's parents have invited her to go camping with them to Brittany." She smiled. "Bless them!"

"Can't her Dad have her for a bit?" Helen asked cautiously. Ruth had told her that she and Simon had separated but had said little beyond that.

Ruth laughed briefly but without humour. "That would be nice but it seems her father has too much else on."

Helen said nothing.

Ruth swung her bag over her shoulder and looked

around to make sure she had left nothing behind. She paused, aware that Helen was looking at her; perhaps expecting more information. She shrugged. "It's only for a few weeks. Not a problem. I'll manage."

Helen believed her. "I'm sure you will." She looked thoughtfully at Ruth. "Not my business of course Ruth, but in these last few weeks you seem to have changed."

Ruth, who had been making her way to the door, stopped and turned in surprise. "Changed? How do you mean?"

"I don't know, but you seem more upbeat; not so stressed." Helen broke off nervously. "Perhaps it's just my imagination."

Ruth did not reply immediately but kept looking at Helen. Then she half smiled. "Must be the weather."

Helen watched as Ruth left and then muttered to herself, "I doubt if it's just the weather."

Dave was in full Pasco flow. "That would make you proper teasy."

"It did. There are several letters of complaint in the Clarion. All from disgruntled passengers off the last London train abandoned at St Erth station with no onward connection to St Ives."

"But you said the London train was only ten minutes late, Prof."

"Indeed. Not an unusual occurrence."

"So why didn't the St Ives train wait?"

"Good question, Pasco."

"It's only a tiddly little train; only goes to St Ives. Wouldn't matter running a bit late. They must have known there'd be us country folk on the London train needing to get to St Ives."

"I'm sure they did Pasco."

"So why couldn't they wait?"

"Different company; different timetables. They don't speak to each other."

"That don't make no sense, Prof."

"Nothing makes much sense on the rail network, Pasco. Different companies run the trains, another one is responsible for the track and someone else for the stations."

"Sounds like a proper dog's breakfast."

"The fruits of privatisation, Pasco."

"So why?"

"I think the idea was to encourage competition."

"That's good isn't it? Bit of competition."

Luke laughed in professorial irony. "Except there is no competition. Now we have the worst of all outcomes. Private monopolies. And who does that benefit, Pasco?"

"You got me there Prof," Dave admitted, as his script required.

"The shareholders, Pasco. That's who."

"So what do ordinary folk get out of it?"

"Higher fares; an unintegrated service."

"Not good, then?"

"We have the highest fares in Europe, Pasco. And the most congested roads."

"Roads?"

"The government pretends to have a green agenda. It claims to want to reduce carbon emissions. One way of making a start on that would be to get people to use their cars less and public transport more."

"Not much chance of that here. Not with our buses. Costs Tamsin more than a fiver just to go and see her Mum in Hayle."

"I expect it does. And it's absurd that even with petrol prices at an all-time high, driving your car to London is still cheaper than taking the train."

"That's barmy, isn't it?"

"Barmy indeed, Paso. Welcome to the mad, mad world of Public Transportation."

Luke held up the cautionary silencing finger for a few

seconds whilst he switched off the recording. That done, he relaxed and leaned back in his chair and smiled at Dave. "Well done. A masterclass as ever."

Dave tossed his script down on the table between them. "You make me more gormless every session."

Luke laughed. "But you capture it so well, Dave."

Dave thought about it. "Not sure if I should take that as a compliment."

"The highest." Luke reached across the table and collected Dave's discarded script.

"So now we've upset the railway companies. The list grows longer."

"They could do with a bit of upsetting," Luke observed as he gathered the scripts together.

"So who's next on your blacklist?" Dave asked, as he got to his feet and began putting on the jacket he had hung over the back of his chair during the recording.

Luke considered the question. "Not sure. In fact, I thought we might take a bit of a break for a week or two."

"Oh." Dave seemed surprised.

"Leave them wanting more," Luke said. "Isn't that what you did in the theatre sometimes?"

"True. Rather than feeling they've had too much," Dave agreed. "I dare say one or two councillors will be happy for you to take a break."

Luke nodded. "Well, it is the holiday season. Rest and recreation and all that."

Dave looked thoughtfully at Luke. "Is this the new, mellow, peace and good will to all men version of the old Luke I am hearing?"

Luke smiled at that but said nothing.

Dave looked quizzically at his friend. "Now I come to think of it you do seem a bit more relaxed of late."

Luke looked surprised. "Really? It must be the weather."

Paula managed a fixed smile as she ushered out the last customers of the day; just giving them a few seconds to be out of earshot before muttering, "Thank God for that," and slamming the café door and reversing the Open sign. She leaned with her back against the door for a moment as if defying anyone to barge it open.

"We'll need more scones for tomorrow, Paula." Esther volunteered this unwelcome information as she began collecting up the used crockery.

Paula let out a theatrical groan as she straightened herself up and moved away from the door. "Just what I wanted to hear." She looked at Esther busying herself at the tables. "Don't ever contemplate a career in catering, Esther."

Esther laughed. "No chance." Then she realised that was less than tactful. "Sorry, Paula, that must have sounded rude."

Paula shrugged dismissively. "Hardly. Merely stating the obvious."

Esther gabbled to make up for her gaffe, "I mean you do a fantastic job here and everyone thinks..."

Paula held up a restraining hand to silence her. "You know what they say, Esther. If you are in a hole stop digging."

Esther blushed and busied herself with cleaning the tables.

Paula seemed in a mood to talk. She pulled out a chair and slumped down wearily on it. "So if catering is a 'no no' what are your career plans: if you have any?"

Esther stopped her tidying up and looked directly at Paula. "I want to be a journalist." She said it almost defiantly as if she expected some withering put-down from Paula.

Paula, however, merely responded with a slight nod and a half smile. "Now I wonder who put that idea in your head?"

Esther rose to the bait. "Not Luke, if that's what you're thinking."

Paula laughed. "It had crossed my mind."

"I did mention it to him once but he tried to put me off; told me it messed with your head."

"Did he say it had messed with his?"

Esther hesitated. "He didn't." She paused. "I wanted to ask but it would have been too nosey."

"But you had your suspicions?" Paula asked teasingly.

Esther put down the tray she had been holding and considered Paula's question seriously. "Luke is a lovely guy. We all think that." She paused uncomfortably.

"But?" Paula prompted.

"But," Esther went on, "I don't think I really know him. He never gives anything away; about himself or what he's thinking. He's like, you know, on his guard all the time."

"Perhaps he's scared," Paula said softly.

"Scared?" Esther looked surprised. "Sacred of what?"

"Of letting go; losing control of events."

Esther frowned at the suggestion. "I don't know if I can get my head around that, Paula."

Paula stood up; her mood changed. "Enough of this soul searching. I have bloody scones to make. After this." Paula pulled her packet of cigarettes out of her apron pocket and made for the kitchen door. "Finish this clearing up and then you'd better get off home. I don't want your mother thinking I'm exploiting child labour."

Paula quickly lit her cigarette and luxuriated in the first lungful of nicotine as she propped herself against the open door and watched Esther begin to load the dishwasher. "I'm a terrible example I'm afraid, Esther."

Esther looked up. "Sorry?"

"This smoking." She waved the cigarette in Esther's

direction. "And the drinking." She pointed the cigarette towards the cider bottle on a kitchen shelf.

Esther laughed but refrained from comment.

"Fortunately the young are more tolerant of such vices, I believe?"

Esther grinned. "There are worse."

Paula smiled. "So they tell me." She drew in another deep smoke-filled breath. Then suddenly she dropped the cigarette half smoked and stamped it under her foot. Esther looked up in some surprise. "Your mother tells me you will be starting at college soon. A levels and so on."

"Yes, that's right."

"Looking forward to it?"

"I am. I won't be a schoolkid anymore." She now spoke with animation. "No more horrible school uniform."

Paula sighed in remembrance. "You think that was bad. We had to wear gym slips!"

Esther stood open-mouthed at the thought of Paula in a gym slip. Paula must have guessed her imagining. "I know: doesn't bear thinking about."

Esther hurried to explain. "No; I was just—"

Paula cut her short. "The point is when you start at College you could be our Saturday Girl." She paused. "If you wanted to, that is."

Esther burst spontaneously into a wide smile. "That would be great Paula. Thank you."

Paula seemed embarrassed by the gratitude. "It will put a few bob in your pocket. Help with the household budget I dare say."

Esther smiled her agreement. "Of course. Mum won't have to sub me. Thanks so much, Paula."

Paula had clearly endured a surfeit of gratitude. "Anyway, get a move on with the washing up now. It won't do itself."

Esther resumed her appointed chore but with the smile still on her face.

TWENTY-FIVE

Luke slumped down gratefully on a slab of convenient rock and exhaled deeply several times before recovering his composure sufficiently to speak. "Good grief," he panted, "I am so unfit." He lay back and gradually allowed his heart beat to slow and his breathing return to normal.

Ruth stood a few paces away on the path and looked down at him in amused concern. "Are you OK?"

Luke nodded and sat up straight. "Getting there." He groaned in mock distress. "Remind me, next time."

"Remind you of what?"

"Never to go on a cliff walk with a fitness instructor."

Ruth laughed and walked over to the rock. Luke shifted along it to create a space for her to sit. For a moment neither of them spoke as they took in the view. The had left Luke's car at a beach car park, where they had been lucky to find a space, and where the beach itself was heaving with holidaymakers making the most of the summer warmth. Within a few minutes of setting off along the coast path the crowds had been left behind and apart from a few fellow walkers they had the world to themselves. The sea was shimmering gently in the late afternoon sun; still and clear enough in the shallows to reveal its bed of sand. Only the occasional cry of a wheeling gull and the gentle suck of shingle, from the inaccessible cove at the foot of the cliffs below, broke the spell of mellow silence.

Ruth spoke first. "I've never been here. Ridiculous really. To have all this," she gestured at the wide encompassing sea, "and not get out in it."

"Must have been difficult: with two young kids."

"True. We did manage the beach a bit when they were small. But even that was a struggle; trying to fit it in with work. And Simon was not really a beach person." She seemed lost for a moment in the tangle of memory; gazing distractedly out at the unanswering sea.

Luke said nothing.

Ruth turned and looked at Luke: her focus regained. "And you? You come here often?" She burst into laughter. "Did I really say that? The corniest of chat up lines."

Luke laughed with her. "I did. When I first came down I spent a lot of time on these cliffs." He smiled reflectively. "Trying to cleanse my soul the psychiatrists would say."

"And did it?" Ruth's question was serious.

Luke shrugged. "Take more than a sea view to do that."

"What would it take, Luke?" Ruth looked hard at him.

Luke looked away. "Not sure on that one, Ruth."

Ruth made to speak again but was distracted by the sight of two walkers suddenly looming into view over the crest of the path. She and Luke swung their legs to one side to allow the couple to pass in front of their rock. They exchanged cheerful greetings; inevitably commenting on the weather and the view. In the few seconds that exchange took the mood had changed. Not for the first time Ruth felt she had got close to Luke only for the moment to dissipate. She thought of the kiss: how it had nearly been so much more and yet neither of them had spoken of it since. She did not dwell on it: calling to mind the tiresome cliché Esther was over fond of quoting at her, 'it is what it is'.

She deliberately switched to safer ground. "Thank God for Brittany."

Luke did not need an explanation. "Sarah enjoying herself?"

"I had a text. They're having a great time." She paused reflectively. "The pony trekking was a big success too. She never stopped talking about it." She sighed. "She's growing up so quickly Luke. Won't be my little girl for too much longer. I suppose I should be glad really."

"Glad?"

"I was afraid she'd be the one most upset about Simon and me splitting up."

"And is she?"

"To begin with she was. But kids are pretty resilient aren't they?"

"Or good at hiding their feelings," Luke said.

Ruth sighed. "As you should know. You and your father."

Luke offered reassurance. "But she sees her Dad."

Ruth looked uncertain. "She did: to begin with. Not much recently."

"Well, she has been away."

"I know. I tell myself that. But Simon hasn't shown any interest: not been about; not asked what she's doing."

"Perhaps he's busy," Luke said.

Ruth looked hard at him. "Busy? Busy doing what?"

Luke shrugged.

Ruth reproved herself. "I know. It's nothing to do with me. I don't know why I should still feel resentful. It's over. I keep telling myself."

"Can't be easy after twenty years: just to let go."

Ruth stared at him with an expression half of amusement and half of exasperation. "You know your problem, Luke?"

Luke smiled. "I have many."

"You are so bloody reasonable." She punched him playfully on the shoulder. "So nice."

Luke laughed but grabbed the arm that had punched him and drew Ruth close so that they were face to face. "Beware the beast that lurks beneath," he intoned melodramatically.

Then they both laughed. A seagull chose that moment to squawk loudly at some imagined slight which broke the spell. They both stood and looked rather sheepishly at each other before setting off again along the path.

The sun was losing its warmth and beginning its descent into the sea by the time they got back to the car park. The beach was now sparsely populated: only a few braving a late barbecue, huddled in anoraks and blankets. Luke had asked Ruth if she had time for a drink and she had readily agreed so they walked across to the beachside pub and Luke brought them both pints. They took the first mouthfuls greedily to quench the walking thirst. Simultaneously they sat back against the high backs of their bench.

"Bliss!" Ruth murmured. She raised her glass to Luke in thanks. "I can't think when I was last in a pub."

"We have Paula to thank."

"I know. Employing Esther. And with my classes on hold for the holidays and Sarah in France, at last I have a chance to please myself for once. Great. And thank you Luke. I wouldn't have known about that walk without you."

"My pleasure. Glad you enjoyed it."

They both drank again; easy in each other's company. Luke finished his pint first. He put down his glass. "Esther seems to be coping OK with Paula."

"I know. I was nervous for her at first; we all know what

Paula can be like and Esther can be outspoken at times: not the most tactful."

Luke smiled. "I think that may be why Paula gets on with her. Birds of a feather."

"You may be right. I hadn't thought of that."

"There's another thing." Luke paused and took another sip of his drink.

"What's that?"Ruth queried.

Luke paused to gather his thoughts. "I think Paula might see in Esther what she was like at her age. Bright; sparky; life ahead of her and all that. Might make her feel a bit protective."

Ruth looked puzzled. "Protecting Esther from what?"

"From throwing it all away."

"How?"

Luke paused only briefly. "By running away with a rock band."

Ruth looked in confusion at Luke. "What? Is that what Paula did?"

"I probably shouldn't have told you that." He looked reproachfully at his glass. "The drink must have loosened my tongue."

Ruth was still digesting the information. "Now that you have told me I suppose I'm not that surprised. When you think what she's like now I guess she must have been a pretty wild teenager."

Luke nodded. "Yes. People don't really change, do they? Just get a bit more complex."

Ruth seemed to be about to reply to that but thought better of it.

Luke sensed her caution and moved the conversation on to safer ground. "Jazz. You said you were a fan."

Ruth took a moment to adjust to the change of tack. "I was," she sighed, "once upon a time."

"You seemed to recognise most of my collection. When you came round to dinner."

The mention of that evening hung between them for a few seconds. Neither of them had made reference since to that brief moment when they had come so close to moving beyond the restraints of nominal friendship. Ruth came back to the present. "Simon introduced me to jazz. We always had it on in the flat." She paused. "Before the kids came along." She was surprised at how easy it was now to talk about the past with Simon without anguish or resentment. Perhaps she really had ' moved on' as the cliché demanded. "But I haven't listened to much jazz for years."

Luke put down his glass. "Would you like to?"

Ruth was taken aback by the question. "I hadn't really thought..."

Luke cut in. "I go to this jazz festival every year." He spoke with unconcealed enthusiasm now. "It's near Brighton; a beautiful site on the South Downs. Three days of it, and all the top names are there. My one annual indulgence: escape across the Tamar."

"Sounds great," Ruth said; amused by his unexpected animation.

"It is," Luke paused: perhaps a little self-conscious of his exuberance. He calmed himself down. "You'd love it, I'm sure."

"I expect I would but—"

"Come with me, then."

Rut looked at him in surprise.

"It's at Easter, but you have to snap up the tickets as soon as they come on sale."

Ruth was still processing this shift in the conversation. "Well, I don't know. There are the girls to think of. I've not left them on their own before."

Luke sighed and sat back. "Of course. Silly of me."

There was a lengthy silence before Ruth spoke; almost as if to herself. "I suppose Esther would cope on her own and perhaps Paula would be there for her in an emergency." She looked at Luke; her brow furrowed in concentration. "Maybe there would be some school trip for Sarah. I'd need to check on that nearer the time."

Luke smiled now and sat forward. "So it might be possible?"

"It might." Ruth smiled at Luke. "I think it really might."

"Great. Let me know when you've checked it all out and, if it looks as if it can work, then I can book the tickets."

Ruth laughed. "Just one thing, Luke."

Luke frowned and looked uneasily at Ruth. "What's that, Ruth?"

"Are you sure you will be able to put up with me for three days?"

Luke took a few seconds to realise Ruth was joking, but his reply was serious. "I think I could manage a lot longer than that, Ruth."

TWENTY-SIX

"Is that really any good, Esther?" Ben asked with some scepticism.

Esther, with her mouth full of a Big Mac Veggie Burger, chewed energetically before she was able to reply. "Great. You should try one."

Ruth laughed. "You forget your uncle grew up in Zimbabwe and now lives in Australia. Steaks from a barbecue are in his DNA."

Esther pulled a face. "Gross!"

Esther's conversion to vegetarianism was a relatively new phenomenon. It coincided with her recent start at the Sixth Form College and Ruth suspected it was not unrelated to her friendship with Tom; the computer geek with whom she had worked on the beach project. He was a militant vegan, which Ruth, to her shame, found rather tiresome when trying to think what to offer him by way of refreshment when he visited: which he did frequently, ostensibly to work with Esther on their new mission. She supposed Tom might be a sort of boyfriend but she had never dared suggest that to Esther.

Ben laughed happily at Esther's verdict on meat eating. "What about you, Sarah? You thinking of joining the lettuce club?"

Sarah considered the question carefully and looked guiltily at the meat-filled bun on her plate. "I know I should but I do like burgers: proper ones." She glanced at her sister guiltily, "Sorry, Esther."

Esther scowled at this admission but Ruth and Ben both laughed. "Never mind, Sarah," Ruth said consolingly, "I expect you'll get there one day." She turned her head and whispered to Ben, "Luke says vegetarianism is a rite of passage for adolescent girls."

The whisper had not escaped Esther. "He'd better not say that to me!"

Her mother merely smiled at her. "I'm sure he wouldn't dare, dear."

Ben pushed away his empty plate and reached for his glass of Coke. "When do I get to meet this Luke guy I hear so much about?" He looked at Ruth for an answer but she was slow to respond.

Esther took over. "I've asked him to come round to-morrow evening." She glanced briefly at Ruth. "If that's OK? To check that Tom and I are setting our stuff out properly." She frowned. "Tom is great on the techie stuff but words aren't really his thing."

"I'm sure you more than make up for that," Ruth joked, and Esther smiled in spite of herself.

"So what is it this time, Esther?" Ben asked. "Your Mum told me all about the plastic pollution survey. Great work there."

"Sewage," Esther said forcefully enough to attract the attention of nearby diners.

"Ah," Ben managed.

Esther leaned forward intently. "Do you know how much raw sewage gets pumped into our bathing water every day?"

Ben smiled. "No; but I guess you're going to tell me."

Ruth intervened before Esther could elaborate further. "Perhaps not now; some of us are still eating."

Reluctantly, Esther sat back.

Ben noticed the two empty plates of his nieces. "Why don't you two go and sort out some ice creams or something. I'm sure you can manage a pudding."

Esther stood. "Thanks. I think I probably could. What about you two?" She looked at Ben and Ruth.

"Not for me," Ruth said. "I'm still struggling to finish this." She gestured at her plate.

"Uncle Ben?" Esther asked.

"Not for me either thanks. But here." He took his wallet out of his inside jacket pocket and handed Esther a ten pound note. "Take it out of that."

Esther took the proffered note. "Thank you." She beckoned to Sarah. "Come on. They've probably got those chocolate Mcflurries you drool over."

The two girls set off to the counter. Ruth finally cleared her plate and smiled at Ben. "They're loving this, Ben; such a wonderful surprise."

"Sorry it was such short notice. There was a problem with a big UK contract. It needed sorting."

"And have you sorted it?"

"Yes; think so. Means a quick turnaround I'm afraid. Fly home in a couple of days."

"Shame. But it's great to see you." Ruth stretched out her hand and took her brother's. "Really great."

Ben looked affectionately at his sister. "And great to see you. Looking so well: so happy." He lowered his voice. "Not like the last time."

Ruth sighed. "Was it that bad?"

"Not good. I didn't say anything but I could tell things were tough."

Ruth turned her head away.

Ben continued "And Simon? What about Simon?"

Ruth shrugged. "Not in our lives anymore."

Ben looked surprised. "Not even for the girls?"

"To begin with; but now hardly ever."

That seemed to puzzle Ben. "That's weird. He was a good dad to them: in his own way."

"He was," Ruth agreed, "I don't know what's going on with Simon." She sighed. "Perhaps just as well."

"I guess. Time to look ahead."

"So everyone tells me."

Ben fiddled with his discarded cutlery and risked a sideways glance at his sister. "And what about Luke?"

Ruth was instantly on her guard. "What about him?"

Ben feigned innocence. "Just asking. Is he special?"

Ruth looked away from her brother's scrutiny. "Well; let's just say he's different."

She was spared further cross examination by the noisy return of her daughters with their calorie-loaded confections.

Luke sat at the end of the kitchen table examining the folder Esther had given him to study. She stood behind him looking anxiously over his shoulder at the page he was reading. "Does it make any sense?"

Luke put the folder down. "It does; but you have to tease it out from amongst all the statistical stuff."

Esther groaned. "That's what I thought, but Tom says we have to have the factual evidence."

"He's right of course but perhaps you could have your prose narrative separate from the graphs and figures. Footnotes and an appendix might be helpful too."

Esther picked up the folder with a sigh. "I'll have to

persuade him; I'll talk to him now." She picked up her phone off the table and made to tap in numbers.

Ruth intervened from the far end of the table. "I think upstairs might be better, Esther."

Esther looked up from her phone in some surprise at the suggestion but did not contest it. "Oh, sure."

"And don't wake Sarah," Ruth asked.

Esther nodded in compliance and carried the folder and her phone to the foot of the stairs; clearly impatient to speak with Tom. She paused and turned quickly. "Thanks, Luke. That was really helpful. Goodnight Mum; Uncle Ben." Courtesies observed she raced up the stairs.

The three adults smiled at her unconcealed enthusiasm. Luke got to his feet. "I'd better be going."

"Already?" Ruth asked. "It's not late."

"I know but I need to get some stuff done for the Clarion." He smiled wryly, "I've been putting it off for too long."

"What is it?" Ruth asked.

"Theatre review; the local AmDram offering."

Ruth laughed. "Be nice to them."

"I'll try: but it will be an effort." Luke began to put on his coat.

Ben got to his feet and walked towards Luke with hand outstretched. "It's been great meeting you at last, Luke. Ruth and the girls are always talking about you."

Luke looked down and fumbled distractedly with the fastenings on his jacket. "Oh, dear," he muttered in embarrassment.

Ben shook Luke's hand. "I need to tell you something else, Luke." He paused and looked at Ruth. "I worry about my big sister here sometimes. I know it hasn't always been easy for her."

"Ben—" Ruth tried to intervene.

Her brother held up a restraining hand, "There's not much I can do to help thousands of miles away so it's great to know she has a good friend to rely on if things get tough."

Ruth rolled her eyes apologetically at Luke from behind her brother's back.

Luke smiled at that but turned his attention back to Ben. "Thanks for that, Ben. I'll do my best." His coat was now secure. "It was good to meet you and have a safe journey back."

"Thanks." Ben paused and looked back at Ruth. "And see if you can persuade my sister to come out to Oz with the girls. They'd be welcome any time."

"OK, Ben. I'll see what I can do."

Luke was ready to go now. He waved a discreet farewell to Ruth who smiled and shrugged apologetically for her brother's presumption.

Ben walked Luke to the front door and opened it for him. "And of course, Luke, if you manage to talk Ruth into it you'd be most welcome to come too."

Luke stepped into the street. Summer's warmth still softened the night air. He reflected on Ben's verdict; 'you are a good friend to Ruth.' Kind words, so why did they cause him pain?

TWENTY-SEVEN

Ben had been gone for nearly a month now. It had been so good to see him, albeit briefly, and Ruth had tried not to let herself get too depressed in the days immediately following his departure, but she had been reminded that her brother was the only person who gave her life context; to whom she would be inextricably tied as long as she lived. Such thinking, she had to reprove herself, was morbidly self-indulgent and as the days passed her mood lightened. The past was not a place to dwell and it was not hard to convince herself that the present was OK and the future, if one dared contemplate it, might not be too bad either. So, she dutifully followed her father's oft prescribed remedy for gloom, 'count your blessings' – a cliché possibly, but effective. She checklisted her 'blessings'; she was healthy and if not wealthy, at least solvent; her two daughters seemed well adjusted and happy to live with her. Ruth had worried that Simon's departure would be traumatic for them but Esther had taken it in her self-absorbed adolescent stride and Sarah, after an initial wobble, had seemed to pick up on her elder sister's unfazed adjustment to a different family life. Perhaps it had helped that there was less tension in the house now. Ruth certainly felt more relaxed; able to be more spontaneous in expressing her feelings: free from the anxiety and frustration of worrying about Simon. Free from wondering what he was doing and where he was and who he was with and whether they could ever mend their broken relationship. Now that was behind her. She need worry about Simon no more. She was free. She had to keep telling herself that. Helen had hinted to her, after a recent class, that now she was free to 'find herself a new man'. That had sounded so trite; the sort of thing a twenty year old might say; not suitable advice for someone near middle age with two growing-up children to contend with. Why did people assume she needed to 'find a man'? She had managed more or less without one for a few years now. Why on earth would she want another one in her life? She was not quite sure what feminism was but Ruth would certainly consider herself a supporter if it proclaimed a woman could be an independent self-sufficient member of the human race without being tied to a man.

This exercise in positive thinking, in the aftermath of Ben's visit, helped Ruth recover her good humour and self-confidence. She offered silent thanks to her father for the advice she had not forgotten. She taught her classes with renewed vigour and enthusiasm and at the café both Paula and Luke commented on how well and happy she looked; Paula quizzically and Luke with a warm smile. Ruth, bolstered by their comments, began to believe her own assurances; it was possible that life was definitely changing for the better and nothing could go wrong.

The holiday crowds had gone now but the weather seemed not to have noticed. People spoke of an 'Indian Summer' and Luke had remarked that he didn't care where it came from as long as it didn't go back there any time soon. It was still just about warm enough to take coffee outside at the beach café even though the beach itself was uncrowded; reclaimed by the local dog walkers. Coffee after work, and before her evening classes, had become almost a habit for them, Ruth told Luke. It gave them a chance to talk, away from Paula's gimlet eye. Not that their talk was searching or agonising. Far from it. They chatted casually and light-heartedly; and sometimes fell happily silent and just enjoyed the view and sound of the sea. Ruth sometimes recalled the first time thy had met at the café, when she had been so wracked with anxiety and uncertainty about what Simon was doing and had needed to ask Luke to stop trying to find out. She glanced at him now; he was leaning back in his chair his eyes closed against the sun. He seemed to sense her surveillance and opened his eyes. He turned to look at Ruth and smiled and she smiled back. It seemed nothing needed to be said.

Ruth had put her phone on the table. She kept it switched on because she had told the girls they could always contact her in an emergency. They laughed at her concern: Esther told her she was in danger of becoming a 'Helicopter Mum,' but Ruth ignored their teasing and now she was quick to pick up the phone as it pinged the arrival of an incoming text. Luke watched her read the text and registered her look of increasing concern. Ruth stared at the message for some time and then looked at Luke in frowning confusion.

"Problem?" Luke asked, now sitting up in his chair.

Ruth did not answer.

Luke tried again. "Is it one of the girls?"

Ruth shook her head. She put down the phone and now focussed on Luke. "No." She paused. "It's Simon."

"Oh." Luke tried to sound non-committal. "Wants to take them out?"

Ruth shook her head. "No. Wants to see me." She looked in confusion at Luke. "He says it's urgent we talk; but not at home."

Now Luke looked confused. "Not at home? Why not?"

"God knows!" Ruth sighed. "He suggests the Morrab Gardens, tomorrow afternoon."

"That sounds a bit weird. Will you go?" Luke asked.

"I'll have to." She gestured at the phone. "I don't really have a choice."

Luke frowned. "What could be so urgent, I wonder?"

Ruth thought about the question. "If it's Simon then it's probably about money." She paused. "What else could it be?"

Luke said nothing.

As if sensing their darkening mood the sun was suddenly hidden by clouds. Ruth stood and picked up her phone and then looked distractedly at her watch. "I'd better get moving."

Luke stood too and pushed his chair back under the table. "Yes. Getting a bit cool here." He looked up at the gathering clouds. "Perhaps summer really is over now."

Ruth was familiar with the Morrab Gardens. Situated in the centre of the town, their sub-tropical plants and trees had offered a tranquil and beautiful oasis for the residents of Penzance and countless visitors for over a hundred years. Ruth had brought her daughters here for picnics when they were little and they had sprawled on rugs on the grass to eat their sandwiches and, on Sundays, be entertained by the musician performing on the venerable bandstand. The gardens held happy memories for Ruth but they were far from her mind as she walked through the ornamental iron gates that guarded the entry. Simon had asked that they meet at the bandstand and now she saw him; hunched on a bench with his anorak tight around him against the chill of the late autumnal afternoon. He was looking at the ground, seemingly oblivious to his surroundings and unaware of Ruth's approach behind him.

Ruth stopped for a few moments some way short of the bench. She was anxious and uncertain and short of sleep; her night disturbed by restless imaginings of what Simon wanted from her. At work it had been hard to hide her preoccupations from Paula, who had asked her on a couple of occasions if she was feeling well. She had bluffed her way through that and had been grateful for Luke tactfully distracting Paula with some fabricated concerns over mundane café issues. When Ruth had excused herself from staying for lunch on the pretext of doing some urgent shopping, Luke had nodded his understanding and offered her a reassuring smile of encouragement.

Ruth composed herself and drew a deep breath before walking close to Simon. "Hello," she said, trying to make the greeting sound routine and neutral.

Simon turned at the sound of her voice. He stood, and Ruth joined him at the bench. For a moment she hesitated; unsure of whether she should offer him a reflex kiss or hug, but the moment passed and they remained apart. Simon sat again and gestured to the space on the bench next to him. Ruth sat alongside him and waited for an explanation. What did he want? Why did they need to meet in a public park? Simon did not speak immediately and, at first, did not look at Ruth but carefully around him as if to ensure no one was close enough to hear whatever it was he had to say. Satisfied their conversation would be private he turned to Ruth. "Thank you," he said.

Ruth waited for more and when nothing was forthcoming, "Thank me for what?"

Simon looked away from her, "For coming. I thought perhaps you wouldn't want to have anything more to do with me."

Ruth considered her response carefully. "If I'm honest Simon—"

Simon broke in. "You're always honest, Ruth. Never any doubt about that."

"Is that a problem?" Ruth tried not to let her resentment show in her question.

Simon looked at her again and managed a weary smile. "No. I suppose not. Not a problem." He paused. "At least not for you."

Ruth had never had much time for word games; for simulated feelings. She remembered Simon used to joke that she had no imagination. He was probably right, which made it easy for her now to say what was on her mind. "Look, Simon. I don't know what you want from me but if you need help; money or whatever; then please say so. If I can help I will. Whatever we had together is over now; but we had twenty years of each other. We have the girls. I can't just walk away from that. I don't love you, Simon; not anymore; not for some time now; but if you are in trouble and I can help I will." Ruth stopped, feeling that perhaps she had said too much; assumed too much.

Simon sighed heavily. "Do I look as if I'm in trouble?"

Ruth paused only briefly. "You look unhappy, Simon. Tormented even. You have done for quite a while. I'm sorry if I've got it wrong but that's what I see."

Simon nodded wearily. "No; you've not got it wrong, Ruth."

Ruth waited in expectation of more but Simon seemed lost in his own thoughts. "So what is the problem, Simon? Why am I here?"

Simon looked around him again, then, satisfied no one was in earshot, spoke softly to Ruth. "The girls. You must tell them."

"Tell them what?" Ruth asked nervously.

"I have to go away."

Ruth frowned in confusion. "Well, you can tell them that yourself surely? That's not such a big deal is it? You have been away quite—"

Simon cut her short. "No, Ruth. I can't; I daren't tell them."

"Why on earth not?"

"Because," and here Simon almost shouted, and then lowered his voice but still spoke with intensity, "because I may never come back."

TWENTY-EIGHT

There was no Marks & Spencer's 'Meal For Two' this time. Luke carried a plate of biscuits in from the kitchen and put them down on the low table in front of Ruth who sat despondently on the settee. She looked at them listlessly. He noticed she had not drunk the coffee he had made for her.

"Thanks," she said, but made no move to eat.

"You sure you wouldn't like a proper drink? Something stronger?" Luke asked anxiously.

Ruth seemed not to register his question for a moment but then made an effort to focus. "No. That's kind of you but I'm not sure that would help." She sighed wearily.

Luke sat next to her. "This is about Simon I imagine? Your meeting in the gardens."

Ruth nodded slowly. "I'm so sorry to involve you, Luke."

Luke placed a reassuring hand on her arm. "Don't be sorry, Ruth. If I can help in any way I hope you know I will."

"Thank you. But I'm not sure if there is anything we can do. It's hopeless." She looked away from Luke to try to hold back unbidden tears.

Luke remained silent; sensing he must wait for Ruth to compose herself.

After a few moments, and taking a deep breath to help

regain her self-control, Ruth looked again at Luke. "You're the only person I can talk to, Luke. And I have to tell someone. Someone I can trust. I can't tell the children; not even Esther. And much as I appreciate what Paula has done for me this would be too much."

Luke risked a smile. "So that leaves me?"

The light touch worked. Ruth relaxed slightly and sat back a little. She managed a wry smile and an apologetic helpless shrug of the shoulders.

Luke picked up the plate of biscuits. He spoke firmly. "Go on. Have a biscuit. And drink your coffee before it gets cold."

Ruth made to protest but Luke held up a commanding hand. "You'll feel better after that; believe me. Then we can talk."

Ruth hesitated for a few seconds but registering Luke's insistence sipped at her coffee and nibbled on a biscuit. Luke too drank his coffee and ate a biscuit. Neither spoke, and only when both cups were empty did Luke turn his attention back to Ruth. "OK. So what did Simon tell you in the gardens this afternoon that was so traumatic?"

Ruth still held on to her empty cup and twisted it around in her hands. When she spoke it was haltingly and softly. "He wants to run away from it all; hide somewhere." She broke off and looked helplessly at Luke. "He doesn't know what else to do."

Luke was silent for a moment, waiting for Ruth to say more but she looked away from him and distractedly put her cup down on the table. "Run away from what, Ruth?" he prompted.

His question regained Ruth's wandering attention. She made an effort to focus on Luke's question. "It started with the London trips. You remember those?"

"Yes. He said he went to sell some of his paintings."

"You never really believed that did you?" Ruth asked resignedly.

Luke took his time to reply. "It didn't matter what I did or didn't believe, Ruth."

Ruth sighed. "I suppose I wanted to believe him: part of my guilt that I was forcing him to find money. But when I knew he was lying I just wanted nothing more to do with it. That's why I gave the money back."

"And told me to stop asking around about Simon in Newlyn."

"Yes. I thought it was over. We would go our own way; lead different lives." She shook her head in despair. "Stupid of me wasn't it?"

"Not at all. It was working. You seemed so much happier; I was pleased for you."

Ruth now turned her head and looked pensively at Luke. "I know you were. I was grateful." She paused awkwardly, "Perhaps more than grateful, Luke." Luke held Ruth's gaze but the still of that moment was quickly lost to Ruth's mounting disquiet. "I was so desperate. I suppose I wanted to believe he had sold his paintings." She shook her head; despairing of her own naivety.

"And what had he sold?" Luke asked quietly but pointedly.

Ruth sighed. "To begin with it was cannabis. He didn't see much harm in that. He's always used it. He still had friends in London who were happy to pay for what he said was 'quality gear': Colombian Gold." She laughed without humour. "He was still talking and thinking like a student." She paused, "But then it got out of control. He was offered money, serious money, to deliver a special load to this dealer in London."

"And did he?" Luke asked.

"Yes. I asked him why he didn't walk away. He said he couldn't."

"Why was that?"

"He didn't really say. I thought perhaps he was scared."

"Possibly," Luke said thoughtfully.

Ruth looked at him questioningly. "What are you thinking, Luke?"

"I'm not sure." He paused. "So that is where the money in the envelope came from?"

"Yes. He admitted it." She closed her eyes in despair. "He said he did it for me."

"Did he now?" Luke could not hide the scepticism in his voice.

Ruth picked up on his tone. "Didn't he?"

Luke would not be drawn. "So where was he getting this stuff from?"

"He said it was better I didn't know."

"I see." Again Luke sounded less than convinced.

"It gets worse, Luke: The last trip to London." Ruth hesitated. "It wasn't cannabis."

"Let me guess. Cocaine?"

"That's dreadful. I told him."

"And what did he say?"

"He more or less broke down. He was crying." Ruth shuddered at the memory. "I felt real pity for him. I know I shouldn't but this is the man I once loved. The girls' father." She looked at Luke. "Do you understand?"

"Of course."

"He's not a bad man, Luke. Weak perhaps, but not bad. And now he's in over his head and he can't get out and he doesn't know what to do." She groaned. "And neither do I."

"Can't he just leave? Get away. Far away?"

"That's what I said," she insisted. "But now it's too late."

"Why?"

"They have him lined up for another trip to London."

"So?"

"Not cocaine this time."

"What then?"

Ruth paused. "People."

Luke stared at Ruth in dismay. "People smuggling? Surely he can't get involved in that?"

"Not like that. Not illegal immigrants."

"Who then?"

"Just three people. Important people he says. Drugs people. They don't tell him much but in a couple of weeks he's supposed to take these men up to London. There'll be big money in it they tell him."

Luke was processing the information. "This is heavy duty stuff, Ruth. This is really police business."

"I know. I told him but he says he can't go to the police without admitting his involvement with drugs. And even if he did tell the police then the gang down here would know it was him and I think he's more scared of them than he is the police."

Luke remembered a conversation with Dave in the bar a few months ago. "I can believe that," he said.

"And if he just runs away, which I thought was the only way out they would suspect his loyalty and get after him. They have long arms and long memories he says."

Neither of them spoke for a while. Ruth looked in despair at Luke who seemed unaware of her as he sat with eyes narrowed in thought. At last he seemed to have reached some cerebral conclusion. He turned to Ruth. "How long before this is supposed to happen?"

Ruth seemed puzzled by the question. "About two weeks I think."

"OK." Luke spoke with crisp authority now. "Make contact with Simon and tell him to sit tight: to carry on as normal for the moment."

"But I thought—"

Luke cut her short. "Ask him if he can find out where these three guys are coming from and how."

Ruth was still lost. "How will that help?"

"I'm not sure, but it might be important. And tell him you will contact him when we have worked out what to do."

"And what are you planning to do, Luke?"

"Never underestimate the power of the Press, Ruth." Luke smiled at her. He looked almost cheerful now; certainly animated.

Ruth was still in total confusion. "I don't know how this will end, Luke." She looked gratefully at him. "But thank you for doing this. For Simon."

Luke smiled at her. "Not for Simon, Ruth."

TWENTY-NINE

"Twice in six months, Luke," Rick's tone was bantering, "I didn't realise life in Penzance was so exciting."

Luke responded in kind. "Thrill a minute, Rick."

"Not another Zimbabwe scoop is it? More from your 'lady friend'."

Luke gritted his teeth but played along with the game. "No. All my own work this time," he lied. "I need a favour."

Rick's tone was now more guarded. "A favour? What sort of favour, Luke?"

"Just information, for the moment. There may be nothing in it."

"But if there is; I'll be the first to know won't I Luke?" Rick said forcibly.

"Speed of light, Rick," Luke said, and crossed his fingers.

Luke had rehearsed what he would say to Rick. He needed to give him enough to secure his co-operation without the specifics which might endanger the fragile plan he was attempting to implement. It was two days since Ruth had come to him in despair with news of Simon's dangerous involvement with people he dare not cross. He had clearly got in over his head and his first instinct had been to run away. Luke had emphasised to Ruth that Simon must be dissuaded from that option: it would be a clear statement of guilt to his unforgiving enforcers. Ruth had arranged to meet Simon a second time in Morrab Gardens and had managed to persuade him to sit tight and give Luke an opportunity to work something out. Ruth had explained that Luke was a 'good friend' they could both trust. She reported, with some embarrassment, that Simon had implied he suspected Luke was more than just a friend but in his powerless situation he accepted the offer of help. He was able to add a few more details about the planned clandestine landing. The three men were Colombians and coming by sea. He was to deliver them to the contact he had used in London. He was given no names. He was told there should be no problems getting them ashore. They would be wearing the same gear as the other crew on the trawler and would make their way individually to the van Simon would drive to London. Luke had to accept it was a plausible operation. The fish market at Newlyn was a hectic place when the boats unloaded. In all the coming and going it was unlikely the three would stand out. Many of the boats had taken on foreign labour so even their appearance would not be untoward. No doubt the legitimate crew on the incoming trawler would have been well rewarded to ask no questions; particularly if they were the ones involved with the previous illicit shipments of drugs. Clearly there was serious money at work here and seriously dangerous people spending it in expectation of earning a great deal more. Luke knew how much was at stake now but was, he had to admit with some relief, not intimidated. He remembered he had clashed with powerful and sinister opponents in the past. Then, of course, he had been emboldened by his belief that the truth must be told. Now, he accepted ironically, it was important the truth did not come out!

"Well," Rick prompted impatiently, "what do you want to know?"

"Probably nothing in it. Rumour, gossip. You know how it is in a small town, Rick."

"I'm happy to say I don't, but cut to the chase, Luke."

Luke paused. "OK then. Colombia, Rick."

Luke said no more and, after a few seconds, Rick responded. "Are we talking movies or the country?"

"With an 'o'."

"The country then. Yes, Luke, I've heard of it, believe it or not."

"I'm sure. But do you have anybody who knows what's going on there?"

"Probably what usually goes on there. Murder and drug trafficking."

"No doubt. But can you be more specific? Who is murdering who at the moment?"

Rick paused. "Not really my pigeon. It's all stale news."

"But," Luke persisted, "you must have someone who's up to speed?"

Rick seemed to be considering the question. "I suppose I could ask Bill Nash. He's our South American guy."

"I'd be grateful, Rick."

"Give me a day. I'll get back to you."

"Thanks, Rick. I'll wait—"

"Hang on," Rick cut in. "What's all this about?"

Luke feigned nonchalance. "As I say, probably nothing. Another Ovanga dead end I expect."

"Literally, in his case," Rick remembered.

Luke laughed. "Quite."

"But if there is something. Luke…"

Luke anticipated the directive. "Of course, Rick. Your exclusive. As always." He ended the call before he was required to tell any more lies.

Ruth was laying tables when Luke entered the café. She raised her eyebrows in silent inquiry.

"Tell you later," Luke mouthed.

Ruth pointed towards the back yard where Paula had repaired for a smoke She whispered to Luke. "She's in a funny mood."

Luke registered that in some surprise and went through to the kitchen to put on his 'pinny'.

"Morning, Paula," he called out.

There was no response but in a few moments Paula came slowly into the kitchen; her cigarette still in her hand. "I need to speak to you, both of you." Her tone was flat with none of its usual energy.

She walked through to the café and checked the Closed sign was still showing. Luke had followed her out from the kitchen and stood with Ruth as they looked anxiously at Paula who registered their concern. "You'd better sit down," she said, "this might come as a bit of a shock."

They both sat. Ruth glanced nervously at Luke as Paula joined them.

Ruth spoke first; her voice betraying her concern. "What is it Paula? Are you OK?"

Paula considered the question. "I suppose; just a bit out of it at the moment."

"Can we do anything to help, Paula?" Luke asked quietly.

"I'm not sure. Can't seem to think straight."

Ruth looked at Luke for reassurance before pressing on. "So what is it, Paula. Are you ill?"

Paula looked at her. "Not me." She laughed without conviction. "I'm never ill." She said no more but shook her head in disbelief.

Ruth would not be deflected. "Then, what is—"

Paula seemed to make an effort to focus. She exhaled deeply. "My mother."

There was a long silence. Ruth and Luke looked at each other in confusion.

Luke was the first to speak "Your mother? But I thought she—"

"Was dead?" Paula completed the sentence for him.

"Well, yes. I suppose I did."

"I never said she was dead, did I?" Paula's voice had now regained something of its familiar bark.

"Perhaps not," Luke admitted.

"Mind you she might just as well have been," Paula conceded. "She severed all links when I ran off with the Jamaican."

Paula paused reflectively and no one spoke for a moment before Ruth attempted to move the narrative on. "But now?"

"She's dying. On her last legs it seems." Paula spoke without emotion.

"I see," Ruth said. "I'm sorry."

"Thank you," Paula managed. "I can't pretend I feel too cut up about it." She directed her next remark to Luke. "Does that make me wicked?"

Luke's reassurance was quick. "Of course not. You have had no contact for years and you parted on bad terms. You can't alter that."

Paula seemed to be considering his verdict.

Ruth spoke almost in spite of herself. "But she was your mother. Sorry, is your mother."

Paula frowned at that but then slowly nodded her agreement. "Dear Ruth." She smiled. "To whom a spade is always a spade."

Ruth blushed apologetically. "I'm sorry; that was tactless of me."

"Not at all." Paula stood. She walked over to the serving counter and fished out another cigarette from a packet she kept under a tea cosy. She lit it and turned to face Ruth and Luke. "She has asked to see me it seems. They contacted me as next of kin; found my details. I had a call this morning."

Ruth was quick to speak. "You must go, Paula."

Paula smiled at that instruction. "What about you, Luke? What do you think? Should I go?"

Luke reflected for a moment. "I can't answer that for you, Paula."

Ruth looked at him in some exasperation but no surprise, but Paula accepted his response. "You're quite right, of course. It is up to me." She stubbed out vigorously the cigarette she had just lit. "I will go."

Ruth could not help herself. "You won't regret it, Paula."

Paula laughed. "But you two might. Can you manage to keep this place going whilst I'm away? I'm not sure how long I'll be gone."

Ruth and Luke looked at each other for a moment. Ruth spoke for them. "I'm sure we can. It's not a busy time of the year. Can't we Luke?"

Luke hesitated only briefly. "No problem. I'll come in early to open up."

"And I can cope with most of the stuff we cook. Not that it will quite be up to your standards, Paula," she added quickly and tactfully.

Paula responded to the flattery with a smile. "And you can probably call on Esther when she's not at college?"

Ruth accepted that and got briskly to her feet. "Well that's all settled. We can run through a checklist before you go, can't we?"

"If I have time."

Ruth looked puzzled. "Time? When were you thinking of going?"

Paula was putting the cigarette packet back under the cosy. "Well, there is a convenient flight tomorrow afternoon."

Luke registered his surprise. "Flight?"

Paula turned to face him. "Yes. Sorry. Didn't I mention it? My mother has lived in the South of France for the last ten years."

THIRTY

Ruth frowned in concentration as she added the spices to the chicken curry. Paula had found time to leave a list of the most popular Daily Specials and Ruth was nervously following the instructions from Paula's collected file of favourite recipes. She tasted the curry and was relieved to find it palatable. There was a fruit crumble in the oven and a sponge she had made first thing cooling on a wire rack. It had been an early start and Luke, after he had fired up the coffee machine, had taken the list Paula had left to the supermarket, to stock up larders and fridges.

With the curry now simmering gently on low heat Ruth allowed herself to relax for the first time that morning. She rolled her shoulders to shake out the tension and sat gratefully at an empty table. There was an hour to go yet before opening time. No doubt at this stage Paula would have been on her second or third cigarette of the day but Ruth simply exhaled deeply and sat back in her chair and attempted to relax. Not easy. Not only had she had to get up early but also put cereal out for the girls and shout upstairs for them to be sure to clear away the breakfast things. Sarah was back at school and needed to be out of the house in good time. Esther kept more irregular college hours but Ruth had charged her with the responsibility of getting her sister organised for school. She had explained to them last night that she was covering full time for Paula and why. Esther had taken that on board and told Ruth not to worry about Sarah; she would 'sort her out'. Ruth now knew enough about her older daughter to accept that assurance.

Ruth had also needed to 'sort out' her classes. She had spent the best part of the evening texting and telephoning class members explaining apologetically that she would need to put the sessions on hold for a week or two due to 'unforeseen family circumstances'. That, she convinced herself, was not actually a lie because she could almost regard Paula as family now. Reflecting on that while the curry and crumble wafted tempting aromas from the kitchen she had to admit that a break from her classes was not unwelcome. She could not deny any more that the physical strain of leading the more energetic and youthful of her clients into their punishing routines was beginning, after nearly twenty years, to take its toll on her body. Aches and pains and strains, no doubt came with the territory as they say, but realistically she wondered how much longer she could withstand the daily assault on her body. She could keep going with the pensioner class no doubt but if she could find ways of earning enough money to abandon the rest she would happily bale out.

Her contemplation of that future was put on hold as Luke returned from his shopping expedition. She helped him struggle in with his laden bags. They put them down on the nearest table and Ruth made to unload the contents but Luke, breathing heavily from his exertion, held up a restraining palm. "Hang on a sec," he asked.

Ruth teased him. "Not fit Luke, that's your problem."

Luke managed a smile but shook his head. "True. But it's not that." He sat at the table and took out his phone. Ruth looked at him in confusion but sat too.

Luke held up the phone in explanation. "Just got a text from Rick. Information."

Ruth was immediately attentive; tense and nervous too. The cooking had briefly taken her mind off Simon and his problems. Now they bore down on her again. "What does he say?"

Luke was looking at the screen of his phone. "There's quite a lot of it."

Ruth waited anxiously and watched Luke, his lips moving silently, as he studied the material Rick had sent him. Eventually he put his phone down and looked at Ruth. He said nothing for a moment. Ruth could not be so restrained. "What is it, Luke. What information?"

Luke gestured at his phone lying on the table. "He spoke to his South American expert: about Colombia." He paused; frowning: still ordering his thoughts.

Ruth prompted him again. "Colombia?"

Luke nodded. "I assumed that this was the connection. Simon spoke of 'Colombian Gold'. It's the main source of drugs that find their way into Europe. Rick's guy told him that the Mexicans had more or less frozen the Colombian cartels out of direct access to the US market so they had diversified into Europe; plenty of routes and harder to police."

"How could Simon have got mixed up with all this dreadful stuff?" Ruth groaned.

Luke seemed about to answer Ruth's question, but hesitated and then moved on. "There's more."

Ruth sighed. "Tell me, then."

"In the last few months the Colombian government have agreed an extradition treaty with the United States. Several of the major gang leaders have been arrested and are awaiting trial in America." Luke paused and looked hard at Ruth. "It seems the rest are running for the exit." He sat back.

Ruth nodded slowly. "So you think the three Simon has to take to London could—" She broke off in despair at what she was suggesting.

Luke's tone was almost apologetic. "I'm only guessing of course; just trying to join up the dots."

Ruth shook her head. "No. It all makes sense. The money involved; the organisation."

"And the timing," Luke said.

"Timing?" Ruth queried.

"Simon said they told him it would be about two weeks before the pick-up, didn't he?"

"Yes. I think so," Ruth remembered.

"Well that would figure. I assume these men will be coming by sea. Presumably on a container ship; probably heading for Antwerp or Rotterdam. That would bring it through the Channel and close to Cornwall. Drop off at sea not a problem."

"But you said something about timing."

"Rick's contact says sailing times to Europe take between sixteen to twenty-one days depending on weather conditions. So assuming they are already under way that only gives us less than two weeks to come up with a plan."

Ruth looked at him in bewilderment. "Plan, Luke? What sort of a plan?"

Dave had looked puzzled when he had been shown the script but Luke had brushed aside his queries with a vague, "I'll explain later," so now he was in full Pasco mode of baffled confusion as Luke lectured him.

"What I have been trying to explain, Pasco, is that the present is just a continuation of the past; and knowledge of our history is the way we understand the present. Do you follow me?"

"Not sure that I do Prof," Dave mumbled. "Never was much good at history."

"Not just factual history, Pasco, popular legend too."

"How do you mean?"

Luke sighed dramatically. "Let's take Cornwall as an example. What, historically, have been the activities which shaped society here?"

Pasco pondered for a few seconds. "Methodism I guess. All those chapels; choirs and hymn singing."

"Excellent, Pasco. But what about the Cornish economy? What were the wealth creators?"

Pasco paused in pretend thought. "Well, tin mining I suppose."

Luke offered encouragement. "Well done, Pasco. That would certainly be one." He paused. "But what else?"

"Fishing?" Dave asked nervously.

"Well done again, Pasco. Fishing and tin mining have certainly been major players in the Cornish economy historically." Luke's tone now became more interrogatory. "But now, Pasco?"

"Well the mining's finished and the fishing is all buggered."

"Eloquently put, Pasco. So what is left?"

"Tourism," Pasco said confidently.

"For a few months of the year. Hard work though and not all good Cornishmen and true want to make tea for holidaymakers or clean chalets."

"Can't blame them."

"Indeed. So what else in Cornwall in days gone by has proved profitable?"

"Dunno, Prof."

"Come on Pasco." Luke paused for a moment. "Think rugby."

"Rugby?" echoed Dave in convincing bafflement.

"Here's a clue. The Cornish what?"

After a pause, "Pirates! Got you, Prof."

"It's deep in Cornish folklore. All those kegs of brandy evading the revenue men. And how many cafés and restaurants and pubs are called the pirates this or the smugglers that?"

"A fair few."

"It was all too easy wasn't it? Dozens of remote and inaccessible coves where the contraband could be landed and willing helpers ashore to spirit the goods away. Tobacco and brandy were the favourites."

Dave laughed. "Not much point in that now. Smoking is on the way out and booze is cheap enough in the supermarkets."

"You're quite right, Pasco." Luke paused and then lowered his voice. "But I think we all know there are rich pickings to be made for those still following in the smugglers' footsteps."

Dave now also lowered his voice in dramatic tension. "Drugs, Prof?"

Luke laughed ironically. "Don't tell me you're surprised Pasco. I think we all know that if you go into certain pubs and ask the right people you can lay your hand on any substances known to man. At a price of course."

"I have heard it said," Dave conceded.

"I'm sure you have."

"But it's a bit chancy isn't it? Been a fair few arrests; boats seized and that."

"Tip of the iceberg, Pasco. Most of this stuff will get through and out onto the streets in our big cities. And those who do get caught are usually the small fry; rarely the bosses."

"Must be worth the risk I suppose?"

"One successful deal would probably bring in more than an honest fisherman could earn in his lifetime."

"Big money then? This drug stuff."

"Huge. But—" Luke paused.

Dave interrupted. "But what Prof?"

"Think Pasco. All the headlines are about it now. What will earn some criminal organisation even more than smuggling drugs?"

Dave feigned a light bulb moment. "People!"

"Correct. A dreadful growth industry."

"But there's nothing like that down here, Prof, is there? That's all up Dover way."

"Yes. Those poor souls packed onto leaking rafts and abandoned in the English Channel."

"Couldn't do that in our seas, Prof."

"No. Not that. But maybe something a little more sophisticated."

"What?" Dave sounded, as required, bemused.

"I seem to remember a few years ago a party of Vietnamese were landed at Newlyn. Am I right?"

Dave laughed. "A right cock up. As if twenty of them walking through Newlyn in broad daylight wouldn't be noticed! Poor sods were all arrested in the back of a lorry on the M5."

"Indeed. The whole business was an organisational disaster. But the fact remains they did land at Newlyn and with more careful planning it might have succeeded."

"How do you mean, Prof?"

"Say, for example, you were bringing in just two or three illegals. You know how busy the market is at landing times. Disguise your clients as deck hands and I doubt anyone would notice them. You could whisk them away unobserved."

Dave pondered that. "Might work I suppose. Still a risk."

"True. But if your customers were, say, for argument sake, rich and powerful criminals on the run, no doubt they would pay well."

Dave scoffed. "That's all James Bond, stuff, Prof." He paused. "Isn't it?"

"Sometimes truth is stranger than fiction, Pasco."

"What? You telling me that this stuff happens? In Newlyn?"

"I am saying it's possible, Pasco, and strictly between ourselves," Luke now articulated slowly and softly, "I don't believe I'm the only one who thinks that."

"What do you mean, Prof?"

"Have you been to the harbour at Newlyn recently, Pasco?"

"Can't say I have."

"Maybe just gossip of course but I am told there are a few strangers about."

"Lots of folk come and go there."

"True. But some find it hard to merge into the background."

Dave laughed. "Those with big feet you mean?"

"Probably nothing in it, but it did make me wonder."

"Coppers? Is that what you're saying?"

"I doubt if just coppers. Border Force, perhaps Special Branch."

"What would they be doing there?"

"They must be acting on some intelligence I imagine. They have infiltrated most of the drug syndicates; some gang member in London must have been leaned on or made an offer he couldn't resist."

"I didn't reckon you were into all this, Prof."

"I keep my finger on the pulse, Pasco. Sources in London; you know how it is."

"Can't say I do, Prof."

"No, I suppose not. Anyway Pasco," Luke offered airily, "as I say, probably just rumour."

"Perhaps Prof. But you know what they say; no smoke without fire."

Luke did the throat cutting mime and after a few

seconds' silence put down his script. Dave still held on to his and looked at it thoughtfully for a moment before putting it down. He looked questioningly at Luke who held his gaze but said nothing.

Dave broke the silence. "Are you going to tell me then?"

Luke feigned surprise. "Tell you what?"

Dave gestured at the script on the table in front of him. "What all that was about?"

"About?" Luke asked innocently.

"Please! I'm not Pasco, now, Luke."

Luke held up his hands in surrender. "Fair enough, Dave, but I think it's safer if you take it at face value."

"Safer?" Dave frowned at Luke. "How do you mean?"

"Then if anyone ask you about it you'll have nothing to tell them."

Dave did not seem satisfied with that. "Ask me? Who's going to ask me?"

Luke sighed and then accepted Dave would not be content with evasion. "OK, Dave. I don't want you to get too involved in this, but I have my reason for that script. It should become clearer in the next few days and then I can explain. You'll just have to trust me I'm afraid and if anyone should ask you, tell them you only read the scripts put in front of you." Luke smiled. "Make it clear you're just a jobbing actor: a voice for hire."

"Is that what I am?"

"For the purposes of this script, yes."

Dave pondered on that and then shrugged. "I've been called worse things."

Luke nodded. "Thanks, Dave. I appreciate that."

Dave stood and pushed his script back across the table to Luke. "So all that stuff about Special Branch and people smuggling. Is any of that true?"

Luke tapped the side of his nose conspiratorially, "All in good time, Dave. All in good time."

THIRTY-ONE

"Are you sure you don't want anything to eat?" Ruth asked, as she put the mug of coffee down in front of Luke.

He shook his head. "No thanks. I seem to have lost my appetite."

Ruth smiled wearily at him and sat cradling her own cup. "Cooking and being around food all day certainly puts you off eating." She sat back wearily in her chair and looked around her kitchen. "And there's a pile of washing and ironing waiting if I can summon the energy."

Luke looked at her. "You're doing a great job. Lots of compliments from the punters."

Ruth allowed herself a small smile. "Three days in and I'm on my knees. Come back Paula!"

"No word?"

"Nothing yet."

They both sipped their coffee in silence; sharing a few easy moments before facing anxieties sharper than physical weariness. Luke needed to explain to Ruth what lay ahead. After finishing at the café he had gone to the Clarion office and left a draft article for Peter to consider. He would go back tomorrow to get a reaction. He had told Ruth, without going into detail, that she would need to play her part in his plan. With Sarah up in her room doing her homework and Esther over at Tom's working on their new project, it was time to discuss strategy.

"You'll need to see Simon again, Ruth."

"I suppose I can. I'll text him."

Luke thought about that. "Tell him you need to make arrangements about taking the girls to the cinema and—"

"What?" Ruth blurted out in astonishment.

Luke held up a restraining hand. "Hold on. Let me explain. Hopefully he'll work out that you really want to see him about something more urgent."

Ruth frowned and considered Luke's request. "Are you telling me, Luke, that his phone might be tapped or whatever they call it?"

Luke shrugged. "Not tapped; but..." and here he paused before deciding to proceed. "I think the people he's involved with are not beyond invading his privacy, to put it politely."

Ruth took a moment to register this. "You know them, Luke? These people?" She could not keep the surprise out of her voice.

Luke sat back in his chair for a moment. He seemed absorbed in his own thoughts.

Ruth asked her question again; this time with more urgency. "You do know don't you? Who Simon is mixed up with."

Luke looked warily at Ruth. "I thought it was over with; that you didn't need to know. You more or less told me that you didn't want to know."

Ruth frowned. "Did I?"

"When I was asking about Simon; asking in Newlyn. You told me to stop: said that it didn't matter anymore."

"You're right; I did," Ruth admitted. "I hoped I could draw a line: start again." She shook her head despairingly.

"Stupid of me." Luke made no comment and Ruth sighed but then forced herself to focus. "So who are they, Luke? Tell me."

Luke held her gaze for a few moments; then he shrugged: accepting that he could prevaricate no more. "The Trebenten family."

Ruth looked at Luke in expectation of more but he sat quietly, absently drumming his fingers on the table top. In exasperation Ruth raised her voice. "Come on, Luke. What about this Trebenten family?"

Luke's reply was guarded: low key; almost monosyllabic. "Newlyn fishing family. Hard cases; almost certainly bringing in drugs."

Ruth seemed more confused than enlightened by this information. "Why on earth would Simon get involved with people like that?" Her question demanded an answer but Luke sat in uncomfortable silence. Ruth persisted. "What are you not telling me, Luke?"

Luke looked away for a moment. "I hoped you would never need to hear this, Ruth."

"Hear what?" Ruth demanded.

Luke hesitated only briefly, then turned his head to face her. "Simon seems to be in some sort of relationship with Elowen; the Trebenten daughter." He looked apologetically at Ruth.

Ruth sat back in shock as she absorbed the information; she looked stricken. There was silence apart from the noise of the reflex tapping of Luke's nervous fingers on the table before he became aware of it and clenched his fist to still the sound. That action distracted Ruth from whatever thoughts were churning in her mind. She exhaled deeply and looked directly at Luke. "What sort of relationship?" Luke seemed discomforted by the question but Ruth spared him the anguish of having to answer it. She forced a wry smile from somewhere. "What a stupid question. Sorry." Her mood and tone were now more positive. "Is she beautiful; this Elowen?"

Luke was surprised by the question. "So they tell me."

Ruth nodded in weary acceptance. "Young too, no doubt. Young and beautiful." She laughed without humour. "No doubt Simon was putty in her hands."

"I think he might have been infatuated," Luke explained. "She is the brains behind the family they tell me. Beautiful and clever: probably manipulative and ruthless too. No doubt Simon found it hard to resist."

"No doubt," Ruth said grimly. "He always had a roving eye."

"More fool him!" Luke's observation was fierce and spontaneous.

Ruth sat back in surprise. Then she smiled at Luke. "Thank you, Luke."

The atmosphere was changed by that moment. Luke was now relaxed and clear-headed. He had shed the burden of carrying the secret of Simon's betrayal of Ruth but he needed to be sure that the disclosure had not altered her commitment to trying to rescue him from the consequences of his infidelity. He put this to Ruth. "Now that you know about Simon, I have to ask. Do you still want to try to help him?"

Ruth looked surprised at the question. "Of course. I know I've said it before and maybe it's hard to believe but Simon is not a bad person; even though he's been sucked into doing horrible stuff. He wants to stop and if I can help I will." She looked thoughtfully at Luke. "Does that make sense, Luke?"

"Of course." He smiled. "You wear your heart on your sleeve, Ruth. Do you know that?"

Ruth looked embarrassed by that. "Do I? Perhaps I haven't got the imagination to hide my feelings." She pointed her finger at Luke. "Unlike some."

Now it was Luke's turn to look embarrassed. He rapidly changed the subject. "Now, when you meet Simon this is what you have to tell him."

THIRTY-TWO

Peter Rawlings frowned as he studied the article Luke had drafted. He put it down on the table and stared questioningly at Luke whose returning gaze was without expression.

Peter was the first to break the silence. He gestured at the document he had just put down. "This is heavy duty, Luke. If it had come from anyone but you I wouldn't touch it with a barge pole."

"It's fireproof, Peter."

Peter picked up the draft and looked at it again. "Carefully worded Luke, I grant you that." He studied the text again for some moments. "'Usually reliable source'; 'anonymous tip-offs'; 'informants who ask not to be named'," he intoned, before slapping the paper back down on the table. "All piss and wind, Luke. Can I believe a word of it?"

Luke shrugged. "Your choice Peter. If you won't run it I still know those who will."

Peter frowned and then seemed to come to a decision. "I expect you do, Luke. Just tell me one thing. Is this kosher?"

Luke smiled. "Why would I make it up?"

Peter nodded. "That's what I ask myself and I can't come up with an answer."

"So you'll print it?"

Peter hesitated only briefly. "All right. You win. I'll lead with it tomorrow." He groaned. "And then keep my head down."

Luke stood. "Thank you, Peter."

Peter stood too. "This source of yours, Luke. No chance of a name, I suppose. Just between ourselves."

Luke's smile was bleak. "No chance at all, Peter."

Ruth managed a smile and some cheerful banter as she thanked the last of the departing lunchtime customers. She stood at the café door for a moment watching as they set off down the street. Then, with a grateful sigh of relief, she closed and locked the door. She turned back to the table where Luke sat with his half eaten bowl of soup cooling in front of him as he studied the front page of the Clarion.

Ruth sat beside him. "Do you think it will work?" she asked anxiously.

Peter put the newspaper down but pointed at the headline.

Ruth read it out loud. " 'People smuggling threat at Newlyn.' " She looked inquiringly at Luke then studied the rest of the article. When she had finished she glanced at Luke again before reading again what he had written. "You make it sound so convincing." She shook her head in disbelief. "I could almost believe it if I didn't know different."

"What matters is whether the Trebentens believe it or not."

Ruth was still studying the newspaper. "I think they might. You have this stuff," and here she read verbatim, "'an unnamed source in Special Branch did not deny their interest in possible criminal involvement in people smuggling by rogue members of the Newlyn fishing community.' "

"Carefully worded," Luke conceded wryly.

Ruth was now reading out loud another section of the article. "'It can be assumed the authorities are acting on insider information from moles embedded within London criminal gangs.'"

"It's important for Simon that the Trebentens believe that," Luke admitted.

Ruth nodded but continued to examine the text and read it out. "'Rumours are circulating in Newlyn that undercover officers are already in place in expectation of an imminent attempt to land illegals.'" She put down the newspaper and looked warily at Luke. "I wonder who started the rumours?"

Luke smiled at her. "I wonder."

"This sounds so convincing even—"

"Even if it's all a pack of lies. Is that what you were going to say?"

Ruth half smiled. "I suppose I was."

"I have said nothing factual: just suggestions and insinuations. No names; no accusations."

"Fake news?" Ruth asked.

Luke groaned. "I suppose it is. I never thought I would be guilty of that."

Ruth instinctively put her hand over his. "I'm so sorry, Luke."

"What for?"

"For getting you into this."

Luke did not release his hand. "Ironic really. I was banished for trying to tell the truth behind the lies and now I am happily using lies to hide the truth."

"Doesn't that upset you?"

Luke thought about that. "Strangely it doesn't. The lies are harmless; they won't damage anyone, except, hopefully., the Trebentens."

"And your lies could let Simon escape them."

Luke agreed. "Let's hope so." He paused. "Have you seen him yet?"

Ruth nodded. "This morning; before I came in. I told him what you said. To stay put and act normally. To seem OK, about the London trip."

"And can he do that?"

"I think so. He doesn't really have a choice."

"And you didn't mention the Trebenten daughter."

Ruth shrugged. "Why would I? He's a free agent now."

Luke looked at her. "A funny sort of freedom, Ruth."

Ruth gave Luke's hand a gentle pat of affection before she stood and looked around the café. "I'd better get back to the kitchen: stuff to do."

Luke stood too. "I'll help clear up." He raised his eye heavenward in mock prayer. "Come back, Paula! All is forgiven."

THIRTY-THREE

"I tell you, Luke, I'm skating on very thin ice here." Even on the end of the phone Luke could sense the barely concealed panic in the voice of the Clarion's editor.

Luke tried to offer reassurance. "Just hold your nerve, Peter. You can tell them you saw it as your public duty to put out the word that a very serious crime was rumoured to be close to execution."

"I'm the one who'll be close to execution if this goes pear-shaped!" Peter protested.

"It won't."

"Can you be sure, Luke? The story has only been out there a day and my phone is red hot."

"That's good isn't it?" Luke suggested cheerfully.

"No! It is not good when the callers are from Special Branch and Devon and Cornwall police amongst others. Demanding to know where my information comes from."

"I hope you read from the Journalist's Bible."

"'I cannot reveal my source'." He sighed. "You can imagine how that went down. Talk of warrants and injunctions."

"Bluff, Peter."

"Are you certain of that Luke? I've had the proprietor breathing down my neck as well."

"What's he complaining about? This should boost your circulation figures sky high."

"He's terrified of getting sued."

"Trust me, Peter, there is nothing you printed that is actionable."

"Because it's speculation and unprovable allegations and hearsay!"

Luke laughed. "Nothing new there then."

"It's only because I know of your reputation, what you did in the past, that I trusted you Luke, but I have this horrible suspicion I might have been taken for a ride."

"Please, Peter. Why would I do that? What possible reason could I have for concocting a bogus story? Do you think I'm that desperate?"

There was a pause on the line as Peter considered the question. "I suppose not," he conceded grudgingly, "but I have this gut feeling I'm not getting the whole truth."

"Truth is a many-sided diamond, Peter," Luke intoned with feigned gravity.

"Oh, please, spare me the *Reader's Digest* philosophy. I can do without that. Not only have I got the police and the proprietor leaning on me but the media crew are banging on my door too."

"No doubt. Look, Peter, I seem to remember you asking that if I had a big story I would bring it to you. Well, I have and people are taking notice. I'm told the TV cameras were in evidence at the harbour this morning; not to mention a visible uniformed police presence."

"Oh, God! Who told you?"

Luke could not help himself. "A usually reliable source." With that he ended the conversation, with Peter in mid expletive.

Ruth wearily closed her front door behind her and for a moment leant back against it to gather her strength.

"We're in here Mum!" Esther called out from the kitchen.

Ruth straightened slowly, hung up her coat and walked through to the kitchen. She paused at the door to take in the sight of her daughters standing on either side of the kitchen table and staring at a large sheet of cardboard spread out in front of them. As Ruth moved closer she saw that Sarah was poised with a felt pen, ready to write.

"What on earth are you two doing?"

Esther turned and smiled cheerfully at her mother. "Don't panic, Mum. Sarah's got better writing than me so I asked her to do it."

"Do what?" Ruth demanded.

Sarah looked up at her mother with the pen still firmly in her grasp. She gestured with it at the blank cardboard. "I'm making Esther a placard."

Ruth shook her head in confusion and pulled out a kitchen chair and slumped down on it. "A placard?" She looked questioningly at Esther who accepted explanations were required. She pulled out a chair from beside the table and plonked it down opposite Ruth. She sat and looked slightly nervously at her mother. "It's for a demo. This weekend. You see—"

Ruth interrupted her sharply. "A demo? What demo? What are you talking about, Esther?"

"Don't panic, Mum. There's a coach organised; Surfers against Sewage. Tom will be with me."

"Am I supposed to find that reassuring? Neither of you are adults yet."

"Maybe, but we're old enough to know what's right and what's wrong," Esther insisted and looked unblinkingly at Ruth.

Ruth said nothing for a moment and then sat back in the chair with a sigh. "So tell me then. Where is this demo thing?"

"Exeter. Outside South West Water's offices."

"And what will you do there?"

Esther looked surprised by the question. "I'm not sure really. March up and down a bit with our banners I suppose; some chanting." She smiled brightly. "I think there's a band organised."

"I see." Ruth shrugged. "And do you think it will do any good. Will it change anything?"

"I don't know. But you've got to try haven't you?"

"I suppose so," Ruth allowed.

"It's all about getting the publicity; raising awareness Tom says. It will probably get on TV and into the papers. Then perhaps people will know the truth won't they?"

"Because it's in the papers?" Ruth said softly, almost to herself, and smiled wryly.

Esther looked at her mother in confusion. "What?"

Ruth affected brightness. "Nothing." She stood up and pushed the chair back against the table. "Just promise me you won't get arrested. Esther. That would be more than I could handle at the moment."

Esther scoffed at the notion. "Of course we won't." She stood too and made to return her attention to the table where Sarah was now carefully printing on the placard, but then she paused and looked back at Ruth who was still standing distractedly by the table. "Are you OK Mum? You look shattered."

Ruth regained her focus and looked at Esther. "Too much cooking I expect. No word about Paula's return yet."

Esther did not look convinced. "Is that it? I thought perhaps there was something else. You've been a bit on edge the last few days haven't you?"

"Have I?" Ruth's reply was guarded. She knew better now than to discount Esther's powers of perception.

Esther persisted. "Everything all right with Luke?"

Ruth was about to respond with her familiar assertion that she and Luke remained good friends and nothing had changed there, when she was saved from this half-truth by Sarah's question to her sister. "Do you think the 'S' is too big?"

Esther leaned over the table to inspect the printing. "No. That's great."

Ruth joined in the inspection, intrigued in spite of her misgivings. "What will it say?"

Sarah paused for a moment from her task. "'Save our Seas'."

"That's clear enough. You're doing a good job there Sarah."

Sarah smiled gratefully. "Thanks Mum." But instead of resuming her task she paused and looked sheepishly at Ruth. "I don't suppose I can go on the demo as well?"

Ruth looked at her in mock horror. "You suppose right!"

Sarah did not seem surprised by the response and frowned in concentration as she began work on the 'A'.

Ruth smiled to herself but then had a final word to Sarah before she began sorting out some supper for them all. "Anyway, Sarah, you have a netball match on Saturday. You can demonstrate your skill at that!"

Dave was polishing glasses and rearranging them on the shelves behind the bar counter when Luke walked in. He turned to greet him. "Thanks for coming."

Luke pulled out a bar stool and sat. Dave remained behind the bar but stopped polishing the glasses and leaned on the counter to face Luke.

"Your text made it seem urgent, Dave."

"I just thought I should bring you up to speed, while it was quiet." He gestured at the empty bar.

"Fine: speed away, Dave. What's the worry?"

Dave paused to perch on a stool leaning forward and speaking in a hushed voice, "The Trebentens." He nodded at Luke as if his words were explanatory enough.

Luke waited for clarification but none came. "What about the Trebentens?"

Dave looked around again at the silent and empty bar but when he spoke it was still with a lowered voice. "They were in here last night: two of the brothers. Both nasty pieces of work." Dave paused as if still disturbed by the recollection.

"And?" Luke inquired patiently.

"They wanted to know. About the podcast. Who was responsible for it."

Luke laughed. "Gratifying they were showing an interest."

Dave frowned. "It was no bloody joke, Luke, I can tell you."

"I'm sorry, Dave. It must have been tough for you," Luke said contritely.

"It was. Luckily, some of the rugby boys were in after their training night and they could see things were getting a bit heavy so they sort of froze them out."

"So what did you tell them, Dave? The Trebentens."

"Just as you suggested. That I was just a jobbing actor paid to read a script someone else had written."

Luke smiled. "If only that were true."

"What?"

"That you were paid."

Dave allowed himself a smile.

"Did you convince them?" Luke continued.

"I'm not sure. I think they would like to have leaned on me a bit if the rugby guys hadn't stepped in."

"So what exactly did you tell them about me?"

"Like you said. That you had close contacts in the Met and I assumed the information had come from them; that someone in London had spilled the beans."

"Well done."

Dave was clearly more relaxed now. "With the rugby boys there I got quite cheeky." He smiled at the memory. "I said as they were so interested perhaps they should approach you and if they had any information then you'd be happy to share it with your friends in the security services and perhaps give the Trebentens a write-up in the paper as a concerned fishing family anxious to protect the good name of Newlyn."

Luke laughed. "Brilliant, Dave. How did that go down?"

"I don't think you can expect a call from them. They must think you're bulletproof with all those friends in law enforcement."

"Let's hope so."

Dave shook his head in wonder. "And yet Luke, I still don't know if any bloody word of it is true."

Luke said nothing.

"Will I ever know?"

"One day, Dave. Trust me. When it's all quietened down."

"No sign of that yet. Reporters; TV Crews; Coppers – everywhere."

"Indeed, the power of the Press, Dave. And our little podcast has not gone unheard it seems."

"That's true."

"Which makes me the bearer of good tidings, Dave."

"Why am I nervous?"

"No need. I have had a fair number of people wanting to do an advertising deal with us and even some wanting to be subscribers."

"Good God!" Dave gasped.

"So, I might even be able to pay you sometime soon."

"Now I've heard it all."

"So when this hurly burley's done I think we might widen our net. See if we can land a few national politicians and the like." Luke laughed. "Give Cornwall Council a breather."

Dave stood. He reached for the whisky bottle on the optic behind him. "Well, Luke, it might only be three o'clock in the afternoon but I think we might raise a glass in anticipation of Pasco's entry onto the world stage."

THIRTY-FOUR

The night was quiet and clear and the huge container ship was sliding easily through the gentle waves, its phosphorescent wake ruffling the moonlit sea. High up on the bridge the Captain stood alongside the Helmsman, scanning the dark, empty ocean ahead. Then he turned and joined the Navigation Officer and they both looked closely at the radar screen. The Captain was pleased with what he saw. There were no other vessels showing in immediate proximity; at least nothing big enough to register but he knew the small trawler was out there and he was now close to the rendezvous. The offload would be tricky but they had done it before; even if this was the first time with a human cargo. He would not be sorry to be rid of his three passengers. Although the crew had been well paid for their silence, the brooding presence of the dangerous fugitives on board had been unsettling to them all for the last two weeks. Well, they would soon be gone, he thought with relief, and where they would be going was not his to know. He barely knew who he would be handing them over to. The bosses at the top told you as little as possible: you were just a link in an anonymous chain and it was not a good idea to ask questions. On the occasions when he had dropped stuff off before there had been barely more than a few words exchanged with the men in the trawler: he had no idea of their names and could hardly distinguish their features in the darkness. It was an arrangement that seemed to suit everyone. The next hour would be tense: not good for the blood pressure his wife nagged him about but the money should stop her nagging. He smiled to himself at the thought but then turned again to the radar and conferred with his Navigating Officer. They agreed on their exact co-ordinates. The captain checked his watch. He left the bridge and walked to stand against a guard rail on the open deck. He muttered a brief thank you to his God that the night was calm. He raised the Aldis lamp and flashed his prearranged Morse identification signal. It was the only secure way of communicating with the trawler. Radio contacts could be picked up by others. Now he waited tensely for an acknowledgement that his message had been seen and the drop-off could go ahead. He fretted when there were no immediate coded recognition flashes of light beaming back to him. Impatiently, he sent his signal again. This time, after only a brief pause, the night was pierced by a sequence of flashing lights. The trawler was acknowledging him. Relieved, the Captain sent his next message asking clearance to proceed to the transfer of his cargo. After a brief pause the returning signal was as unwelcome as it was unexpected. Shocked, he asked for the message to be repeated. It was, and the message was the same. Abort. It was the agreed emergency code and there could be no questioning it. Managing to control his inner frustration and anger he sent the brief signal that he had received the signal and understood it. There was nothing more he could do. A decision had been taken somewhere by someone that it was not safe to proceed. With a mounting sense of apprehension he turned away from the rail. He now would have to face telling three angry and dangerous men that things had not gone according to plan and they would have to stay on board until they reached Rotterdam. He shuddered to think what that would do for his blood pressure.

Ruth sat staring at the note in her hand. She had found it on the mat when she had returned wearily from work. The front doorbell jolted her into action and she put down the note and went to let Luke in.

"Your text seemed urgent," Luke said, as he followed Ruth to the kitchen.

Ruth did not reply but handed him the note. He studied it for a few moments and then looked questioningly at her.

"It was here when I got home. He must have dropped it off this afternoon."

Luke nodded in agreement. "Makes sense. He wouldn't want to risk a phone call or a meeting. Not at this stage."

Ruth sat and looked nervously at Luke. "What do you think?"

Luke looked again at the note and then pulled a chair alongside Ruth's. He smiled. "I think it's worked."

Ruth took the note from him. "'Everything cancelled'," she intoned, "but nothing else."

"That would figure," Luke said. "He would be careful not to write more in case someone else got to look at it."

Ruth pondered that for a moment. "Yes. I suppose so."

They sat in silence for a moment: the note between them.

Ruth picked it up again and looked at the brief message. She frowned and put the note down and looked questioningly at Luke. "So what do we do now, Luke?"

"Nothing. We do nothing. In a day or two the bubble will burst. The press will move on to something else and the forces of law and order will congratulate themselves on thwarting a serious crime."

Ruth thought about that. "Well, I suppose they have; in a way, Luke."

"So everyone's a winner," he said with a wry smile.

Ruth looked at him: not quite convinced by his confidence. "But not the Trebentens."

"I agree. Not the Trebentens. But what can they do about it without risking showing their hand? I suspect they will lie low for a bit." He laughed. "Perhaps concentrate on catching fish."

Ruth seemed uncertain about his apparent confidence. "Aren't you scared, Luke? That they might come after you?"

Luke shrugged. "It's possible I suppose, but unlikely. They seem to have swallowed the bait: that I am on best mate terms with the forces of law and order."

Ruth still did not seem convinced. "I hope you're right." She looked at Luke unable to conceal her anxiety.

Luke put his hand over hers reassuringly. "Don't worry about me, Ruth. I've taken on more dangerous characters than the Trebentens in my time and lived to tell the tale."

Ruth tried to look reassured. She smiled nervously but placed her other hand over Luke's. For a moment neither of them spoke. When Ruth broke the silence she spoke softly and looked directly at Luke. "You're a brave man, Luke. Did you know that?"

Luke considered her words in some surprise and then shook his head and laughed in denial. "I wish, Ruth. I've been called many things but never brave."

Ruth was insistent. She leaned closer to him and held his gaze. "First time for everything, Luke," and she stopped talking and kissed him gently but not briefly. Then she sat back and smiled broadly at him. Luke returned her smile but felt no need to speak. Ruth laughed and got to her feet. "Tea, Luke? Isn't that what the English do at moments of drama?"

Luke considered the question in mock seriousness. "So I believe."

Ruth walked over to the sink and filled the electric kettle. She plugged it in and stood waiting for it to boil but suddenly switched it off and looked back at Luke; her face betraying a new anxiety.

Luke registered her change of mood. "What's the matter?"

"Simon. What happens to Simon?"

"Hopefully nothing. You told him the plan?"

"Yes. To stay put; even try to seem disappointed that the chance of making big money was gone; ask them why it had been called off."

"Good. That should work. I think we flagged up the betrayal as coming from the London end of the operation. They should have no reason to suspect Simon. Provided he doesn't panic and run away." He paused briefly in thought. "Maybe at Christmas he could go. Say he was visiting his parents or something. It's what people do at that time of the year isn't it?"

Ruth nodded her agreement. "I'll tell him again."

"How? You need to be careful. Perhaps give it a few days; let things settle down."

"Of course. Then I'll text him to say we need to talk about Esther's university application. Something routine like that."

"And he'll read between the lines?" Luke queried.

"I'm sure. That's what we arranged at our last meeting. He'll fix a time to come to the gardens again."

"Good. That should work, Ruth."

Reassured, Ruth turned her attention back to the kettle and switched it on again but before it came to the boil there was the distraction of a noisy entry at the front door.

The empty tea pot and drained cups lay neglected on the

kitchen table. Esther took a hungry bite out of another biscuit and, still munching, resumed her angry monologue. Ruth and Luke, with only a brief shared conspiratorial smile, waited patiently. "Tom wanted to chain himself to the railings," Esther exclaimed through a mouthful of biscuit crumbs.

"Good grief! I hope you stopped him?" Ruth asked anxiously.

"I did. I was scared they would beat him up."

"Who?"

"The Police. They had these riot shields and batons, can you believe it?" Esther demanded.

"I thought it was supposed to be a peaceful protest," Luke said.

"It was!" Esther hesitated. "At least it started that way." She paused and reached absently for another biscuit.

"And then what happened?" Luke prompted.

Esther said nothing for a moment as she recollected events. "Well," she begun, "it was fine to begin with. We held up our banners and walked up and down. There was a band playing. A couple of the organizers made speeches and we all cheered and clapped. The cops were quite chilled." She smiled briefly. "It was even fun, I suppose." She stopped smiling. "Then it changed. We wanted to take petitions into the Offices of the Water Board but the police wouldn't let us get near the building. There was a bit of pushing and shoving. I was getting scared: and then someone threw a bottle." She broke off and shook her head in exasperation. "Not one of us; but these other guys had shown up. I think they were just looking for a fight. Tom said they were anarchists. It ruined everything. We just got out as quickly as we could." She sighed despairingly. "Can you believe it, Luke?"

Luke did not reply immediately. Esther's account of her day had taken him back in memory to Trafalgar Square all those years ago. "Yes, Esther," he said quietly, "I can believe it."

Esther now sat forward and glared directly at Luke. "Now you know why I want to be a journalist. If they won't let you protest; if they keep you away from the people with the power then writing about it is the only way to get the truth out. Isn't it?" She demanded, still looking unblinkingly at Luke.

Luke held her gaze. "In theory, Esther. Although it doesn't always work like that." He turned his head and half smiled at Ruth.

Ester seemed confused by his reply. "I don't understand. Why doesn't it—"

Luke was spared further cross examination by another noisy entry at the front door before Sarah burst into the kitchen: still red-faced from the exertions of netball. She flung her sports bag down amidst the cups on the kitchen table before slumping into a chair. "Hi, Mum, Luke. I'm starving, is there anything to eat?" Ruth laughed and got up and walked towards the kitchen cupboards in search of food. Sarah looked hopeful and then appeared, belatedly, to register her sister's presence. "So, Esther. How was your demo? Did they like my placard?"

THIRTY-FIVE

Ruth took a careful look around the empty café. For a second time that afternoon she went from table to table re-straightening the flower vases and checking again that the condiment pots were full. She was looking around for any other adjustments that might be required when Luke, who had been assiduously cleaning and then polishing the coffee machine, laughed.

"I know," Ruth admitted sheepishly, "this is all a bit over the top."

Luke gave the machine a final buffing with his duster and then came and stood alongside Ruth and they both surveyed the pristine state of their workplace. "She will be impressed."

It was now Ruth's turn to laugh; albeit wryly. "Impressed? She's only been away a fortnight. Have you forgotten what she's like?"

Luke indicated the empty room. "She can hardly complain, Ruth. The place is sparkling and you've managed all the cooking brilliantly."

"Hm." Ruth did not sound convinced. "What time will she be here?"

Luke looked at his watch. "Unless the train is late, any time now."

"What did she say? On the phone?"

Luke pondered for a moment. "Only that she was on the train and could we be here when she arrived."

"I wonder why she wanted us here."

"Not sure. I expect she just wanted to grill us about how we had coped."

"Probably," Ruth said, not entirely convinced. She paused for a moment. "Do you think we should tell her about what's been going on? About Simon, and the rest of it?"

Luke shook his head. "I think not. The fewer people who know the truth about that the better."

Ruth sighed. "I expect you're right but I will feel guilty about keeping it from her."

Luke instinctively put his arm around Ruth's shoulder and gave her a hug. "That's your trouble Ruth."

"What?"

"Feeling guilty. It's your default position."

Ruth made to protest but then smiled in acceptance of the charge. "It must be the Jewish mother syndrome."

They both laughed at that but were distracted by the sound of a car pulling up outside the café. Like guilty children discovered in some misdemeanour they quickly moved apart and composed themselves to face whatever drama lay in store.

Paula did not disappoint them. She burst through the door, slammed it behind her and let the small suitcase she was carrying fall to her feet. She stood immobile, breathing heavily. "Bloody hell!" she said: nothing more.

Luke recovered first. He picked up her case and carried it to the back of the room. Ruth made as if to give Paula a welcoming embrace but held back indecisively: unsure if Paula would respond kindly.

"Bloody hell!" Paula said again. She still did not move.

Luke was brave enough to try to move things on. "Tiring journey, Paula?"

Paula looked at him as if aware of his presence for the first time. "No smoking on the plane, no smoking on the train and even the sodding taxi driver asked me not to smoke in his cab."

"Ah." Luke tried to make the sound sympathetic.

Ruth managed to suppress a nervous giggle, "Would you like a coffee, or tea or something?"

"No." Paula seemed to be recovering some sort of motor skills. She walked over to the serving counter and fumbled beneath. Ruth and Luke exchanged glances and Luke winked.

Paula found what she had been looking for. She quickly had the cigarette alight and drew heavily on it. The result was transformative. She leaned back against the counter and looked around the café and then looked at Ruth. "You seem to have everything under control here."

"I hope so, Paula."

Luke looked at Paula and gestured at Ruth. "She's done a fantastic job," he said.

Ruth was quick to deny it. "Not really, Paula. Not the sane without you."

"Hm." Paula considered that and inhaled deeply on her cigarette. The effect was calming. "Thank you: both of you. I'm grateful."

Luke managed to hide his surprise, "Not a problem, Paula. Glad to help."

Rut felt she should respond too. "It was fine, Paula. I actually quite enjoyed it."

This remark seemed to jolt Paula's reactions into a new direction. "Did you now?" She muttered almost to herself. Then, surprisingly, she stubbed out her cigarette and bent to put it in a bin. Luke and Ruth watched silently; unsure if any further comment from them was wise. Paula straightened up and became aware of them staring at her. "We need to talk.

Things to sort out. I thought we could do it now but I'm too knackered. Tomorrow I might be human again."

Luke and Ruth looked questioningly at each other. Ruth nodded nervously.

Luke responded. "Yes. Tomorrow then."

Paula snatched another cigarette from the cache under the counter and put it between her lips but refrained from lighting it for the moment. "I need a long hot bath and then bed. Sorry to have kept you hanging about."

"That's fine, Paula. Get a good night's rest," Ruth said encouragingly.

Paula grunted and picked up her suitcase; ready to head upstairs to her bed. She had the energy for one pleasantry. "Anything exciting happened in my absence?" She could not suppress a yawn as she asked the question.

Luke turned to Ruth and smiled briefly before turning back to Paula. "Oh, you know Paula. Same old, same old."

Sarah peered inside her lunch box. "Cheese and tomato again, Mum."

Ruth looked up from the end of the kitchen table where she had been nursing a cup of coffee distractedly for some time. "Not complaining I hope."

Sarah closed the lid on her sandwiches. She grinned at her mother. "My favourite."

Ruth managed a smile. "Flattery will get you everywhere." She sipped at her coffee but it had got too cold to be palatable. She put the cup down with a grimace and a sigh.

Sarah studied her mother for a moment. "Are you feeling alright, Mum?"

Ruth composed herself. "Of course I am. Why?"

Sarah hesitated. "It's just that I thought you seemed a bit quiet that's all. Last night too. Esther noticed as well."

Ruth feigned brightness. "Well, sometimes a bit of quiet goes down well." She forced a laugh. "You can tell Esther that."

Sarah did not seemed entirely convinced but gathering her school things together she walked to the end of the table and gave Ruth a quick kiss. "I'll be home a bit later tonight."

Ruth nodded. "I know. Netball practice. I expect you'll be starving again."

Sarah made for the door but held up her lunch box as she went. "Not with these lovely sandwiches," she laughed, as she closed the door behind her.

Ruth sat for a moment, smiling at Sarah's parting shot. It reminded her again how her younger daughter was no longer a child; in the last few months she had grown not only physically but also in confidence. Ruth's fears that she would be badly affected by Simon leaving had not been borne out. She seemed to have accepted, like her older sister, that – to quote Esther, 'it was no big deal.' Even when Simon's contact with his daughters became increasingly sporadic it seemed to cause them no grief. Ruth sometimes felt guilty about that but then she recalled Luke's verdict yesterday that guilt was her default position.

Recalling that, and Paula's rather surreal return, caused Ruth to ponder again on what turn events might now take. This explained her preoccupation, which had not escaped the notice of her daughters. Paula wanted to talk. But about what? She had tried to ask Luke if he had any idea what she might have in mind but he could offer no insight. He teased her not to fret and to be patient, which made her cross and him laugh. She had protested it was easy for him to be relaxed about the matter; he had his podcast, which might become seriously popular it seemed, and his stuff for the Clarion. But if Paula were to close the café (and Ruth feared that was what she might be about to tell them), then Luke would only miss out on a free lunch but she would have to try to find more work again, at a time when restarting her more active classes would perhaps be asking too much of her body. Quite apart from that, Ruth was depressed at the thought that she would no longer be working with Paula and Luke on a daily basis. Covering for Paula's absence had been a challenge but one she had risen to and actually enjoyed. She knew now she could do that work and make a success of it. It had boosted her self-esteem and, of course, working with Luke had brought them even closer. Everything seemed, at last in her life, to be set fair. Now it looked as if the clouds were rolling in. Wearily, Ruth got to her feet and carried her cup across to the sink and swilled the cold coffee away.

It had been a busy lunchtime and Paula, obviously recovered from her journey, was in good form; bantering with her regulars who were pleased to see her back and not rising to the bait when some told her in jest that Ruth had managed very well without her!

Now that the door had been locked and the Open sign reversed, Paula was able to light up and join Ruth and Luke who sat at a table in expectation; Ruth nervously and Luke quizzically.

Paula plonked herself down opposite them. She took a deep drag on her newly lit cigarette and then wastefully stubbed it out. "Right. You must be wondering what all this is about."

"Just a bit," Luke ventured.

"Things have changed," was Paula's reply.

Ruth feared the worst and looked anxiously at Luke who attempted to move things on. "In what way, Paula?" he asked.

"My mother's death." Paula picked up her recently discarded cigarette and looked at it thoughtfully.

"We didn't know how, I mean, or—" Ruth stopped, unsure of how to go on.

Paula helped her out. "Very peacefully; as they say, she didn't suffer."

"That's something I suppose," Ruth said and immediately regretted the banality of her observation.

Luke was more focussed. "Did you get to see her? To talk?"

Paula nodded. "Yes." She laughed mirthlessly. "She had the courtesy to hang on for a few days after I arrived. I was with her in the hospice most of the time until the end."

Ruth instinctively reached across the table and held Paula's hand. "That must have been awful for you, Paula."

Paula did not move her hand away and she looked at Ruth and smiled. "Actually it wasn't. Quite the opposite really."

"Did she recognise you?" Luke asked.

Paula sat back and Ruth let go of her hand. "She was drugged up to the eyeballs of course but she had moments of lucidity. We could talk."

"What did you talk about?"

"The past, mostly," Paula said softly. "Happy memories of when I was child; family holidays, that sort of thing."

Nobody spoke for a moment.

"That must have been a comfort to her," Ruth said.

"I hope so," Paula replied. "I tried to cheer her up; tried to make up for all those wasted years when we never spoke. I even reminded her of the Jamaican Rock Guitarist and said I was sorry that had caused her pain."

"How did she react to that?" Luke asked.

Paula smiled at him. "She laughed. I took that as a sign that I was forgiven." She could no longer resist the cigarette but before she lit it she looked across the table at both Ruth and Luke. "That was how I will remember her: laughing." She lit the cigarette.

Luke and Ruth said nothing.

Paula sucked in some nicotine. It energised her and she now spoke with her usual brisk vigour. "You must be wondering why I am telling you all this."

"Of course not—" Ruth protested but was not allowed to finish.

"It appears that I am now a rich woman."

Ruth and Luke looked at each in some confusion and then back at Paula, who surveyed them through a haze of tobacco smoke.

"Rich?" Luke echoed.

"It turns out my mother had invested my father's money profitably. And the house. A villa on Cap d'Antibes; I've been advised to ask a ridiculous sum of money for it but apparently people are already queuing up to buy it."

There was silence while Luke and Ruth digested this information and Paula tapped out ash on a convenient saucer.

Ruth could guess what was coming next. As she had feared, Paula would now surely sell up and enjoy a lavish retirement. Ruth tried not to let her anxiety make her begrudge Paula her unexpected wealth. It would mean having to find another job of course and face taking on more classes again but needs must. Perhaps she had expected too much; it had been too good to last. The relief she had felt in rescuing Simon would now be eroded by nagging worries about her own future. But she could not let Paula see that. It would be too selfish to allow her concerns to detract from Paula's good fortune if, she asked herself, the death of your mother could be deemed good fortune. She put that conundrum to one side and managed to smile cheerfully at Paula. "So a life of leisure now Paula. What have you got planned?"

"That's what the solicitor asked me when he told me I never need work again."

"He was right of course," Luke said.

"Indeed," Paula accepted, and took in another mouthful of smoke. She then blew most of it out languidly, "And for about ten seconds I almost agreed with him."

"Sorry?" Luke asked in confusion.

Paula stubbed out the half-finished cigarette to join the earlier casualties in the saucer. She leaned forward and looked intently at Ruth and Luke. "Retirement. What would I do with that?" The question was clearly a rhetorical one. "You know what would happen." She gestured at the discarded cigarettes in the saucer. "Too much of that and too much of my many other vices. I would destroy myself."

Ruth valiantly tried to protest. "Surely not, Paula, you—"

She was not allowed to finish as Paula raised a restraining hand. "Kind of you to think so Ruth but I know myself too well. I need to be occupied and in touch with normal people: not rich freeloaders." She sat back and looked inquiringly at them.

Luke coughed nervously before offering an opinion. "By normal people, Paula, do you—"

Again Paula cut the speaker short. "Yes. Believe it or not I mean people like you and Ruth." And then, as an apparent afterthought, she gestured at the empty tables. "And my customers: or at least some of them."

Ruth and Luke looked uncertainly at each other. Ruth plucked up the courage to speak. "So if you aren't going to retire, are you just carrying on as normal?"

Paula laughed loudly. "Normal? Is that what I am? Normal?"

Ruth blushed but struggled on. "What I mean, Paula: is everything going to be the same?" Her tone was hopeful.

But that hope was soon dashed. "The same! Certainly not."

Ruth shrugged helplessly, unsure of what to say or whether it would be wise to say anything.

Paula put her out of her misery. She stood up, with both arms outstretched indicatively, inviting Ruth and Luke to take in the empty café space. Neither of them felt emboldened to speak. "Well?" Paula rasped.

"Well what, Paula?" Luke finally managed.

Paula stared at him reproachfully; like a teacher who had expected a better answer from her star pupil, but she appeared to accept that perhaps she could have asked a more detailed question. She sat down again and fumbled in the pocket of her apron and pulled out a sheet of paper. Luke and Ruth stared at in bemusement; seeing nothing but sketchy lines and jumbled numbers. Paula flattened out the paper. "It's only a rough sketch. It gave me something to do on that bloody train. I'll need to find an architect of course and a reliable builder – if such a creature exists – but I think it can be done." She looked up at Ruth and Luke. "What do you two think?"

Neither replied immediately, as they stared at Paula, open-mouthed.

"A partner? She wants you to be a partner?" Esther could not keep disbelief out of her voice.

Ruth thrust a scuffed piece of paper across the table to Esther who picked it up and studied it intently. "She cobbled something together on the train; she said if I agree she'll have it drawn up by a solicitor."

Esther put down the paper and looked at her mother. "And why wouldn't you agree? From what I can make out she provides the money and you manage the café."

Ruth nodded. "But not the café as you know it, Esther. Have a look at this." Ruth took another sheet of paper from her shoulder bag and passed it over to Esther. "I copied it from her plans. It's only a rough outline but you can see what she has in mind."

Ester studied the plan for a moment and then looked in puzzlement at her mother. "But this is really mega. It would cost thousands."

Ruth smiled. "True. But it seems she now has thousands. From her mother."

Esther digested that information but did not look convinced. She frowned at Ruth. "But why does she want to spend it on the café? When you think what else she could do with it."

"I think that's the problem. She's scared of what she might do to herself without the discipline of the café."

Esther smiled. "I think I get that. She'd be on a perpetual rave!"

"She told us she needed to be around normal people."

"Like us?" Esther laughed.

"I think by her standards we're probably pretty normal."

Esther paused in thought for a moment. "You might be right. When we're clearing up on Saturdays she seems quite interested in what we're up to. Me and Sarah." She grinned at her mother. "And of course she's always grilling me about you and Luke."

Ruth covered her embarrassment by changing the subject. "I think she realised what a sad mistake it was to cut all ties with her mother: ten wasted years, she said."

"And she won't get those back."

"So maybe she accepts she needs people around her. Maybe close friends she never had."

"Like calling to like then, Mum," Esther suggested.

"What?"

"You've never had close friends have you? It was just us. Sarah and me and Dad. And not Dad for long."

Ruth was silent for a moment. "That's how it was, Esther. Remember, I came here from Africa. No family around me; no old school friends to keep in touch with; no relatives to support me when the two of you were babies."

"I know, Mum. It must have been tough," Esther agreed quietly.

"I'm not complaining." She managed a wry smile. "Well, perhaps I am a bit, but it was my choice. My Dad would have said 'just get on with it, don't bay for the moon'."

Esther laughed. "I wish I could have met my Grandfather. He sounds a straight talker."

"I think you may have inherited some of his character. 'Don't sit about complaining: just get up and get on.' He would have approved of you."

"And of you," Esther countered, "taking on this partnership."

Ruth hesitated. "I haven't said I would yet."

Esther looked at her in exasperation "What? Why on earth wouldn't you?"

"I feel a bit guilty, I suppose."

"There you go again!" Esther threw up her hands in despair. "Feeling guilty. Luke always teases you about that but he's right. What have you got to feel guilty about this time?"

Ruth shrugged. "I suppose because I can't bring any money into this partnership so why should I share the profit?" She managed a half-hearted laugh. "That is, if we make any."

Esther groaned in exasperation. "Look, Paula obviously doesn't need your money. What she wants is someone on her side. Someone honest, hard-working and, above all, someone she likes." Esther pointed a finger at her mother. "And that, Mum, is you. Believe me." Having delivered her judgement Esther sat back in her chair and stared challengingly at Ruth: daring her to disagree.

THIRTY-SIX

"I don't see much trickling in these parts," Dave protested.

"Nor are you likely to, Pasco," Luke responded. "I think the trickling stops just south of Kensington."

"But, if I've got the hang of what you've been going on about, Prof, letting these Bankers and the like pay less tax benefits all of us."

"That's the theory, Pasco. The Trickle Down effect. We all get richer because as the few get wealthier the money they spend finds its way into our pockets."

"But they spend it on posh holidays in foreign parts or flash cars or, I don't know, sending their kids to private schools or something. How's that going to trickle my way so that I can pay my electric bill? Because if it doesn't trickle my way pretty soon me and Tamsin will have to buy extra vests and sit in the dark to eat our dry crust."

"A dismal prospect indeed, Pasco, and one sure to break the heart of our caring political masters."

"You taking the piss, Prof?"

"As if I would. No, Pasco. I am simply trying to help you grasp the economic theories that underlie the government's policies. Theories they have derived from years of study at the most prestigious centres of learning. The Cabinet is packed with people of great intelligence with strings of academic qualification to their name."

"Is that so? Then why do they make such a cock up of everything they touch?"

"That, Pasco, is one of life's mysteries and one I hope we can return to in our next little chat when I plan to shine a light for you on another of the glittering jewels in our Government's treasure chest."

"What Jewel would that be, Prof?"

"Levelling Up," Luke said emphatically as he ended the recording.

Dave waited a few seconds before putting down his script. "So when will that be, Luke? Before Christmas?"

Luke stood and began gathering in the scripts. "I thought we'd leave it until the New Year. This is the season of Good Will to all men after all."

Dave laughed at that. "If you say so."

Luke fumbled in his jacket pocket and produced an envelope which he handed to Dave. "Talking of Christmas, here's your present." He passed the envelope over to Dave.

Dave looked puzzled but slit open the envelope and removed its content. He looked at the cheque for a moment. "Blimey, Luke, real money."

"Not much, but a start. I hope there might be more to come."

Dave tucked the cheque away in an inside pocket. "Thanks, Luke." He paused. "But it's not really about the money for you, is it?"

Luke hesitated. He looked at Dave. "Probably not."

Dave nodded. "You're back doing what you're good at. Trying to get at the truth."

Luke shrugged. "Whatever that is."

Dave would not be deflected. "Don't knock yourself. It's important. It matters."

Luke smiled. "Thanks, Dave." He put the scripts into his document case and put on his overcoat.

Dave stood too and put on a woolly hat and a scarf. "Bit nippy out there."

"Seasonal, Dave."

Luke walked towards the door with Dave following but before they got there Dave tapped Luke on the shoulder and he turned and looked at him in some surprise. "What, Dave?"

"Talking of truth just then reminded me."

"Reminded you of what?"

"That Trebenten business. You never did tell me what that was all about."

Luke showed no flicker of emotion. "Really, Dave, how remiss of me." Then, with no further comment, he turned and walked out of the door.

It was the shortest day of the year and even in mid-afternoon the light in the Morrab Gardens was fading fast. Ruth looked at her watch anxiously. They would be closing the gates in half an hour. Why was Simon late? It was too cold to sit on the bench which had become their meeting place so Ruth had wandered distractedly around the gardens for a few minutes but the trees and plants were dispiritingly winter drab and did nothing to lighten her mood. Simon had texted her to arrange to meet so why wasn't he here? She would give him five more minutes and then go. No sooner had Ruth made that decision than Simon came hurrying down the path towards her. He raised his hand in recognition.

"Sorry I'm late. There was a long queue in the Post Office."

"Post Office?"

"Yes. I had to get currency," Simon explained.

Ruth looked at him in surprise. "You're going away?"

Simon looked around before answering but there was no one in sight. "I'll explain. Let's walk."

Ruth fell into step with him. "Where are you going, Simon?"

"India," Simon replied emphatically.

Ruth could not hide her astonishment. "India!"

They both stopped. Simon looked at Ruth. "Why not? It's far enough away isn't it? From everything."

Ruth was still trying to process the information. "How long are you going for?"

Simon resumed walking and Ruth trailed after him. "I don't know. As long as the money lasts I suppose."

Ruth could not change her nature and ignore the practicalities. "Have you got somewhere to stay? What will you do?"

Simon laughed. "You don't have to worry about me now, Ruth, but since you ask, one of my college mates has settled near Calcutta; hooked up with an Indian girl. I can stay with them to start with and then travel around; try to get back into painting and put some work together."

"Does anyone else know, Simon?"

Simon stopped again and, as if by reflex, looked cautiously about. Satisfied he would be unheard by anyone but Ruth he spoke quietly to her. "I told people I was going home to Wales for Christmas: to visit my parents."

"And they believed you?"

Simon shrugged and spoke as they walked on. "I don't think they cared. Not anymore."

Ruth could not help herself. "Not even Elowen?"

Simon paused momentarily. He looked hard at Ruth; a momentary look of anger quickly dissolving into one of weary resignation. He walked on slowly. "You knew about that, then?"

"Sort of," Ruth said nervously, "I believe she's very beautiful."

"She is," Simon said flatly. "At least, to look at."

"But?" Ruth asked.

Simon did not look at Ruth now as they walked. It was as if he was talking to himself. "There's always a 'but' isn't there. She used me of course; while I was useful to them. I see that now, but I suppose I was happy to be used. Not just for the money, not even mostly for the money, but to please her." Now he did stop and look at Ruth. "Pathetic aren't I? Believing I meant anything to her."

Ruth considered the question. "You won't be the first or the last, Simon, to have gone down that road."

"'A sadder and a wiser man'. Isn't that what they say?"

"Well, India will give you a chance to start again." Ruth wondered if that was too patronising but then another thought distracted her. "The girls, Simon. What will you tell them?"

"The truth; or at least part of it; that I am going to India and I don't know when I'll be coming back and when I do it won't be back to Cornwall."

"That'll be hard on them. Simon."

"Not so hard, Ruth. The last time I saw them it was clear they were coping fine without me. You too, they said; you and Luke."

Now it was Ruth's turn to stop in shock. She spoke angrily, "They had no right to say that. Luke and I—"

Simon held up his hand to stop her. "No need, Ruth. No need for apologies or explanations. We're free now; both of us, and although I don't know anything about this Luke guy I owe him. Without him I might not be getting this chance to start again."

Before Ruth could respond a bell broke the silence as a

warning the gardens were about to close. For a moment she looked at Simon and he smiled ruefully at her but neither moved to embrace the other. Simon turned quickly and made towards the gate. He turned briefly to wave a brisk farewell to Ruth and called out, "I'll send you a postcard from Calcutta," Then the dusk swallowed him up.

THIRTY-SEVEN

Sarah studied the slip of paper in her hand and then addressed the assembled company. "What do mice send each other at Christmas?"

No one seemed to know. Esther broke the silence. "Come on, Sarah, I know you're dying to tell us."

Sarah read from her script. "Cross mouse cards!"

There were groans of despair from the celebrants. Ruth held up both hands in surrender. "Please Sarah, we give in. No more cracker jokes."

Sarah laughed. "Only if I can have a bit more of the champagne." She pushed her empty glass across the laden table towards Paula.

Ruth looked uncertainly towards Paula who poured a very small measure into Sarah's glass. "And that's your lot unless you want to end up like me."

Ruth laughed and looked happily around the table. It was the first time Paula had come to the house which, Ruth confessed, had filled her with nervous apprehension but Paula had told her not be silly: after all they were partners now and the meal had been a great success, she had to admit. She had been nervous about cooking the turkey that Paula had insisted on buying for them, but it had been well received.

Even Esther had teetered on the brink of her vegetarian principles before consoling herself with the nut roast Paula had provided for her. They had not sat down for the meal until late afternoon which had given Ruth time to clear away the cooking debris and set out the table with her best (that is, not chipped or stained) cutlery and glasses. Sarah had spent hours decorating the Christmas tree which Luke had delivered to them on Christmas Eve. Ruth had found some old fairy lights in the attic which, to her great surprise, still worked, and they now twinkled cheerfully on the tree, supplementing the flickering light from the candles Esther had demanded to be the accompaniment to their meal Everyone wore paper hats and they had joked and laughed their way through the destruction of all the delicious food. Only after Paula had flamed the brandy under the Christmas pudding and instructed them to make a wish whilst they ate it, did they admit defeat and slump back replete and contented.

Ruth did not remember when she had last felt so relaxed: even happy. It had been nearly a year since the tentative interview at the café which had brought Paula and, of course, Luke into her life. So much had changed since then. Her emotions had been through the wringer. She had plunged into darkest despair at times but perhaps now she could at last, what do they say, 'move on'. She smiled at the prospect and Luke, at the end of the table, noticed her smile and raised his glass in acknowledgement. They silently toasted each other. Ruth was aware of Paula in earnest conversation with Sarah about netball! It was hard to imagine that Paula had been her school netball captain; a fact she had let slip after a couple of glasses of the champagne she had insisted on supplying. Esther was now showing Luke something on her laptop: no doubt relevant to her ongoing battle with the Water Board. That was another development Ruth had come to accept over the last year: her daughters were growing up fast, immersed increasingly in their own lives. Simon had taken them out for coffee in the town it seemed, and told them of his decision to take himself off to India. Neither of the girls showed any distress at the news. If Esther had any inkling of the real motive for Simon's departure she made no mention of it. Of course, Ruth still felt protective of her girls but she was aware that she must try not to show it too much. That is why, when Ben had phoned on Christmas Eve to wish them a happy Christmas she had promised to discuss with Sarah and Esther the offer he had made to fly them over for the Easter holidays; even though, as she had explained, she would be too tied up with the re-opening of the café to be able to come herself.

The prospect of the café make-over did not, to her surprise, make Ruth nervous. In fact she was excited about it. Paula had been quick to employ an architect and a builder and work would start in the New Year. The café would need to close and the dining area and the kitchen would be completely refurbished and extended out in the back yard. Even Nosey Nicholson had been involved, advising on the correct materials and kitchen layout from his Health and Safety viewpoint. Paula said she preferred to have him in the tent pissing out rather than the alternative. Ruth would need to be a sort of Clerk of the works; keeping daily watch over the builders. They had agreed, at Ruth's request, that she would be able to carry on with her one senior fitness class but other than that her focus would need to be on the cafe as Paula herself would have to go back to France for a while to sort out her mother's estate. When she returned she and Ruth would work on the new menus and cook experimental dishes. Paula was determined not to employ a chef, claiming they often drank too much and were temperamental: a verdict

Ruth managed to accept with a straight face. However they would need to take on a couple of kitchen and waiting staff and Ruth was entrusted with that. Paula told her 'she was better at that sort of thing'. The hope was that the café could re-open after Easter, and Luke was sternly warned by Paula that if he expected to still get a free lunch he would need to write a glowing review in the Clarion.

Ruth's daydreaming was interrupted as Paula announced she needed to get moving. Christmas or not she had a mountain of 'bloody paperwork' to get through before she went back to France. She thanked Ruth profusely for the meal and gave her and the girls an enveloping hug. Luke insisted, in spite of her indignant protests, that he would walk her home. "Who do you think is going to attack an ugly old bat like me?" Her question went unanswered as Luke ushered her away.

Ruth watched them go and then forced herself reluctantly to her feet to confront the washing up. Sarah, looking a little sleepy after her first exposure to champagne, said she would like to help but needed to lie down for a bit. Ruth did not press her; it was Christmas after all. Esther made a half-hearted effort to move a few dirty plates to the sink but after the first load looked apologetically at her mother.

"Can this wait a bit, Mum?"

Ruth shrugged. "I'll just do it gradually. There's no hurry."

Esther held up her phone. "Tom has just texted me. He wants me to go round. He's desperate. They are trying to make him play charades."

Ruth laughed. "Not Tom's thing I should imagine. You'd better go and rescue him."

Esther smiled gratefully at her mother. "Thanks."

Ruth slowly began to pile up plates. "Luke will give me a hand when he gets back."

Esther registered that but made no move to leave. Instead she had another question for her mother. "Luke?"

Ruth stopped organising the plates. "What about him?"

"You won't send him home, will you? Not on Christmas night."

Ruth stood and looked hard at her daughter. "What are you saying, Esther?"

Esther was not abashed. "You know what I'm saying, Mum."

Ruth made as if to reply but then didn't. She turned and began running hot water into the sink; Esther stayed where she was. After a moment Ruth turned off the tap and then looked back at Esther. "We'll see. Anyway, you'd better go, Esther: save Tom in his hour of need."

Esther nodded slowly, as if confirming that she understood that her mother was implying more than she was saying. She smiled. "See you, Mum."

Ruth watched Esther go and accepted, not for the first time in recent months, that her teenage daughter sometimes understood her better than she understood herself.

Luke took the proffered plate and after drying placed it on top of the pile on the draining board. "Nearly there," he said.

"Just these glasses." Ruth indicated the washing up bowl in the sink. "Are you sure she enjoyed it?" she asked Luke.

"Loved it. Said she hadn't spent Christmas with a family since she was a kid." Luke cleared some space for the glasses, then stood in thought for a moment. "Nor me, for that matter. I was usually working on Christmas Day and since then it didn't really seem worth bothering."

"That sounds so sad, Luke," Ruth sympathised. "So what did you do?"

"Usually bought myself a decent bottle of something and

went for a walk if it wasn't raining and then listened to some music." He smiled at Ruth. "Not so sad, really."

"No friends or relatives to spend it with?"

"Just my sister and it didn't seem worth trekking all the way up there." He sighed. "Too lazy I suppose."

"Friends, then?"

Luke shook his head. "In my job you didn't really have close friends, just sources. The people you worked with were more competitors than colleagues."

Ruth grimaced, as she handed Luke the last glass. "Sounds grim." She handed him the last glass.

Luke polished the glass with a tea towel and put it with the others. He turned and smiled at Ruth. "And how were your Christmases?"

Ruth thought about it. "In Zim it was never like the Christmas on the cards. Midsummer and blazing hot. My father used to light the barbecue but no turkey or such like." She was lost in her memories for a moment before turning to look at Luke. "Anyway, if he was anything he was Jewish, so no church going or carols or anything like that." She laughed wearily. "I guess Christmas was really a non-event for us. I used to be a bit envious of the other girls at school with all their Christmas presents and parties."

"But when you came to England?"

"I used to try to make it a bit special for Esther and Sarah but we never had much money to spend on presents for them. Simon was not a fan of Christmas, said it was just 'commercialising paganism', so insisted we didn't waste money buying each other presents."

"Oh, dear," Luke said sheepishly.

Ruth looked at him in surprise. "It wasn't that bad; not having a present."

"Well then; I hope this won't be too much of a shock."

He took an envelope out of his jacket pocket and handed it to Ruth.

Ruth looked in surprise at Luke and then took the envelope. Slowly she opened it and took out the contents and studied them, then she looked at Luke in confusion. "Luke; you shouldn't—"

Luke moved closer to her and put a finger over her lips to silence her protest. "I dare say I shouldn't have but I have. Tickets were selling out fast and when I heard the girls might be going to Australia for Easter I took a chance that you might be able to come with me." He took his hand away from Ruth's lips but pulled her close to him. "If you can, will you?" he asked quietly. Ruth kissed him gently. "Of course I will, Luke," she answered, and kissed him again, this time more urgently.

THIRTY-EIGHT

From the main stage the sound of a soulful Blues number just carried, above the heads of the packed crowd, to a shaded grassy area when Ruth lay on a rug and looked up at the puffs of white cloud drifting across the blue canopy of the sky. She was glad to rest. The two days of the festival had been both exhilarating and exhausting. They had gone to bed late, in the glamping tent Luke had booked for them, and spent the days and late evenings absorbed in the music. Tomorrow Ruth knew she would have to face her real world again but for the moment she could savour this time of magic with Luke. When she had seen the luxury tent she thought momentarily of the last occasion she had camped, with Simon on their trip around Europe. That small tent belonged now to a past so distant it seemed unreal. She could hardly recognise herself as the young girl who had spent months in wild love-making under a hot sun. She knew that with Luke there would perhaps never be that frantic passion but what they had instead was a deep contentment and affection for each other which made their physical relationship just as satisfying as the unrestrained desires of youth. Thinking of Luke, she sat up and shaded her eyes to look for his approach. He had gone to the beer tent for thirst-quenching pints and now she saw him, cautiously manoeuvring through the crowd, the cardboard cartons held gingerly out in front of him in each hand. She smiled as she saw him frowning in concentration; determined not to spill a drop of his precious cargo. He looked up and saw her: nodded and smiled in recognition. She made space for him on the rug and he sat carefully down beside her and handed her one of the beers. They raised their drinks to each other in a mutual toast.

Ruth took a few sips and then with her free hand pointed towards the soaring ridge of the South Downs which provided a dramatic backdrop to the festival site. She turned to Luke. "This is how I thought England would look."

Luke looked puzzled. "What?"

Ruth laughed. "All the books we had as kids were about English children having adventures in the countryside; and all the illustrations showed fields and woods and streams. Green grass, rolling hills and so on." She gestured again towards the Downs. "Just like this."

Luke smiled. "The reality must have been a shock."

"Everything was a shock, Luke," Ruth sighed.

Luke said nothing.

They sat in silence for a moment; absorbed in their own thoughts. Ruth drained the last of her drink and then took Luke's hand. They looked at each other and smiled. "That was then, Luke. This is now." Luke leaned forward and kissed her gently.

A roar of applause and thunderous clapping announced the end of the performance on the main stage.

Luke stood and helped Ruth to her feet. They joined in the applause as the musician left the stage. The clapping and shouts of 'more!' continued and grew louder. "I expect they'll come back for one more. That's how it works." As if on cue the band returned and launched into another number. The crowd roared their approval. Luke punched the air in appreciation and then, immediately, and somewhat sheepishly, lowered his arm to his side and looked at Ruth with an apologetic grin. Ruth laughed and punched the air too. Reassured, Luke turned to face the stage; his concentration on the music now was total but he managed to point towards the stage to indicate that he needed to get closer. Ruth nodded that she had got the message and stooped to fold up the rug and gather the cardboard mugs. When she straightened up she saw that Luke had positioned himself at the back of the crowd and had joined with them in clapping his hand above his head in time with the music as instructed by the band leader.

Ruth almost wished she had a camera with her, or her phone, so that later she could tease Luke with this reminder that he could let himself go when need be. But now she knew that anyway. Not just, to put it bluntly, in bed, but in the way he had settled so easily into the lives of her family. The way they felt about each other made it senseless for Luke to carry on living alone in his flat; so he had let it and moved in with Ruth. She did have some initial misgivings about how Esther and Sarah would react but, when she put it to them that Luke might move in, they had welcomed the idea. Esther, of course, had been the one to encourage the arrangement in the first place, and Sarah saw no problem. It helped, after he had moved in, that Luke made it clear by his words and actions that he would not pretend to be a surrogate father. His friendly and unthreatening presence reinforced that and Ruth, gradually, could believe that her home might at last be a place free of tension and anxiety. She had found it hard to hold back tears when Esther and Sarah had hugged Luke so warmly before they boarded the plane at Heathrow. Remembering that, Ruth also recalled the text from Esther which had arrived a couple of days ago accompanied by pictures of her and Sarah on Bondi Beach with their cousins. Ben had phoned to reassure Ruth that the girls had arrived safely. He said they talked a lot about Luke and clearly liked him. Ben had reassured Ruth that they would, when she first told him that she and Luke would be living together; he reminded her that he had only met Luke briefly but long enough to see that they were right for other; 'I guess I knew before you did' was how he had put it. Ben asked about Simon but all Ruth could tell him was that they had received a postcard from Calcutta to say India was an inspiration and Ben's only reaction to that was to say that it sounded as if he had no plans for a quick return. He had tried, unsuccessfully, not to sound too pleased.

Ruth looked around for a bin to dispose of the cardboard. She spotted one a short distance away and strolled over to it and dropped in the mugs. She paused and looked again at the sentinel Downs. She would keep the memory; at least until next year when they had agreed they must come again. A year? She could only pray that it would be less traumatic than the last and was hopeful that might be the case. Luke had encouraged her to think of what lay ahead as an opportunity not a problem and he had only been half joking. It had certainly been challenging to get the café ready for next week's opening. Paula had needed to stay longer in France than she anticipated, dealing with what she described as 'mountains of bloody Gallic bumf'. This had left Ruth with hands-on supervision of the builders, whom she edged towards the finishing line with a mixture of cajolery, pleading, demanding, insisting, and frequent cups of tea. They seem to have parted on reasonably good terms with the work completed even to Paula's satisfaction. Ruth had also had to take on new staff and had settled on a couple of middle-aged Cornish ladies whom, she thought, were unlikely to be blown off course by

Paula's temperamental gusts. Not that Paula had been in bad humour of late. She seemed to be looking forward to the road ahead. She and Ruth had tried out a variety of dishes before deciding on their new menus. Luke had been reminded again by Paula, possibly in jest, if he expected to carry on getting a free lunch he would need to write a glowing review of the restaurant (Paula had upgraded it in her mind from a café) in the Clarion. He had responded, possibly also in jest, that he would see if he could find the time now that he was so busy with his podcast.

Ruth was still enjoying the memory of that exchange when she became aware that the music had stopped and the spectators were dispersing. She looked to see if Luke had spotted her. At first she could not pick him out amongst the thinning crowds and then she glimpsed him, by the grassy area where they had drunk their beers, looking around in some confusion clearly wondering where she had gone. Loath to shout, Ruth waved her hand to catch his attention. After a few seconds he registered her signal. She saw him wave and head towards her. As she watched him approach she felt her mood lighten; any worries about the future banished. He reached her and took her hand. They did not speak but smiled broadly at each other.